Men of the Deep Waters by William Hope Hodgson

William Hope Hodgson was born in Essex, England on November 15th, 1877.

Over his short career he produced a large body of work which explored and covered many genres. From horror, to science fiction, to stories on the sea, where he had spent much of his early life.

In 1899, at the age of 22, he opened W. H. Hodgson's School of Physical Culture, in Blackburn, England, offering tailored exercise regimes for personal training.

Eventually the business shut down and he immersed himself in writing. An article in 1903 "Physical Culture versus Recreative Exercises" seems to be one of the first and the following year came his first short story "The Goddess of Death". It was the beginning of an intensely creative period in his life.

When war drew its shadow over Europe Hodgson received a commission as a Lieutenant in the Royal Artillery. In 1916 he was thrown from a horse and suffered a serious head injury; he received a mandatory discharge, and returned to writing.

Hodgson recovered sufficiently to re-enlist but at the Battle of Ypres in April 1918 he was killed by an artillery shell.

Index of Contents

PREFACE

Directly afterwards, a shrill, yelling noise seemed to fill the whole sky with a deafening, piercing sound. I glanced hastily over the port quarter. In that direction the whole surface of the ocean seemed to be torn up into the air in monstrous clouds of spray. The yelling sound passed into a vast scream, and the next instant the cyclone was upon us.

"Through the Vortex of a Cyclone,"

For Wa-ha! I am hale,
And when I make sail
My thundering bulk roars over the tides,
Roars over the tides,
And everything hides,
Save the Albicore-fool! a-splitting his sides—
A fish kangaroo a-jumping the tides.
For he's naught but a fish and a half,
Wa! Ha!
A haddock far less than a young bull calf!
With me Wa! Ha! Ha!
He has far too much side
For a bit of a haddock a-jump in the tide!
Yea, I am the Great Bull Whale!
I have shattered the moon when asleep
On the face of the deep, by a stroke of my sweep
I have shattered its features pale.
Like the voice of a wandering gale
Is the smite of my sounding tail,
For Wa-ha! I am hale,
And when I make sail
My thundering bulk roars over the tide,
Roars over the tide,
And scatters it wide,
And laughs at the moon afloat on its side—
'Tis naught but a star that hath died!
For 'tis naught but a star that hath died,
Wa! Ha!
A matter of cinders afloat in the Wide!
With me Wa! Ha! Ha!
It has far too much side
For a bit of a cinder afloat in the tide!

ON THE BRIDGE

(The 8 to 12 watch, and ice was in sight at nightfall)

IN MEMORY OF
APRIL 14, 1912.
LAT. 41 deg. 16 min. N.
LONG. 50 deg. 14 min. W.

Two-bells has just gone. It is nine o'clock. You walk to wind'ard and sniff anxiously. Yes, there it is, unmistakably, the never-to-be-forgotten smell of ice ... a smell as indescribable as it is unmistakable.

You stare, fiercely anxious (almost incredibly anxious), to wind'ard, and sniff again and again. And you never cease to peer, until the very eye-balls ache, and you curse almost insanely because some door has been opened and lets out a shaft of futile and dangerous light across the gloom, through which the great ship is striding across the miles.

For the least show of light about the deck, "blinds" the officer of the watch temporarily, and makes the darkness of the night a double curtain of gloom, threatening hatefully. You curse, and 'phone angrily for a steward to go along and have the door shut or the window covered, as the case may be; then once again to the dreadful strain of watching.

Just try to take it all in. You are, perhaps, only a young man of twenty-six or twenty-eight, and you are in sole charge of that great bulk of life and wealth, thundering on across the miles. One hour of your watch has gone, and there are three to come, and already you are feeling the strain. And reason enough, too; for though the bridge-telegraph pointer stands at Half-Speed, you know perfectly well that the engine-room has its private orders, and speed is not cut down at all.

And all around, to wind'ard and to loo'ard, you can see the gloom pierced dimly in this place and that, everlastingly, by the bursts of phosphorescence from breaking sea-crests. Thousands and tens of thousands of times you see this ... ahead, and upon either beam. And you sniff, and try to distinguish between the coldness of the half-gale and the peculiar and what I might term the "personal," brutal, ugly Chill-of-Death that comes stealing down to you through the night, as you pass some ice-hill in the darkness.

And then, those countless bursts of dull phosphorescence, that break out eternally from the chaos of the unseen waters about you, become suddenly things of threatening, that frighten you; for any one of them may mean broken water about the unseen shore of some hidden island of ice in the night ... some half-submerged, inert Insensate Monster-of-Ice, lurking under the wash of the seas, trying to steal unperceived athwart your hawse.

You raise your hand instinctively in the darkness, and the cry "Hard a Starboard!" literally trembles on your lips; and then you are saved from making an over-anxious spectacle of yourself; for you see now that the particular burst of phosphorescence that had seemed so pregnant of Ice, is nothing more than any one of the ten thousand other bursts of sea-light, that come and go among the great moundings of the sea-foam in the surrounding night.

And yet there is that infernal ice-smell again, and the chill that I have called the Chill-of-Death, is stealing in again upon you from some unknown quarter of the night. You send word forrard to the look-outs, and to the man in the "nest," and redouble your own care of the thousand humans who sleep so trustfully in their bunks beneath your feet ... trusting you—a young man—with their lives ... with everything. They, and the great ship that strides so splendid and blind through the Night and the Dangers of the Night, are all, as it were, in the hollow of your hand ... a moment of inattention, and a thousand deaths upon the head of your father's son! Do you wonder that you watch, with your very heart seeming dry with anxiety, on such a night as this!

Four bells! Five bells! Six bells! And now there is only an hour to go; yet, already, you have nearly given the signal three times to the Quartermaster to "port" or "starboard," as the case may be; but each time the conjured terror of the night, the dree, suggestive foam-lights, the infernal ice-smell, and the Chill-of-Death have proved to be no true Prophets of Disaster in your track.

Seven bells! My God! Even as the sweet silver sounds wander fore and aft into the night, and are engulfed by the gale, you see something close upon the starboard bow.... A boil of phosphorescent lights, over some low-lying, sea-buried thing in the darkness. Your night-glasses are glaring at it; and then, even before the various look-outs can make their reports, you KNOW. "My God!" your spirit is crying inside of you. "My God!" But your human voice is roaring words that hold life and death for a thousand sleeping souls:—"Hard a Starboard!" "Hard a Starboard!" The man in the Wheel-house leaps at your cry ... at the fierce intensity of it; and then, with a momentary loss of nerve, whirls the wheel the wrong way. You make one jump, and are into the Wheel-house. The glass is tinkling all about you, and you do not know in that instant that you are carrying the frame of the shattered Wheel-house door upon your shoulders. Your fist takes the frightened helmsman under the jaw, and your free hand grips the spokes, and dashes the wheel round toward you, the engine roaring, away in its appointed place. Your junior has already flown to his post at the telegraph, and the engine-room is answering the order you have flung at him as you leapt for the Wheel-house. But You ... why, you are staring, half-mad, through the night, watching the monster bows swing to port, against the mighty background of the night. . . . The seconds are the beats of eternity, in that brief, tremendous time.... And then, aloud to the wind and the night, you mutter, "Thank God!" For she has swung clear. And below you the thousand sleepers sleep on.

A fresh Quartermaster has "come aft" (to use the old term) to relieve the other, and you stagger out of the Wheel-house, becoming conscious of the inconvenience of the broken woodwork around you. Someone, several people, are assisting you to divest yourself of the framework of the door; and your junior has a queer little air of respect for you, that, somehow, the darkness is not capable of hiding.

You go back to your post then; but perhaps you feel a little sick, despite a certain happy elation that stimulates you.

Eight bells! And your brother officer comes up to relieve you. The usual formula is gone through, and you go down the bridge steps, to the thousand sleeping ones.

Next day a thousand passengers play their games and read their books, and talk their talks and make their usual sweepstakes, and never even notice that one of the officers is a little weary-looking.

The carpenter has replaced the door; and a certain Quartermaster will stand no more at the wheel. For the rest, all goes on as usual, and no one ever knows. . . . I mean no one outside of official circles, unless an odd rumour leaks out through the stewards.

And a certain man has no deaths to the name of his father's son.

And the thousand never know. Think of it, you people who go down to the sea in floating palaces of steel and electric light. And let your benedictions fall silently upon the quiet, grave, neatly-uniformed man in blue upon the bridge. You have trusted him unthinkingly with your lives; and not once in ten thousand times has he ever failed you. Do you understand better now?

CHAPTER I

"An' we's under the sea, b'ys,
Where the Wild Horses go,
Horses wiv tails
As big as ole whales
All jiggin' around in a row,
An' when you ses Whoa!
Them divvils does go!"

"How was it you catched my one, granfer?" asked Nebby, as he had asked the same question any time during the past week, whenever his burly, blue-guernseyed grandfather crooned out the old Ballade of the Sea-Horses, which, however, he never carried past the portion given above.

"Like as he was a bit weak, Nebby b'y; an' I gev him a smart clip wiv the axe, 'fore he could bolt off," explained his grandfather, lying with inimitable gravity and relish.

Nebby dismounted from his curious-looking go-horse, by the simple method of dragging it forward from between his legs. He examined its peculiar, unicorn-like head, and at last put his finger on a bruised indentation in the black paint that covered the nose.

"'S that where you welted him, granfer?" he asked, seriously.

"Aye," said his granfer Zacchy, taking the strangely-shaped go-horse, and examining the contused paint. "Aye, I shore hit 'm a tumble welt."

"Are he dead, granfer?" asked the boy.

"Well," said the burly old man, feeling the go-horse all over with an enormous finger and thumb, "betwixt an' between, like." He opened the cleverly hinged mouth, and looked at the bone teeth with which he had fitted it, and then squinted earnestly, with one eye, down the red-painted throat. "Aye," he repeated, "betwixt an' between, Nebby. Don't you never let 'm go to water, b'y; for he'd maybe come alive ag'in, an' ye'd lose 'm sure."

Perhaps old Diver-Zacchy, as he was called in the little sea-village, was thinking that water would prove unhealthy to the glue, with which he had fixed-on the big bonito's tail, at what he termed the starn-end of the curious looking beast. He had cut the whole thing out of a nice, four-foot by ten-inch piece of soft, knot-less yellow pine; and, to the rear, he had attached, thwart-ship, the afore-mentioned bonito's tail; for the thing was no ordinary horse, as you may think; but a gen-u-ine (as Zacchy described it) Sea-Horse, which he had brought up from the sea bottom for his small grandson, whilst following his occupation as diver.

The animal had taken him many a long hour to carve, and had been made during his spell-ohs, between dives, aboard the diving-barge. The creature itself was a combined production of his own extremely fertile fancy, plus his small grandson's Faith. For Zacchy had manufactured unending and peculiar stories of what he saw daily at the bottom of the sea, and during many a winter's evening, Nebby had "cut boats" around the big stove, whilst the old man smoked and yarned the impossible yarns that were so marvellously real and possible to the boy. And of all the tales that the old diver told in his whimsical fashion, there was none that so stirred Nebby's feelings as the one about the Sea-Horses.

At first it had been but a scrappy and a fragmentary yarn, suggested as like as not, by the old ballade which Zacchy so often hummed, half-unconsciously. But Nebby's constant questionings had provided so many suggestions for fresh additions, that at last it took nearly the whole of a long evening for the Tale of the Sea-Horses to be told properly, from where the first Horse was seen by Zacchy, eatin' sea-grass as nat'rel as ye like, to where Zacchy had seen li'l Martha Tullet's b'y ridin' one like a reel cow-puncher; and from that tremendous effort of imagination, the Horse Yarn had speedily grown to include every child that wended the Long Road out of the village.

"Shall I go ridin' them Sea-Horses, Granfer, when I dies?" Nebby had asked, earnestly.

"Aye," Granfer Zacchy had replied, absently, puffing at his corn-cob. "Aye, like's not, Nebby. Like as not."

"Mebbe I'll die middlin' soon, Granfer?" Nebby had suggested, longingly. "There's plenty li'l boys dies 'fore they gets growed up."

"Husht! b'y! Husht!" Granfer had said, wakening suddenly to what the child was saying.

Later, when Nebby had many times betrayed his exceeding high requirement of death, that he might ride the Sea-Horses all round his Granfer at work on the sea-bottom, old Zacchy had suddenly evolved a less drastic solution of the difficulty.

"I'll ketch ye one, Nebby, sure," he said, "an' ye kin ride it round the kitchen."

The suggestion pleased Nebby enormously, and practically nullified his impatience regarding the date of his death, which was to give him the freedom of the sea and all the Sea-Horses therein.

For a long month, old Zacchy was met each evening by a small and earnest boy, desirous of learning whether he had "catched one" that day, or not. Meanwhile, Zacchy had been dealing honestly with that four-foot by ten-inch piece of yellow pine, already described. He had carved out his notion of what might be supposed to constitute a veritable Sea-Horse, aided in his invention by Nebby's illuminating questions as to whether Sea-Horses had tails like a real horse or like real fishes; did they wear horse-shoes; did they bite?

These were three points upon which Nebby's curiosity was definite; and the results were definite enough in the finished work; for Granfer supplied the peculiar creature with "reel" bone teeth and a workable jaw; two squat, but prodigious legs, near what he termed the "bows"; whilst to the "starn" he affixed the bonito-tail which has already had mention, setting it the way Dame Nature sets it on the bonito, that is, "thwart-ships," so that its two flukes touched the ground when the go-horse was in position, and thus steadied it admirably with this hint taken direct from the workmanship of the Great Carpenter.

There came a day when the horse was finished and the last coat of paint had dried smooth and hard. That evening, when Nebby came running to meet Zacchy, he was aware of his Grandfather's voice in the dusk, shouting:—"Whoa, Mare! Whoa, Mare!" followed immediately by the cracking of a whip.

Nebby shrilled out a call, and raced on, mad with excitement, towards the noise. He knew instantly that at last Granfer had managed to catch one of the wily Sea-Horses. Presumably the creature was somewhat intractable; for when Nebby arrived, he found the burly form of Granfer straining back tremendously upon stout reins, which Nebby saw vaguely in the dusk were attached to a squat, black monster:—

"Whoa, Mare!" roared Granfer, and lashed the air furiously with his whip. Nebby shrieked delight, and ran round and round, whilst Granfer struggled with the animal.

"Hi! Hi! Hi!" shouted Nebby, dancing from foot to foot. "Ye've catched 'm, Granfer! Ye've catched 'm, Granfer!"

"Aye," said Granfer, whose struggles with the creature must have been prodigious; for he appeared to pant. "She'll go quiet now, b'y. Take a holt!" And he handed the reins and the whip over to the excited, but half-fearful Nebby. "Put y'r hand on 'er, Neb," said old Zacchy. " That'll quiet 'er."

Nebby did so, a little nervously, and drew away in a moment.

"She's all wet 's wet!" he cried out.

"Aye," said Granfer, striving to hide the delight in his voice. "She'm straight up from the water, b'y."

This was quite true; it was the final artistic effort of Granfer's imagination; he had dipped the horse overside, just before leaving the diving barge. He took his towel from his pocket, and wiped the horse down, hissing as he did so.

"Now, b'y," he said, "welt 'er good, an' make her take ye home."

Nebby straddled the go-horse, made an ineffectual effort to crack the whip, shouted:—"Gee-up! Gee-up!" And was off—two small, lean bare legs twinkling away into the darkness at a tremendous rate, accompanied by shrill and recurrent "Gee-ups!"

Granfer Zacchy stood in the dusk, laughing happily, and pulled out his pipe. He filled it slowly, and as he applied the light, he heard the galloping of the horse, returning. Nebby dashed up, and circled his Granfer in splendid fashion, singing in a rather breathless voice:—

"An' we's under the sea, b'ys.
Where the Wild Horses go,
Horses wiv tails
As big as ole whales
All jiggin' around in a row,
An' when you ses Whoa!
Them debbils does go!"
And away he went again at the gallop.

This had happened a week earlier; and now we have Nebby questioning Granfer Zacchy as to whether the Sea-Horse is really alive or dead.

"Should think they has Sea-Horses 'n heaven, Granfer?" said Nebby, thoughtfully, as he once more straddled the go-horse.

"Sure," said Granfer Zacchy.

"Is Martha Tullet's li'l b'y gone to heaven?" asked Nebby.

"Sure," said Granfer again, as he sucked at his pipe.

Nebby was silent a good while, thinking. It was obvious that he confused heaven with the Domain of the Sea-Horses; for had not Granfer himself seen Martha Tullet's li'l b'y riding one of the Sea-Horses. Nebby had told Mrs. Tullet about it; but she had only thrown her apron over her head, and cried, until at last Nebby had stolen away, feeling rather dumpy.

"Has you ever seed any angels wiv wings on the Sea-Horses, Granfer?" Nebby asked, presently; determined to have further information with which to assure his ideas.

"Aye," said Granfer Zacchy. "Shoals of 'em. Shoals of 'em, b'y."

Nebby was greatly pleased.

"Could they ride some, Granfer?" he questioned.

"Sure," said old Zacchy, reaching for his pouch.

"As good 's me?" asked Nebby, anxiously.

"Middlin' near. Middlin' near, b'y," said Granfer Zacchy. "Why, Neb," he continued, waking up with a sudden relish to the full possibilities of the question, "thar's some of them lady ayngels as c'ud do back-somersaults an' never take a throw, b'y."

It is to be feared that Granfer Zacchy's conception of a lady angel had been formed during odd visits to the circus. But Nebby was duly impressed, and bumped his head badly the same day, trying to achieve the rudiments of a back-somersault.

CHAPTER II

Some evenings later, Nebby came running to meet old Zacchy, with an eager question:—

"Has you seed Jane Melly's li'l gel ridin' the Horses, Granfer?" he asked, earnestly.

"Aye," said Granfer. Then, realising suddenly what the question portended:—

"What's wrong wiv Mrs. Melly's wee gel?" he queried.

"Dead," said Nebby, calmly. "Mrs. Kay ses it's the fever come to the village again, Granfer."

Nebby's voice was cheerful; for the fever had visited the village some months before, and Granfer Zacchy had taken Nebby to live on the barge, away from danger of infection. Nebby had enjoyed it all enormously, and had often prayed God since to send another fever, with its attendant possibilities of life again aboard the diving-barge.

"Shall we live in the barge, Granfer?" he asked, as he swung along with the old man.

"Maybe! Maybe!" said old Zacchy, absently, in a somewhat troubled voice.

Granfer left Nebby in the kitchen, and went on up the village to make inquiries; the result was that he packed Nebby's clothes and toys into a well-washed sugar-bag, and the next day took the boy down to the barge, to live. But whereas Granfer walked, carrying the sack of gear, Nebby rode all the way, most of it at an amazing gallop. He even rode daringly down the narrow, railless gang-plank. It is true that Granfer Zacchy took care to keep close behind, in as unobtrusive a fashion as possible; but of this, or the need of such watchfulness, Nebby was most satisfactorily ignorant. He was welcomed in the heartiest fashion by Ned, the pump-man, and Binny, who attended to the air-pipe and life-line when Granfer Zacchy was down below.

CHAPTER III

Life aboard the diving-barge was a very happy time for Nebby. It was a happy time also for Granfer Zacchy and his two men; for the child, playing constantly in their midst, brought back to them an adumbration of their youth. There was only one point upon which there arose any trouble, and that was Nebby's forgetfulness, in riding across the air-tube, when he was exercising his Sea-Horse.

Ned, the pump-man, had spoken very emphatically to Nebby on this point, and Nebby had promised to remember; but, as usual, soon forgot. They had taken the barge outside the bar, and anchored her over the buoy that marked Granfer's submarine operations. The day was gloriously fine, and so long as the weather remained fixed, they meant to keep the barge out there, merely sending the little punt ashore for provisions.

To Nebby, it was all just splendid! When he was not riding his Sea-Horse, he was talking to the men, or waiting at the gangway eagerly for Granfer's great copper head-piece to come up out of the water, as the air-tube and life-line were slowly drawn aboard. Or else his shrill young voice was sure to be heard, as he leant over the rail and peered into the depths below, singing:—

"An' we's under the sea, b'ys.
Where the Wild Horses go,
Horses wiv tails
As big as ole whales
All jiggin' around in a row.
An' when you ses Whoa!
Them debbils does go!"
Possibly, he considered it as some kind of charm with which to call the Sea-Horses up to view.

Each time the boat went ashore, it brought sad news, that first this and then that one had gone the Long Road; but it was chiefly the children that interested Nebby. Each time that his Granfer came up out of the depths, Nebby would dance round him impatiently, until the big helmet was unscrewed; then would come his inevitable, eager question:—Had Granfer seen Carry Andrew's li'l gel; or had Granfer seen Marty's li'l b'y riding the Sea-Horses? And so on.

"Sure," Granfer would reply; though, several times, it was his first intimation that the child mentioned had died; the news having reached the barge through some passing boat, whilst he was on the sea-bottom.

"Look you, Nebby!" shouted Ned, the pump-man, angrily. "I'll shore break that horse of yours up for kindlin' next time you goes steppin' on the air-pipe."

It was all too true; Nebby had forgotten, and done it again; but whereas, generally, he took Ned's remonstrances in good part, and promised better things, he stood now, looking with angry defiance at the man. The suggestion that his Sea-Horse was made of wood, bred in him a tempest of bitterness. Never for one moment to himself had he allowed so horrible a thought to enter his own head; not even when, in a desperate charge, he had knocked a chip off the nose of the Sea-Horse, and betrayed the merciless wood below. He had simply refused to look particularly at the place; his fresh, child's imagination allowing him presently to grow assured again that all was well; that he truly rode a "gen-u-ine" Sea-Horse. In his earnestness of determined make-believe, he had even avoided showing Granfer Zacchy the place, and asking him to mend it, much as he wanted it mended. Granfer always mended his toys for him; but this could not be mended. It was a real Sea-Horse; not a toy. Nebby resolutely averted his thoughts from the possibility of any other Belief; though it is likely that such mental processes were more subconscious than conscious.

And now, Ned had said the deadly thing, practically in so many naked words. Nebby trembled with anger and a furious mortification of his pride of Sea-Horse-Ownership. He looked round swiftly for the surest way to avenge the brutish insult, and saw the air-pipe; the thing around which the bother had been made. Yes, that would make Ned angry! Nebby turned his strange steed, and charged straight away back at the pipe. There, with an angry and malicious deliberateness, he halted, and made the big front hoofs of his extraordinary monster, stamp upon the air-pipe.

"You young devil!" roared Ned, scarcely able to believe the thing he saw. "You young devil!"

Nebby continued to stamp the big hoofs upon the pipe, glaring with fierce, defiant, blue eyes at Ned. Whereupon, Ned's patience arose and departed, and Ned himself arrived bodily in haste and with considerable vigour. He gave one kick, and the Sea-Horse went flying across the deck, and crashed into the low bulwarks. Nebby screamed; but it was far more a scream of tremendous anger, than of fear.

"I'll heave the blamed thing over the side!" said Ned, and ran to complete his dreadful sacrilege. The following instant, something clasped his right leg, and small, distinctly sharp teeth bit his bare shin, below the up-rolled trousers. Ned yelled, and sat rapidly and luridly upon the deck, in a fashion calculated to shock his system, in every sense of the word.

Nebby had loosed from him, the instant his bite had taken effect; and now he was nursing and examining the black monster of his dreams and waking moments. He knelt there, near the bulwarks, looking with burning eyes of anger and enormous distress at the effects of Ned's great kick; for Ned wore his bluchers on his bare feet. Ned himself still endured a sitting conjunction with the deck; he had not yet finished expressing himself; not that Nebby was in the least interested ... anger and distress had built a wall of fierce indifference about his heart. He desired chiefly Ned's death.

If Ned, himself, had been less noisy, he would have heard Binny even earlier than he did; for that sane man had jumped to the air-pump, luckily for Granfer Zacchy, and was now, as he worked, emptying his soul of most of its contents upon the derelict Ned. As it was, Ned's memory and ears did duty together, and he remembered that he had committed the last crime in the Pumpman's Calendar ... he had left the pump, whilst his diver was still below water. Powder ignited in quite a considerable quantity beneath him, could scarcely have moved Ned more speedily. He gave out one yell, and leaped for the pump; at the same instant he discovered that Binny was there, and his gasp of relief was as vehement as prayer. He remembered his leg, and concluded his journey to the pump, with a limp. Here, with one hand he pumped, whilst with the other, he investigated Nebby's teeth-marks. He found that the skin was barely broken; but it was his temper that most needed mending; and, of course, it had been very naughty of Nebby to attempt such a familiarity.

Binny was drawing in the life-line and air-pipe; for Granfer Zacchy was ascending the long rope-ladder, that led up from the sea-bottom, to learn what had caused the unprecedented interruption of his air-supply.

It was a very angry Granfer who, presently, having heard a fair representation of the facts, applied a wet but horny hand to Nebby's anatomy, in a vigorous and decided manner. Yet Nebby neither cried nor spoke; he merely clung on tightly to the Sea-Horse; and Granfer whacked on. At last Granfer grew surprised at the continued absence of remonstrance on Nebby's part, and turned that young man the other end about, to discover the wherefore of so determined a silence.

Nebby's face was very white, and tears seemed perilously near; yet even the nearness of these, did not in any way detract from the expression of unutterable defiance that looked out at Granfer and all the world, from his face. Granfer regarded him for a few moments with earnest attention and doubt, and decided to cease whipping that atom of blue-eyed stubbornness. He looked at the Sea-Horse that Nebby clutched so tightly, in his silence, and perceived the way to make Nebby climb down ... Nebby must go and beg Ned's pardon for trying to eat him (Granfer smothered a chuckle), or else the Sea-Horse would be taken away.

Nebby's face, however, showed no change, unless it was that the blue eyes shone with a fiercer defiance, which dried out of them that suspicion of tears. Granfer pondered over him, and had a fresh idea. He would take the Sea-Horse back again to the bottom of the sea; and it would then come alive once more and swim away, and Nebby would never see it again, if Nebby did not go at once to Ned and beg Ned's pardon, that very minute. Granfer was prodigiously stern.

There came, perhaps, the tiniest flash of fright into the blue eyes; but it was blurred with unbelief; and, anyway, it had no power at that stage of Nebby's temper to budge him from his throne of enormous anger. He decided, with that fierce courage of the burner of boats, that if Granfer did truly do such a dreadful thing, he (Nebby) would "kneel down proper" and pray God to kill Ned. An added relish of vengeance came to his child's mind.... He would kneel down in front of Ned; he would pray to God "out loud." Ned should thus learn beforehand that he was doomed.

In that moment of inspired Intention, Nebby became trebly fixed into his Aura of Implacable Anger. He voiced his added grimness of heart in the most tremendous words possible:

"It's wood!" said Nebby, glaring at Granfer, in a kind of fierce, sick, horrible triumph. "It carn't come back alive again!"

Then he burst into tears, at this dreadful act of disillusionment, and wrenching himself free from Granfer's gently-detaining hand, he dashed away aft, and down the scuttle into the cuddy, where for an hour he hid himself under a bunk, and refused, in dreary silence, any suggestion of dinner.

After dinner, however, he emerged, tear-stained but unbroken. He had brought the Sea-Horse below with him; and now, as the three men watched him, unobtrusively, from their seats around the little cuddy-table, it was plain to them that Nebby had some definite object in view, which he was attempting to mask under an attitude of superb but ineffectual casualness.

"B'y," said Granfer Zacchy, in a very stern voice, "come you an' beg Ned's pard'n, or I'll shore take th' Sea-Horse down wiv me, an' you'll never see 'm no more, an' I'll never ketch ye another, Nebby."

Nebby's reply was an attempted dash for the scuttle-ladder; but Granfer reached out a long arm, that might have been described as possessing the radius of the small cuddy. As a result, Nebby was put with his face in a corner, whilst Granfer Zacchy laid the Sea-Horse across his knees, and stroked it meditatively, as he smoked a restful after-dinner pipe.

Presently, he knocked out his pipe, and, reaching round, brought Nebby to stand at his knee.

"Nebby, b'y," he said, in his grave, kindly fashion, "go you an' beg Ned's pard'n, an' ye shall hev this right back to play wiv."

But Nebby had not been given time yet to ease himself clear of the cloud of his indignation; and even as he stood there by Granfer, he could see the great bruise in the paint, where Ned's blucher had taken effect; and the broken fluke of the tail, that had been smashed when the poor Sea-Horse brought up so violently against the low bulwarks of the barge.

"Ned's a wicked pig man!" said Nebby, with a fresh intensity of anger against the pump-hand.

"Hush, b'y!" said Granfer, with real sternness. "Ye've had fair chance to come round, an' ye've not took it, an' now I'll read ye a lesson as ye'll shore mind!"

He stood up, and put the Sea-Horse under his arm; then, with one hand on Nebby's shoulder, he went to the ladder, and so in a minute they were all on the deck of the barge. Presently, Granfer was once more transformed from a genial and burly giant, into an india rubber-covered and dome-ended monster. Then, with a slowness and solemnity befitting so terrible an execution of justice, Granfer made a fathom, or so, of spunyard fast about the Sea-Horse's neck, whilst Nebby looked on, white-faced.

When this was accomplished, Granfer stood up and marched with ponderous steps to the side, the Sea-Horse under his arm. He began to go slowly down the wooden rungs of the rope-ladder, and presently there were only his shoulders and copper headpiece visible. Nebby stared down in an anguish; he could see the Sea-Horse vaguely. It seemed to waggle in the crook of Granfer's arm. It was surely about to swim away. Then Granfer's shoulders, and finally his great copper head disappeared from sight, and there was soon only the slight working of the ladder, and the paying out of the air-pipe and life-line, to tell that any one was down there in all that greyness of the water-dusk; for Granfer had often explained to Nebby that it was always "evenin' at th' sea-bottom."

Nebby sobbed once or twice, in a dry, horrid way, in his throat; then, for quite half an hour, he lay flat on his stomach in the gangway, silent and watchful, staring down into the water. Several times he felt quite sure he saw something swimming with a queer, waggling movement, a little under the water; and presently he started to sing in a low voice:—

"An' we's under the sea, b'ys,
Where the Wild Horses go,

Horses wiv tails
As big as ole whales
All jiggin' around in a row,
An' when you ses Whoa!
Them debbils does go!"
But it seemed to have no power to charm the Sea-Horse up to the surface; and he fell silent, after singing it through, maybe a dozen times. He was waiting for Granfer. He had a vague hope, which grew, that Granfer had meant to tie it up with the spunyard, so that it could not swim away; and perhaps Granfer would bring it up with him when he came. Nebby felt that he would really beg Ned's pardon, if only Granfer brought the Sea-Horse up with him again.

A little later, there came the signal that Granfer was about to ascend, and Nebby literally trembled with excitement, as the life-line and air-pipe came in slowly, hand over hand. He saw the big dome of the helmet come vaguely into view, with the line of the air-pipe leading down at the usual "funny" angle, right into the top of the dome (it was an old type of helmet). Then the helmet broke the water, and Nebby could not see anything, because the "rimples" on the water stopped him seeing. Granfer's big shoulders came into view, and then sufficient of him for Nebby to see that the Sea-Horse was truly not with him. Nebby whitened. Granfer had really let the Sea-Horse go. As a matter of fact, Granfer Zacchy had tethered the Sea-Horse to some tough marine weed-rootlets at the sea-bottom, so as to prevent it floating traitorously to the surface; but to Nebby it was plain only that the Sea-Horse had truly "come alive" and swum away.

Granfer stepped on to the deck, and Binny eased off the great helmet, whilst Ned ceased his last, slow revolution of the pump-handle.

It was at this moment that Nebby faced round on Ned, with a white, set, little face, in which his blue eyes literally burned. Ned was surely doomed in that instant! And then, even in the Moment of his Intention, Nebby heard Granfer say to Binny:

"Aye, I moored it wiv the spunyarn safe enough."

Nebby's anger lost its deadliness abruptly, under the sudden sweet chemistry of hope. He oscillated an instant between a new, vague thought, and his swiftly-lessening requirement of vengeance. The new, vague thought became less vague, and he swayed the more toward it; and so, in a moment, had rid himself of his Dignity, and run across to Granfer Zacchy:

"Has it comed alive, Granfer?" he asked, breathlessly, with the infinite eagerness and expectancy of a child.

"Aye!" said Granfer Zacchy, with apparent sternness. "Ye've sure lost it now, b'y. 'Tis swimmin' an' swimmin' roun' an' roun' all the time."

Nebby's eyes shone with sudden splendour, as the New Idea took now a most definite form in his young brain.

Granfer, looking at him with eyes of tremendous sternness, was quite non-plussed at the harmless effect of his expectedly annihilative news concerning the final and obvious lostness of the Sea-Horse. Yet, Nebby said never a word to give Granfer an inkling of the stupendous plan that was settling fast in his daring child's-mind. He opened his mouth once or twice upon a further question; then relapsed into the safety of silence again, as though instinctively realising that he might ask something that would make Granfer suspicious.

Presently, Nebby had stolen away once more to the gangway, and there, lying on his stomach, he began again to look down into the sea. His anger now was almost entirely submerged in the great, glorious New Idea, that filled him with such tremendous exaltation that he could scarcely lie quiet, or cease from singing aloud at the top of his voice.

A few moments earlier, he had meant to "kneel down proper" and pray God "out loud" for Ned to be killed quickly and painfully; but now all was changed. Though, in an indifferent sort of way, in his healthily-savage child's-mind, he did not forgive Ned.... Ned's sin had, of course, been unforgivable, presumably "for ever and ever and ever"—Certainly until to-morrow! Meanwhile, Nebby never so much as thought of him, except it might be as one whose bewilderment should presently be the last lustre of the glory of his (Nebby's) proposed achievement. Not that Nebby thought it all out like this into separate ideas; but it was all there in that young and surging head ... in what I might term a Chaos of Determination, buoying up (as it might be a lonesome craft) one clear, vigorous Idea.

Granfer Zacchy went down twice more before evening, and each time that he returned, Nebby questioned him earnestly as to the doings of the Sea-Horse; and each time, Granfer told the same tale (in accents of would-be sternness) that the Sea-Horse was "jest swimmin' roun' an' roun'; an' maybe ye wish now ye'd begged Ned's pardon, when ye was bid!"

But, in his heart, Granfer decided that the Sea-Horse might be safely re-caught on the morrow.

CHAPTER V

That night, when the three men were asleep in the little cuddy, Nebby's small figure slipped noiselessly out of the bunk that lay below Granfer Zacchy's. He flitted silently to the ladder, and stole up into the warm night, his shirt (a quaint cut-down of Granfer's) softly flicking his lean, bare legs, as he moved through the darkness, along the barge's decks.

Nebby came to a stop where Granfer's diving-suit was hung up carefully on the "frame"; but this was not what Nebby wanted. He stooped to the bottom of the "frame," and pulled up the small hatch of a square locker, where reposed the big, domed, copper helmet, glimmering dully in the vague starlight.

Nebby reached into the locker, and lugged the helmet out bodily, hauling with both hands upon the air-pipe. He carried it across clumsily to the gangway, the air-pipe unreeling off the winch, with each step that he took.

He found the helmet too clumsy and rotund to lift easily on to his own curly head, and so, after an attempt or two, evolved the method of turning the helmet upon its side, and then kneeling down and thrusting his head into it; after which, with a prodigious effort, he rose victoriously to his knees, and began to fumble himself backwards over the edge of the gangway, on to the wooden rungs of Granfer's rope-ladder, which had not been hauled up. He managed a firm foot-hold with his left foot, and then with his right; and so began to descend, slowly and painfully, the great helmet rocking clumsily on his small shoulders.

His right foot touched the water at the fourth rung, and he paused, bringing the other foot down beside the first. The water was pleasantly warm, and Nebby hesitated only a very little while, ere he ventured the next step. Then he stopped again, and tried to look down into the water. The action swayed the big helmet backwards, so that—inside of it—Nebby's delightfully impudent little nose received a bang that made his determined blue eyes water. He loosed his left hand from the ladder, holding on with his right, and tried to push the clumsy helmet forward again into place.

He was, as you will understand, up to his knees in the water, and the rung, on which he perched, was slippery with that peculiar slipperiness, that wood and water together know so well how to breed. One of Nebby's bare feet slipped, and immediately the other. The great helmet gave a prodigious wobble, and completed the danger; for the sudden strain wrenched his grip from the rope between the rungs. There was a muffled little cry inside the helmet, and Nebby swung a small, desperate hand through the darkness towards the ladder; but it was too late; he was falling. There was a splash; not a very big splash for so big a boy's-heart and courage; and no one heard it, or the little bubbling squeak that came out of the depths of the big copper helmet. And then, in a moment, there was only the vaguely disturbed surface of the water, and the air-pipe was running out smoothly and swiftly off the drum.

CHAPTER VI

It was in the strange, early-morning light, when the lemon and gold-of-light of dawn was in the grey East, that Granfer discovered the thing which had happened. With the wakefulness that is so often an asset of healthy age, he had turned-out in the early hours, to fill his pipe, and had discovered that Nebby's bunk was empty.

He went swiftly up the small ladder. On the deck, the out-trailed air-pipe whispered its tale in silence, and Granfer rushed to it, shouting in a dreadful voice for Binny and Ned, who came bounding up, sleepily, in their heavy flannel drawers.

They hauled in the air-pipe, swiftly but carefully; but when the great dome of the helmet came up to them, there was no Nebby; only, tangled from the thread of one of the old-fashioned thumb-screws, they found several golden, curly strands of Nebby's hair.

Granfer, his great muscular hands trembling, began to get into his rubber suit, the two men helping him, wordless. Within a hundred and fifty seconds, he was dwindling away down under the quiet sea that spread, all grey and lemon-hued and utterly calm, in the dawn. Ned was turning the pump-handle, and wiping his eyes undisguisedly from time to time with the back of one hairy, disengaged hand. Binny, who was of a sterner type, though no less warm-hearted, was grimly silent, giving his whole attention to the air-pipe and the life-line; his hand delicate upon the line, awaiting the signal. He could tell from the feel and the coming-up and going-out of the pipe and the line, that Granfer Zacchy was casting round and round, in ever largening circles upon the sea-bottom.

All that day, Granfer quartered the sea-bottom; staying down so long each time, that at last Binny and Ned were forced to remonstrate. But the old man turned on them, and snarled in a kind of speechless anger and agony that forced them to be silent and let him go his own gait.

For three days, Granfer continued his search, the sea remaining calm; but found nothing. On the fourth day, Granfer Zacchy was forced to take the barge in over the bar; for the wind breezed up hard out of the North, and blew for a dreary and savage fortnight, each day of which found Granfer, with Binny and Ned, searching the shore for the "giving up" of the sea. But the sea had one of its secret moods, and gave up nothing.

At the end of the fortnight of heavy weather, it fell calm, and they took the barge out again, to start once more their daily work. There was little use now in searching further for the boy. The barge was moored again over the old spot, and Granfer descended; and the first thing he saw in the grey half-light of the water, was the Sea-Horse, still moored securely by the length of spunyarn to the rootlets of heavy weed at the sea-bottom.

The sight of the creature, gave old Zacchy a dreadful feeling; it was, at once, so familiar of Nebby, as to give him the sensation and unreasoning impression that the "b'y" must be surely close at hand; and yet, at the same time, the grotesque, inanimate creature was the visible incarnation of the Dire Cause of the unspeakable loneliness and desolation that now possessed his old heart so utterly. He glared at it, through the thick glass of his helmet, and half raised his axe to strike at it. Then, with a sudden revulsion, he reached out, and pulled the silent go-horse to him, and hugged it madly, as if, indeed, it were the boy himself.

Presently, old Granfer Zacchy grew calmer, and turned to his work; yet a hundred times, he would find himself staring round in the watery twilight towards it—staring eagerly and unreasoningly, and actually listening, inside his helmet, for sounds that the eternal silence of the sea might never bring through its dumb waters, that are Barriers of Silence about the lonesome diver in the strange underworld of the waters. And then, realising freshly that there was no longer One who might make the so-craved-for sounds, Granfer would turn again, grey-souled and lonely, to his work. Yet, in a while, he would be staring and listening once more.

In the course of days, old Zacchy grew calmer and more resigned; yet he kept the motionless Sea-Horse tethered, in the quiet twilight of the water, to the weed-rootlets at the sea-bottom. And more and more, he grew to staring round at it; and less and less did it seem a futile or an unreasonable thing to do.

In weeks, the habit grew to such an extent, that he had ceased to be aware of it. He prolonged his hours under water, out of all reason, so far as his health was concerned; and turned queerly "dour" when Ned and Binny remonstrated with him, warning him not to stay down so long, or he would certainly have to pay the usual penalty.

Only once did Granfer say a word in explanation, and then it was obviously an unintentional remark, jerked out of him by the intensity of his feelings:—

"Like as I feel 'm nigh me, w'en I'm below," he had muttered, in a half coherent fashion. And the two men understood; for it was just what they had vaguely supposed. They had no reply to make; and the matter dropped.

Generally now, on descending each morning, Granfer would stop near the Sea-Horse, and "look it over." Once, he discovered that the bonito-tail had come unglued; but this he remedied neatly, by lashing it firmly into position with a length of roping-twine. Sometimes, he would pat the head of the horse, with one great hand, and mutter a quite unconscious:— "Whoa, mare!" as it bobbed silently under his touch. Occasionally, as he swayed heavily past it, in his clumsy dress, the slight swirl of the water in his "wake" would make the Horse slue round uncannily towards him; and thereafter, it would swing and oscillate for a brief time, slowly back into quietness; the while that Granfer would stand and watch it, unconsciously straining his ears, in that place of no-sound.

Two months passed in this way, and Granfer was vaguely aware that his health was failing; but the knowledge brought no fear to him; only the beginnings of an indefinite contentment—a feeling that maybe he would be "soon seein' Nebby." Yet the thought was never definitely conscious; nor ever, of course, in any form, phrased. Yet it had its effect, in the vague contentment which I have hinted at, which brought a new sense of ease round Granfer's heart; so that, one day, as he worked, he found himself crooning unconsciously the old Ballade of the Sea Horses.

He stopped on the instant, all an ache with memory; then turned and peered towards the Sea-Horse, which loomed, a vague shadow, silent in the still water. It had seemed to him, in that moment, that he had heard a subtile echo of his crooned song, in the quiet deeps around him. Yet, he saw nothing, and presently assured himself that he heard nothing; and so came round again upon his work.

A number of times in the early part of that day, old Granfer caught himself crooning the old Ballade, and each time he shut his lips fiercely on the sound, because of the ache of memory that the old song bred in him; but, presently, all was forgotten in an intense listening; for, abruptly, old Zacchy was sure that he heard the song, coming from somewhere out of the eternal twilight of the waters. He slued himself round, trembling, and stared towards the Sea-Horse; but there was nothing new to be seen, neither was he any more sure that he had ever heard anything.

Several times this happened, and on each occasion Granfer would heave himself round ponderously in the water, and listen with an intensity that had in it, presently, something of desperateness.

In the late afternoon of that day, Granfer again heard something; but refused now to credit his hearing, and continued grimly at work. And then, suddenly, there was no longer any room for doubt ... a shrill, sweet child's voice was singing, somewhere among the grey twilights far to his back. He heard it with astounding clearness, helmet and surrounding water notwithstanding. It was a sound, indeed, that he would have heard through all the Mountains of Eternity. He stared round, shaking violently.

The sound appeared to come from the greyness that dwelt away beyond a little wood of submarine growths, that trailed up their roots, so hushed and noiseless, out of a near-by vale in the sea-bottom.

As Granfer stared, everything about him darkened into a wonderful and rather dreadful Blackness. This passed, and he was able to see again; but somehow, as it might be said, newly. The shrill, sweet, childish singing had ceased; but there was something beside the Sea-Horse ... a little, agile figure, that caused the Sea-Horse to bob and bound at its moorings. And, suddenly, the little figure was astride the Sea-Horse, and the Horse was free, and two twinkling legs urged it across the sea-bottom towards Granfer.

Granfer thought that he stood up, and ran to meet the boy; but Nebby dodged him, the Sea-Horse curvetting magnificently; and immediately Nebby began to gallop round and round Granfer, singing:—

"An' we's under the sea, b'ys,
Where the Wild Horses go,
Horses wiv tails
As big as ole whales
All jiggin' around in a row,
An' when you ses Whoa!
Them debbils does go!"
The voice of the blue-eyed mite was ineffably gleeful; and, abruptly, tremendous youth invaded Granfer, and a glee beyond all understanding.

CHAPTER VII

On the deck of the barge, Ned and Binny were in great doubt and trouble. The weather had been growing heavy and threatening, during all the late afternoon; and now it was culminating in a tremendous, black squall, which was coming swiftly down upon them.

Time after time, Binny had attempted to signal Granfer Zacchy to come up; but Granfer had taken a turn with his life-line round a hump of rock that protruded out of the sea-bottom; so that Binny was powerless to do aught; for there was no second set of diving gear aboard.

All that the two men could do, was to wait, in deep anxiety, keeping the pump going steadily, and standing-by for the signal that was never to come; for by that time, old Granfer Zacchy was sitting very quiet and huddled against the rock, round which he had hitched his line to prevent Binny from signalling him, as Binny had become prone to do, when Granfer stayed below, out of all reason and wisdom.

And all the time, Ned kept the un-needed pump going, and far down in the grey depth, the air came out in a continual series of bubbles, around the big copper helmet. But Granfer was breathing an air of celestial sweetness, all unwotting and un-needing of the air that Ned laboured faithfully to send to him.

The squall came down in a fierce haze of rain and foam, and the ungainly old craft swung round, jibbing heavily at her kedge-rope, which gave out a little twanging sound, that was lost in the roar of the wind. The unheard twanging of the rope, ended suddenly in a dull thud, as it parted; and the bluff old barge fell off, broadside on to the weight of the squall. She drifted with astonishing rapidity, and the life-line and the air-pipe flew out, with a buzz of the unwinding drums, and parted, with two differently toned reports, that were plain in an instant's lull in the roaring of the squall.

Binny had run forrard to the bows, to try to get over another kedge; but now he came racing aft again, shouting. Ned still pumped on mechanically, with a look of dull, stunned horror in his eyes; the pump driving a useless jet of air through the broken remnant of the air-pipe. Already, the barge was a quarter of a mile to leeward of the diving-ground, and the men could do no more than hoist the foresail, and try to head her in safely over the bar, which was now right under their lee.

Down in the sea, old Granfer Zacchy had altered his position; the jerk upon the air-pipe had done that. But Granfer was well enough content; not only for the moment; but for Eternity; for as Nebby rode so gleefully round and round him, there had come a change in all things; there were strange and subtle lights in all the grey twilights of the deep, that seemed to lead away and away into stupendous and infinitely beautiful distances.

"Is you listenin', Granfer?" Old Zacchy heard Nebby say; and discovered suddenly that Nebby was insisting that he should race him across the strangely glorified twilights, that bounded them now eternally.

"Sure, b'y," said Granfer Zacchy, undismayed; and Nebby wheeled his charger.

"Gee-Up!" shouted Nebby, excitedly, and his small legs began to twinkle ahead in magnificent fashion; with Granfer running a cheerful and deliberate second.

And so passed Granfer Zacchy and Nebby into the Land where little boys may ride Sea-Horses for ever, and where Parting becomes one of the Lost Sorrows.

And Nebby led the way at a splendid gallop; maybe, for all that I have any right to know, to the very Throne of the Almighty, singing, shrill and sweet:—

"An' we's under the sea, b'ys,
Where the Wild Horses go,
Horses wiv tails
As big as ole whales
All jiggin' around in a row,
An' when you ses Whoa!
Them debbils does go!"

And overhead (was it only a dozen fathoms!) there rushed the white-maned horses of the sea, mad with the glory of the storm, and tossing ruthless from crest to crest, a wooden go-horse, from which trailed a length of broken spunyarn.

THE DERELICT

"It's the Material," said the old ship's doctor.... "The Material, plus the Conditions; and, maybe," he added slowly, "a third factor—yes, a third factor; but there, there...." He broke off his half-meditative sentence, and began to charge his pipe.

"Go on, Doctor," we said, encouragingly, and with more than a little expectancy. We were in the smoke-room of the Sand-a-lea, running across the North Atlantic; and the Doctor was a character. He concluded the charging of his pipe, and lit it; then settled himself, and began to express himself more fully:—

"The Material," he said, with conviction, "is inevitably the medium of expression of the Life-Force— the fulcrum, as it were; lacking which, it is unable to exert itself, or, indeed, to express itself in any form or fashion that would be intelligible or evident to us.

"So potent is the share of the Material in the production of that thing which we name Life, and so eager the Life-Force to express itself, that I am convinced it would, if given the right Conditions, make itself manifest even through so hopeless-seeming a medium as a simple block of sawn wood; for I tell you, gentlemen, the Life-Force is both as fiercely urgent and as indiscriminate as Fire—the Destructor; yet which some are now growing to consider the very essence of Life rampant.... There is a quaint seeming paradox there," he concluded, nodding his old grey head.

"Yes, Doctor," I said. "In brief, your argument is that Life is a thing, state, fact, or element, call-it-what-you-like, which requires the Material through which to manifest itself, and that given the Material, plus the Conditions, the result is Life. In other words, that Life is an evolved product, manifested through Matter and bred of Conditions—eh?"

"As we understand the word," said the old Doctor. "Though, mind you, there may be a third factor. But, in my heart, I believe that it is a matter of chemistry; Conditions and a suitable medium; but given the Conditions, the Brute is so almighty that it will seize upon anything through which to manifest itself. It is a Force generated by Conditions; but nevertheless this does not bring us one iota nearer to its explanation, any more than to the explanation of Electricity or Fire. They are, all three, of the Outer Forces—Monsters of the Void. Nothing we can do will create any one of them; our power is merely to be able, by providing the Conditions, to make each one of them manifest to our physical senses. Am I clear?"

"Yes, Doctor, in a way you are," I said. "But I don't agree with you; though I think I understand you. Electricity and Fire are both what I might call natural things; but Life is an abstract something—a kind of all-permeating Wakefulness. Oh, I can't explain it; who could! But it's spiritual; not just a thing bred out of a Condition, like Fire, as you say, or Electricity. It's a horrible thought of yours. Life's a kind of spiritual mystery...."

"Easy, my boy!" said the old Doctor, laughing gently to himself; "or else I may be asking you to demonstrate the spiritual mystery of life of the limpet, or the crab, shall we say."

He grinned at me, with ineffable perverseness. "Anyway," he continued, "as I suppose you've all guessed, I've a yarn to tell you in support of my impression that Life is no more a mystery or a miracle than Fire or Electricity. But, please to remember, gentlemen, that because we've succeeded in naming and making good use of these two Forces, they're just as much mysteries, fundamentally, as ever. And, anyway, the thing I'm going to tell you, won't explain the mystery of Life; but only give you one of my pegs on which I hang my feeling that Life is, as I have said, a Force made manifest through Conditions (that is to say, natural Chemistry), and that it can take for its purpose and Need, the most incredible and unlikely Matter; for without Matter, it cannot come into existence—it cannot become manifest...."

"I don't agree with you, Doctor," I interrupted. "Your theory would destroy all belief in life after death. It would...."

"Hush, sonny," said the old man, with a quiet little smile of comprehension. "Hark to what I've to say first; and, anyway, what objection have you to material life, after death; and if you object to a material framework, I would still have you remember that I am speaking of Life, as we understand the word in this our life. Now do be a quiet lad, or I'll never be done:—

"It was when I was a young man, and that is a good many years ago, gentlemen. I had passed my examinations; but was so run down with overwork, that it was decided that I had better take a trip to sea. I was by no means well off, and very glad, in the end, to secure a nominal post as Doctor in a sailing passenger-clipper, running out to China.

"The name of the ship was the Bheotpte, and soon after I had got all my gear aboard, she cast off, and we dropped down the Thames, and next day were well away out in the Channel.

"The Captain's name was Gannington, a very decent man; though quite illiterate. The First Mate, Mr. Berlies, was a quiet, sternish, reserved man, very well-read. The Second Mate, Mr. Selvern, was, perhaps, by birth and upbringing, the most socially cultured of the three; but he lacked the stamina and indomitable pluck of the two others. He was more of a sensitive; and emotionally and even mentally, the most alert man of the three.

"On our way out, we called at Madagascar, where we landed some of our passengers; then we ran Eastward, meaning to call at North West Cape; but about a hundred degrees East, we encountered very dreadful weather, which carried away all our sails and sprung the jibboom and fore t'gallant mast.

"The storm carried us Northward for several hundred miles, and when it dropped us finally, we found ourselves in a very bad state. The ship had been strained, and had taken some three feet of water through her seams; the main topmast had been sprung, in addition to the jibboom and fore t'gallant mast; two of our boats had gone, as also one of the pigsties (with three fine pigs), this latter having been washed overboard but some half hour before the wind began to ease, which it did quickly; though a very ugly sea ran for some hours after.

"The wind left us just before dark, and when morning came, it brought splendid weather; a calm, mildly undulating sea, and a brilliant sun, with no wind. It showed us also that we were not alone; for about two miles away to the Westward, was another vessel, which Mr. Selvern, the Second Mate, pointed out to me.

"'That's a pretty rum looking packet, Doctor,' he said, and handed me his glass. I looked through it, at the other vessel, and saw what he meant; at least, I thought I did.

"'Yes, Mr. Selvern,' I said, 'she's got a pretty old-fashioned look about her.'

"He laughed at me, in his pleasant way.

"'It's easy to see you're not a sailor, Doctor,' he remarked. 'There's a dozen rum things about her. She's a derelict, and has been floating round, by the look of her, for many a score of years. Look at the shape of her counter, and the bows and cutwater. She's as old as the hills, as you might say, and ought to have gone down to Davy Jones a long time ago. Look at the growths on her, and the thickness of her standing rigging; that's all salt encrustations, I fancy, if you notice the white colour. She's been a small barque; but don't you see she's not a yard left aloft. They've all dropped out of the slings; everything rotted away; wonder the standing rigging hasn't gone too. I wish the Old Man would let us take the boat, and have a look at her; she'd be well worth it.'

"There seemed little chance, however, of this; for all hands were turned-to and kept hard at it all day long, repairing the damage to the masts and gear, and this took a long while, as you may think. Part of the time, I gave a hand, heaving on one of the deck-capstans; for the exercise was good for my liver. Old Captain Gannington approved, and I persuaded him to come along and try some of the same medicine, which he did; and we grew very chummy over the job.

"We got talking about the derelict, and he remarked how lucky we were not to have run full tilt on to her, in the darkness; for she lay right away to leeward of us, according to the way that we had been drifting in the storm. He also was of the opinion that she had a strange look about her, and that she was pretty old; but on this latter point, he plainly had far less knowledge than the Second Mate; for he was, as I have said, an illiterate man, and knew nothing of sea-craft, beyond what experience had taught him. He lacked the book-knowledge which the Second Mate had, of vessels previous to his day, which it appeared the derelict was.

"'She's an old 'un, Doctor' was the extent of his observations in this direction.

"Yet, when I mentioned to him that it would be interesting to go aboard, and give her a bit of an overhaul, he nodded his head, as if the idea had been already in his mind, and accorded with his own inclinations.

"'When the work's over, Doctor,' he said. 'Can't spare the men now, ye know. Got to get all shipshape an' ready as smart as we can. But we'll take my gig, an' go off in the Second Dog Watch. The glass is steady, an' it'll be a bit of gam for us.'

"That evening, after tea, the captain gave orders to clear the gig and get her overboard. The Second Mate was to come with us, and the Skipper gave him word to see that two or three lamps were put into the boat, as it would soon fall dark. A little later, we were pulling across the calmness of the sea, with a crew of six at the oars, and making very good speed of it.

"Now, gentlemen, I have detailed to you with great exactness, all the facts, both big and little, so that you can follow step by step each incident in this extraordinary affair; and I want you now to pay the closest attention.

"I was sitting in the stern-sheets, with the Second Mate, and the Captain, who was steering; and as we drew nearer and nearer to the stranger, I studied her with an ever growing attention, as, indeed, did Captain Gannington and the Second Mate. She was, as you know, to the Westward of us, and the sunset was making a great flame of red light to the back of her, so that she showed a little blurred and indistinct, by reason of the halation of the light, which almost defeated the eye in any attempt to see her rotting spars and standing-rigging, submerged as they were in the fiery glory of the sunset.

"It was because of this effect of the sunset, that we had come quite close, comparatively, to the derelict, before we saw that she was all surrounded by a sort of curious scum, the colour of which was difficult to decide upon, by reason of the red light that was in the atmosphere; but which afterwards we discovered to be brown. This scum spread all about the old vessel for many hundreds of yards, in a huge, irregular patch, a great stretch of which reached out to the Eastward, upon our starboard side, some score, or so, fathoms away.

"'Queer stuff,' said Captain Gannington, leaning to the side, and looking over. 'Something in the cargo as 'as gone rotten an' worked out through 'er seams.'

"'Look at her bows and stern,' said the Second Mate; 'just look at the growth on her.'

"There were, as he said, great clumpings of strange looking sea-fungi under the bows and the short counter astern. From the stump of her jib-boom and her cutwater, great beards of rime and marine-growths hung downward into the scum that held her in. Her blank starboard side was presented to us, all a dead, dirtyish white, streaked and mottled vaguely with dull masses of heavier colour.

"'There's a steam or haze rising off her,' said the Second Mate, speaking again; 'you can see it against the light. It keeps coming and going. Look!'

"I saw then what he meant—a faint haze or steam, either suspended above the old vessel, or rising from her; and Captain Gannington saw it also:—

"'Spontaneous combustion!' he exclaimed. 'We'll 'ave to watch w'en we lift the 'atches; 'nless it's some poor devil that's got aboard of 'er; but that ain't likely.'

"We were now within a couple of hundred yards of the old derelict, and had entered into the brown scum. As it poured off the lifted oars, I heard one of the men mutter to himself:—'dam treacle!' and, indeed, it was something like it. As the boat continued to forge nearer and nearer to the old ship, the scum grew thicker and thicker; so that, at last, it perceptibly slowed us.

"'Give way, lads! Put some beef to it!' sung out Captain Gannington; and thereafter there was no sound, except the panting of the men, and the faint, reiterated suck, suck, of the sullen brown scum upon the oars, as the boat was forced ahead. As we went, I was conscious of a peculiar smell in the evening air, and whilst I had no doubt that the puddling of the scum, by the oars, made it rise, I felt that in some way, it was vaguely familiar; yet I could give it no name.

"We were now very close to the old vessel, and presently she was high above us, against the dying light. The Captain called out then to:—'in with the bow oars, and stand-by with the boathook,' which was done.

"'Aboard there! Ahoy! Aboard there! Ahoy!' shouted Captain Gannington; but there came no answer, only the flat sound of his voice going lost into the open sea, each time he sung out.

"'Ahoy! Aboard there! Ahoy!' he shouted, time after time; but there was only the weary silence of the old hulk that answered us; and, somehow as he shouted, the while that I stared up half expectantly at her, a queer little sense of oppression, that amounted almost to nervousness, came upon me. It passed; but I remember how I was suddenly aware that it was growing dark. Darkness comes fairly rapidly in the tropics; though not so quickly as many fiction-writers seem to think; but it was not that the coming dusk had perceptibly deepened in that brief time, of only a few moments, but rather that my nerves had made me suddenly a little hyper-sensitive. I mention my state particularly; for I am not a nervy man, normally; and my abrupt touch of nerves is significant, in the light of what happened.

"'There's no one aboard there!' said Captain Gannington. 'Give way, men!' For the boat's crew had instinctively rested on their oars, as the Captain hailed the old craft. The men gave way again; and then the Second Mate called out excitedly:—'Why, look there, there's our pigsty! See, it's got Bheotpte painted on the end. It's drifted down here, and the scum's caught it. What a blessed wonder!'

"It was, as he had said, our pigsty that had been washed overboard in the storm; and most extraordinary to come across it there.

"'We'll tow it off with us, when we go,' remarked the Captain, and shouted to the crew to get-down to their oars; for they were hardly moving the boat, because the scum was so thick, close in around the old ship, that it literally clogged the boat from going ahead. I remember that it struck me, in a half-conscious sort of way, as curious that the pigsty, containing our three dead pigs, had managed to drift in so far, unaided, whilst we could scarcely manage to force the boat in, now that we had come right into the scum. But the thought passed from my mind; for so many things happened within the next few minutes.

"The men managed to bring the boat in alongside, within a couple of feet of the derelict, and the man with the boathook, hooked on.

""Ave ye got 'old there, forrard?' asked Captain Gannington.

"'Yessir!' said the bow-man; and as he spoke, there came a queer noise of tearing.

"'What's that?' asked the Captain.

"'It's tore, Sir. Tore clean away!' said the man; and his tone showed that he had received something of a shock.

"'Get a hold again then!' said Captain Gannington, irritably. 'You don't s'pose this packet was built yesterday! Shove the hook into the main chains.' The man did so, gingerly, as you might say; for it seemed to me, in the growing dusk, that he put no strain on to the hook; though, of course, there was no need; you see, the boat could not go very far, of herself, in the stuff in which she was embedded. I remember thinking this, also, as I looked up at the bulging side of the old vessel. Then I heard Captain Gannington's voice:—

"'Lord! but she's old! An' what a colour, Doctor! She don't half want paint, do she! . . . Now then, somebody, one of them oars.'

"An oar was passed to him, and he leant it up against the ancient, bulging side; then he paused, and called to the Second Mate to light a couple of the lamps, and stand-by to pass them up; for darkness had settled down now upon the sea.

"The Second Mate lit two of the lamps, and told one of the men to light a third, and keep it handy in the boat; then he stepped across, with a lamp in each hand, to where Captain Gannington stood by the oar against the side of the ship.

"'Now, my lad,' said the Captain, to the man who had pulled stroke, 'up with you, an' we'll pass ye up the lamps.'

"The man jumped to obey; caught the oar, and put his weight upon it, and as he did so, something seemed to give a little.

"'Look!' cried out the Second Mate, and pointed, lamp in hand . . . 'It's sunk in!'

"This was true. The oar had made quite an indentation into the bulging, somewhat slimy side of the old vessel.

"'Mould, I reckon,' said Captain Gannington, bending towards the derelict, to look. Then, to the man:—

"'Up you go, my lad, and be smart. . . . Don't stand there waitin'!'

"At that, the man, who had paused a moment as he felt the oar give beneath his weight, began to shin up, and in a few seconds he was aboard, and leant out over the rail for the lamps. These were passed up to him, and the Captain called to him to steady the oar. Then Captain Gannington went, calling to me to follow, and after me the Second Mate.

"As the Captain put his face over the rail, he gave a cry of astonishment:—

"'Mould, by gum! Mould. . . . Tons of it! . . . Good Lord!'

"As I heard him shout that, I scrambled the more eagerly after him, and in a moment or two, I was able to see what he meant—— Everywhere that the light from the two lamps struck, there was nothing but smooth great masses and surfaces of a dirty white mould.

"I climbed over the rail, with the Second Mate close behind, and stood upon the mould-covered decks. There might have been no planking beneath the mould, for all that our feet could feel. It gave under our tread, with a spongy, puddingy feel. It covered the deck-furniture of the old ship, so that the shape of each article and fitment was often no more than suggested through it.

"Captain Gannington snatched a lamp from the man, and the Second Mate reached for the other. They held the lamps high, and we all stared. It was most extraordinary, and, somehow, most abominable. I can think of no other word, gentlemen, that so much describes the predominant feeling that affected me at the moment.

"'Good Lord!' said Captain Gannington, several times. 'Good Lord!' But neither the Second Mate nor the man said anything, and for my part I just stared, and at the same time began to smell a little at the air; for there was again a vague odour of something half familiar, that somehow brought to me a sense of half-known fright.

"I turned this way and that, staring, as I have said. Here and there, the mould was so heavy as to entirely disguise what lay beneath; converting the deck-fittings into indistinguishable mounds of mould, all dirty-white, and blotched and veined with irregular, dull purplish markings.

"There was a strange thing about the mould, which Captain Gannington drew attention to—it was that our feet did not crush into it and break the surface, as might have been expected; but merely indented it.

"'Never seen nothin' like it before! . . . Never!' said the Captain, after having stooped with his lamp to examine the mould under our feet. He stamped with his heel, and the stuff gave out a dull, puddingy sound. He stooped again, with a quick movement, and stared, holding the lamp close to the deck. 'Blest, if it ain't a reg'lar skin to it!' he said.

"The Second Mate and the man and I all stooped, and looked at it. The Second Mate progged it with his forefinger, and I remember I rapped it several times with my knuckles, listening to the dead sound it gave out, and noticing the close, firm texture of the mould.

"'Dough!' said the Second Mate. 'It's just like blessed dough! ... Pouf!' He stood up with a quick movement. 'I could fancy it stinks a bit,' he said.

"As he said this, I knew suddenly what the familiar thing was, in the vague odour that hung about us—It was that the smell had something animal-like in it; something of the same smell, only heavier, that you will smell in any place that is infested with mice. I began to look about with a sudden very real uneasiness.... There might be vast numbers of hungry rats aboard.... They might prove exceedingly dangerous, if in a starving condition; yet, as you will understand, somehow I hesitated to put forward my idea as a reason for caution; it was too fanciful.

"Captain Gannington had begun to go aft, along the mould-covered maindeck, with the Second Mate; each of them holding his lamp high up, so as to cast a good light about the vessel. I turned quickly and followed them, the man with me keeping close to my heels, and plainly uneasy. As we went, I became aware that there was a feeling of moisture in the air, and I remembered the slight mist, or smoke, above the hulk, which had made Captain Gannington suggest spontaneous combustion, in explanation.

"And always, as we went, there was that vague, animal smell; and, suddenly, I found myself wishing we were well away from the old vessel.

"Abruptly, after a few paces, the Captain stopped and pointed at a row of mould-hidden shapes on either side of the maindeck ... 'Guns,' he said. 'Been a privateer in the old days, I guess; maybe worse! We'll 'ave a look below, Doctor; there may be something worth touchin'. She's older than I thought. Mr. Selvern thinks she's about three hundred year old; but I scarce think it.'

"We continued our way aft, and I remember that I found myself walking as lightly and gingerly as possible; as if I were subconsciously afraid of treading through the rotten, mould-hid decks. I think the others had a touch of the same feeling, from the way that they walked. Occasionally, the soft mould would grip our heels, releasing them with a little, sullen suck.

"The Captain forged somewhat ahead of the Second Mate; and I know that the suggestion he had made himself, that perhaps there might be something below, worth the carrying away, had stimulated his imagination. The Second Mate was, however, beginning to feel somewhat the same way that I did; at least, I have that impression. I think, if it had not been for what I might truly describe as Captain Gannington's sturdy courage, we should all of us have just gone back over the side very soon; for there was most certainly an unwholesome feeling abroad, that made one feel queerly lacking in pluck; and you will soon perceive that this feeling was justified.

"Just as the Captain reached the few, mould-covered steps, leading up on to the short half-poop, I was suddenly aware that the feeling of moisture in the air had grown very much more definite. It was perceptible now, intermittently, as a sort of thin, moist, fog-like vapour, that came and went oddly, and seemed to make the decks a little indistinct to the view, this time and that. Once, an odd puff of it beat up suddenly from somewhere, and caught me in the face, carrying a queer, sickly, heavy odour with it, that somehow frightened me strangely, with a suggestion of a waiting and half-comprehended danger.

"We had followed Captain Gannington up the three, mould-covered steps, and now went slowly aft along the raised after-deck.

"By the mizzenmast, Captain Gannington paused, and held his lantern near to it....

"'My word, Mister,' he said to the Second Mate, 'it's fair thickened up with the mould; why, I'll g'antee it's close on four foot thick.' He shone the light down to where it met the deck. 'Good Lord!' he said, 'look at the sea-lice on it!' I stepped up; and it was as he had said; the sea-lice were thick upon it, some of them huge; not less than the size of large beetles, and all a clear, colourless shade, like water, except where there were little spots of grey in them, evidently their internal organisms.

"'I've never seen the like of them, 'cept on a live cod!' said Captain Gannington, in an extremely puzzled voice. 'My word! but they're whoppers!' Then he passed on; but a few paces farther aft, he stopped again, and held his lamp near to the mould-hidden deck.

"'Lord bless me, Doctor!' he called out, in a low voice, 'did ye ever see the like of that? Why, it's a foot long, if it's a hinch!'

"I stooped over his shoulder, and saw what he meant; it was a clear, colourless creature, about a foot long, and about eight inches high, with a curved back that was extraordinarily narrow. As we stared, all in a group, it gave a queer little flick, and was gone.

"'Jumped!' said the Captain. 'Well, if that ain't a giant of all the sea-lice that ever I've seen! I guess it's jumped twenty-foot clear.' He straightened his back, and scratched his head a moment, swinging the lantern this way and that with the other hand, and staring about us. 'Wot are they doin' aboard 'ere!' he said. 'You'll see 'em (little things) on fat cod, an' suchlike.... I'm blowed, Doctor, if I understand.'

"He held his lamp towards a big mound of the mould, that occupied part of the after portion of the low poop-deck, a little fore-side of where there came a two-foot high 'break' to a kind of second and loftier poop, that ran away aft to the taffrail. The mound was pretty big, several feet across, and more than a yard high. Captain Gannington walked up to it:—

"'I reck'n this 's the scuttle,' he remarked, and gave it a heavy kick. The only result was a deep indentation into the huge, whitish hump of mould, as if he had driven his foot into a mass of some doughy substance. Yet, I am not altogether correct in saying that this was the only result; for a certain other thing happened—From a place made by the Captain's foot, there came a little gush of a purplish fluid, accompanied by a peculiar smell, that was, and was not, half-familiar. Some of the mould-like substance had stuck to the toe of the Captain's boot, and from this, likewise, there issued a sweat, as it were, of the same colour.

"'Well!' said Captain Gannington, in surprise; and drew back his foot to make another kick at the hump of mould; but he paused, at an exclamation from the Second Mate:—

"'Don't, Sir!' said the Second Mate.

"I glanced at him, and the light from Captain Gannington's lamp showed me that his face had a bewildered, half-frightened look, as if he were suddenly and unexpectedly half-afraid of something, and as if his tongue had given away his sudden fright, without any intention on his part to speak.

"The Captain also turned and stared at him:—

"'Why, Mister?' he asked, in a somewhat puzzled voice, through which there sounded just the vaguest hint of annoyance. 'We've got to shift this muck, if we're to get below.'

"I looked at the Second Mate, and it seemed to me that, curiously enough, he was listening less to the Captain, than to some other sound.

"Suddenly, he said in a queer voice:—'Listen, everybody!'

"Yet, we heard nothing, beyond the faint murmur of the men talking together in the boat alongside.

"'I don't hear nothin',' said Captain Gannington, after a short pause. 'Do you, Doctor?'

"'No,' I said.

"'Wot was it you thought you heard?' asked the Captain, turning again to the Second Mate. But the Second Mate shook his head, in a curious, almost irritable way; as if the Captain's question interrupted his listening. Captain Gannington stared a moment at him; then held his lantern up, and glanced about him, almost uneasily. I know I felt a queer sense of strain. But the light showed nothing, beyond the greyish dirty-white of the mould in all directions.

"'Mister Selvern,' said the Captain at last, looking at him, 'don't get fancying things. Get hold of your bloomin' self. Ye know ye heard nothin'?'

"'I'm quite sure I heard something, Sir!' said the Second Mate. 'I seemed to hear——' He broke off sharply, and appeared to listen, with an almost painful intensity.

"'What did it sound like?' I asked.

"'It's all right, Doctor,' said Captain Gannington, laughing gently. 'Ye can give him a tonic when we get back. I'm goin' to shift this stuff.'

"He drew back, and kicked for the second time at the ugly mass, which he took to hide the companionway. The result of his kick was startling; for the whole thing wobbled sloppily, like a mound of unhealthy-looking jelly.

"He drew his foot out of it, quickly, and took a step backward, staring, and holding his lamp towards it:—

"'By gum!' he said; and it was plain that he was genuinely startled, 'the blessed thing's gone soft!'

"The man had run back several steps from the suddenly flaccid mound, and looked horribly frightened. Though, of what, I am sure he had not the least idea. The Second Mate stood where he was, and stared. For my part, I know I had a most hideous uneasiness upon me. The Captain continued to hold his light towards the wobbling mound, and stare:—

"It's gone squashy all through!' he said. 'There's no scuttle there. There's no bally woodwork inside that lot! Phoo! what a rum smell!'

"He walked round to the after-side of the strange mound, to see whether there might be some signs of an opening into the hull at the back of the great heap of mould-stuff. And then:—

"'Listen!' said the Second Mate, again, in the strangest sort of voice.

"Captain Gannington straightened himself upright, and there succeeded a pause of the most intense quietness, in which there was not even the hum of talk from the men alongside in the boat. We all heard it—a kind of dull, soft Thud! Thud! Thud! Thud! somewhere in the hull under us; yet so vague that I might have been half doubtful I heard it, only that the others did so, too.

"Captain Gannington turned suddenly to where the man stood:—

"'Tell them——' he began. But the fellow cried out something, and pointed. There had come a strange intensity into his somewhat unemotional face; so that the Captain's glance followed his action instantly. I stared, also, as you may think. It was the great mound, at which the man was pointing. I saw what he meant.

"From the two gapes made in the mould-like stuff by Captain Gannington's boot, the purple fluid was jetting out in a queerly regular fashion, almost as if it were being forced out by a pump. My word! but I stared! And even as I stared, a larger jet squirted out, and splashed as far as the man, spattering his boots and trouser-legs.

"The fellow had been pretty nervous before, in a stolid, ignorant sort of way; and his funk had been growing steadily; but, at this, he simply let out a yell, and turned about to run. He paused an instant, as if a sudden fear of the darkness that held the decks, between him and the boat, had taken him.

He snatched at the Second Mate's lantern; tore it out of his hand, and plunged heavily away over the vile stretch of mould.

"Mr. Selvern, the Second Mate, said not a word; he was just standing, staring at the strange-smelling twin streams of dull purple, that were jetting out from the wobbling mound. Captain Gannington, however, roared an order to the man to come back; but the man plunged on and on across the mould, his feet seeming to be clogged by the stuff, as if it had grown suddenly soft. He zigzagged, as he ran, the lantern swaying in wild circles, as he wrenched his feet free, with a constant plop, plop; and I could hear his frightened gasps, even from where I stood.

"'Come back with that lamp!' roared the Captain again; but still the man took no notice, and Captain Gannington was silent an instant, his lips working in a queer, inarticulate fashion; as if he were stunned momentarily by the very violence of his anger at the man's insubordination. And in the silence, I heard the sounds again:—Thud! Thud! Thud! Thud! Quite distinctly now, beating, it seemed suddenly to me, right down under my feet, but deep.

"I stared down at the mould on which I was standing, with a quick, disgusting sense of the terrible all about me; then I looked at the Captain, and tried to say something, without appearing frightened. I saw that he had turned again to the mound, and all the anger had gone out of his face. He had his lamp out towards the mound, and was listening. There was a further moment of absolute silence; at least, I know that I was not conscious of any sound at all, in all the world, except that extraordinary Thud! Thud! Thud! Thud! down somewhere in the huge bulk under us.

"The Captain shifted his feet, with a sudden, nervous movement; and as he lifted them, the mould went plop! plop! He looked quickly at me, trying to smile, as if he were not thinking anything very much about it:—'What do you make of it, Doctor?' he said.

"'I think—' I began. But the Second Mate interrupted with a single word; his voice pitched a little high, in a tone that made us both stare instantly at him:—

"'Look!' he said, and pointed at the mound. The thing was all of a slow quiver. A strange ripple ran outward from it, along the deck, like you will see a ripple run inshore out of a calm sea. It reached a mound a little fore-side of us, which I had supposed to be the cabin-skylight; and in a moment, the second mound sank nearly level with the surrounding decks, quivering floppily in a most extraordinary fashion. A sudden, quick tremor took the mould, right under the Second Mate, and he gave out a hoarse little cry, and held his arms out on each side of him, to keep his balance. The tremor in the mould, spread, and Captain Gannington swayed, and spread his feet, with a sudden curse of fright. The Second Mate jumped across to him, and caught him by the wrist:—

"'The boat, Sir!' he said, saying the very thing that I had lacked the pluck to say. 'For God's sake——'

"But he never finished; for a tremendous, hoarse scream cut off his words. They hove themselves round, and looked. I could see without turning. The man who had run from us, was standing in the waist of the ship, about a fathom from the starboard bulwarks. He was swaying from side to side, and screaming in a dreadful fashion. He appeared to be trying to lift his feet, and the light from his swaying lantern showed an almost incredible sight. All about him the mould was in active movement. His feet had sunk out of sight. The stuff appeared to be lapping at his legs; and abruptly his bare flesh showed. The hideous stuff had rent his trouser-legs away, as if they were paper. He gave out a simply sickening scream, and, with a vast effort, wrenched one leg free. It was partly destroyed. The next instant he pitched face downward, and the stuff heaped itself upon him, as if it were actually alive, with a dreadful savage life. It was simply infernal. The man had gone from sight.

Where he had fallen was now a writhing, elongated mound, in constant and horrible increase, as the mould appeared to move towards it in strange ripples from all sides.

"Captain Gannington and the Second Mate were stone silent, in amazed and incredulous horror; but I had begun to reach towards a grotesque and terrific conclusion, both helped and hindered by my professional training.

"From the men in the boat alongside, there was a loud shouting, and I saw two of their faces appear suddenly above the rail. They showed clearly, a moment, in the light from the lamp which the man had snatched from Mr. Selvern; for, strangely enough, this lamp was standing upright and unharmed on the deck, a little way fore-side of that dreadful, elongated, growing mound, that still swayed and writhed with an incredible horror. The lamp rose and fell on the passing ripples of the mould, just— for all the world—as you will see a boat rise and fall on little swells. It is of some interest to me now, psychologically, to remember how that rising and falling lantern brought home to me, more than anything, the incomprehensible, dreadful strangeness of it all.

"The men's faces disappeared, with sudden yells, as if they had slipped, or been suddenly hurt; and there was a fresh uproar of shouting from the boat. The men were calling to us to come away; to come away. In the same instant, I felt my left boot drawn suddenly and forcibly downward, with a horrible, painful gripe. I wrenched it free, with a yell of angry fear. Forrard of us, I saw that the vile surface was all a-move; and abruptly I found myself shouting in a queer frightened voice:—

"'The boat, Captain! The boat, Captain!'

"Captain Gannington stared round at me, over his right shoulder, in a peculiar, dull way, that told me he was utterly dazed with bewilderment and the incomprehensibleness of it all. I took a quick, clogged, nervous step towards him, and gripped his arm and shook it fiercely.

"'The boat!' I shouted at him. 'The boat! For God's sake, tell the men to bring the boat aft!'

"Then the mould must have drawn his feet down; for, abruptly, he bellowed fiercely with terror, his momentary apathy giving place to furious energy. His thick-set, vastly muscular body doubled and writhed with his enormous effort, and he struck out madly, dropping the lantern. He tore his feet free, something ripping as he did so. The reality and necessity of the situation had come upon him, brutishly real, and he was roaring to the men in the boat:—

"'Bring the boat aft! Bring 'er aft! Bring 'er aft!'

"The Second Mate and I were shouting the same thing, madly.

"For God's sake be smart, lads!' roared the Captain, and stooped quickly for his lamp, which still burned. His feet were gripped again, and he hove them out, blaspheming breathlessly, and leaping a yard high with his effort. Then he made a run for the side, wrenching his feet free at each step. In the same instant, the Second Mate cried out something, and grabbed at the Captain:—

"'It's got hold of my feet! It's got hold of my feet!' he screamed. His feet had disappeared up to his boot-tops; and Captain Gannington caught him round the waist with his powerful left arm, gave a mighty heave, and the next instant had him free; but both his boot-soles had almost gone.

"For my part, I jumped madly from foot to foot, to avoid the plucking of the mould; and suddenly I made a run for the ship's side. But before I could get there, a queer gape came in the mould, between us and the side, at least a couple of feet wide, and how deep I don't know. It closed up in an instant, and all the mould, where the gape had been, went into a sort of flurry of horrible ripplings, so that I ran back from it; for I did not dare to put my foot upon it. Then the Captain was shouting at me:—

"'Aft, Doctor! Aft, Doctor! This way, Doctor! Run!' I saw then that he had passed me, and was up on the after, raised portion of the poop. He had the Second Mate thrown like a sack, all loose and quiet, over his left shoulder; for Mr. Selvern had fainted, and his long legs flogged, limp and helpless, against the Captain's massive knees as the Captain ran. I saw, with a queer, unconscious noting of minor details, how the torn soles of the Second Mate's boots flapped and jigged, as the Captain staggered aft.

"'Boat ahoy! Boat ahoy! Boat ahoy!' shouted the Captain; and then I was beside him, shouting also. The men were answering with loud yells of encouragement, and it was plain they were working desperately to force the boat aft, through the thick scum about the ship.

"We reached the ancient, mould-hid taffrail, and slewed about, breathlessly, in the half-darkness, to see what was happening. Captain Gannington had left his lantern by the big mound, when he picked up the Second Mate; and as we stood, gasping, we discovered suddenly that all the mould between us and the light was full of movement. Yet, the part on which we stood, for about six or eight feet forrard of us, was still firm.

"Every couple of seconds, we shouted to the men to hasten, and they kept on calling to us that they would be with us in an instant. And all the time, we watched the deck of that dreadful hulk, feeling, for my part, literally sick with mad suspense, and ready to jump overboard into that filthy scum all about us.

"Down somewhere in the huge bulk of the ship, there was all the time that extraordinary, dull, ponderous Thud! Thud! Thud! Thud! growing ever louder. I seemed to feel the whole hull of the derelict beginning to quiver and thrill with each dull beat. And to me, with the grotesque and monstrous suspicion of what made that noise, it was, at once, the most dreadful and incredible sound I have ever heard.

"As we waited desperately for the boat, I scanned incessantly so much of the grey-white bulk as the lamp showed. The whole of the decks seemed to be in strange movement. Forrard of the lamp, I could see, indistinctly, the moundings of the mould swaying and nodding hideously, beyond the circle of the brightest rays. Nearer, and full in the glow of the lamp, the mound which should have indicated the skylight, was swelling steadily. There were ugly, purple veinings on it, and as it swelled, it seemed to me that the veinings and mottlings on it, were becoming plainer—rising, as though embossed upon it, like you will see the veins stand out on the body of a powerful, full-blooded horse. It was most extraordinary. The mound that we had supposed to cover the companionway, had sunk flat with the surrounding mould, and I could not see that it jetted out any more of the purplish fluid.

"'A quaking movement of the mould began, away forrard of the lamp, and came flurrying away aft towards us; and at the sight of that, I climbed up on to the spongy-feeling taffrail, and yelled afresh for the boat. The men answered with a shout, which told me they were nearer; but the beastly scum was so thick that it was evidently a fight to move the boat at all. Beside me, Captain Gannington was shaking the Second Mate furiously, and the man stirred and began to moan. The Captain shook him again.

"'Wake up! Wake up, Mister!' he shouted.

"The Second Mate staggered out of the Captain's arms, and collapsed suddenly, shrieking:—'My feet! Oh, God! My feet!' The Captain and I lugged him up off the mould, and got him into a sitting position upon the taffrail, where he kept up a continual moaning.

"'Hold 'im, Doctor,' said the Captain, and whilst I did so, he ran forrard a few yards, and peered down over the starboard quarter rail. 'For God's sake, be smart, lads! Be smart! Be smart!' he shouted down to the men; and they answered him, breathless, from close at hand; yet still too far away for the boat to be any use to us on the instant.

"I was holding the moaning, half-unconscious officer, and staring forrard along the poop decks. The flurrying of the mould was coming aft, slowly and noiselessly. And then, suddenly, I saw something closer:—

"'Look out, Captain!' I shouted; and even as I shouted, the mould near to him gave a sudden peculiar slobber. I had seen a ripple stealing towards him through the horrible stuff. He gave an enormous, clumsy leap, and landed near to us on the sound part of the mould; but the movement followed him. He turned and faced it, swearing fiercely. All about his feet there came abruptly little gapings, which made horrid sucking noises.

"'Come back, Captain!' I yelled. 'Come back, quick!'

"As I shouted, a ripple came at his feet—lipping at them; and he stamped insanely at it, and leaped back, his boot torn half off his foot. He swore madly with pain and anger, and jumped swiftly for the taffrail.

"'Come on, Doctor! Over we go!' he called. Then he remembered the filthy scum, and hesitated; roaring out desperately to the men to hurry. I stared down, also.

"'The Second Mate?' I said.

"'I'll take charge, Doctor,' said Captain Gannington, and caught hold of Mr. Selvern. As he spoke, I thought I saw something beneath us, outlined against the scum. I leaned out over the stern, and peered. There was something under the port quarter.

"'There's something down there, Captain!' I called, and pointed in the darkness.

"He stooped far over, and stared.

"'A boat, by gum! A Boat!' he yelled, and began to wriggle swiftly along the taffrail, dragging the Second Mate after him. I followed.

"'A boat it is, sure!' he exclaimed, a few moments later; and, picking up the Second Mate clear of the rail, he hove him down into the boat, where he fell with a crash into the bottom.

"'Over ye go, Doctor!' he yelled at me, and pulled me bodily off the rail, and dropped me after the officer. As he did so, I felt the whole of the ancient, spongy rail give a peculiar, sickening quiver, and begin to wobble. I fell on to the Second Mate, and the Captain came after, almost in the same instant; but fortunately, he landed clear of us, on to the fore thwart, which broke under his weight, with a loud crack and splintering of wood.

"'Thank God!' I heard him mutter. 'Thank God! . . . I guess that was a mighty near thing to goin' to hell.'

"He struck a match, just as I got to my feet, and between us we got the Second Mate straightened out on one of the after thwarts. We shouted to the men in the boat, telling them where we were, and saw the light of their lantern shining round the starboard counter of the derelict. They called back to us, to tell us they were doing their best; and then, whilst we waited, Captain Gannington struck another match, and began to overhaul the boat we had dropped into. She was a modern, two-bowed boat, and on the stern, there was painted 'Cyclone Glasgow.' She was in pretty fair condition, and had evidently drifted into the scum and been held by it.

"Captain Gannington struck several matches, and went forrard towards the derelict. Suddenly he called to me, and I jumped over the thwarts to him.

"'Look, Doctor,' he said; and I saw what he meant—a mass of bones, up in the bows of the boat. I stooped over them, and looked. There were the bones of at least three people, all mixed together, in an extraordinary fashion, and quite clean and dry. I had a sudden thought concerning the bones; but I said nothing; for my thought was vague, in some ways, and concerned the grotesque and incredible suggestion that had come to me, as to the cause of that ponderous, dull Thud! Thud! Thud! Thud! that beat on so infernally within the hull, and was plain to hear even now that we had got off the vessel herself. And all the while, you know, I had a sick, horrible, mental-picture of that frightful wriggling mound aboard the hulk.

"As Captain Gannington struck a final match, I saw something that sickened me, and the Captain saw it in the same instant. The match went out, and he fumbled clumsily for another, and struck it. We saw the thing again. We had not been mistaken. . . . A great lip of grey-white was protruding in over the edge of the boat—a great lappet of the mould was coming stealthily towards us; a live mass of the very hull itself. And suddenly Captain Gannington yelled out, in so many words, the grotesque and incredible thing I was thinking:—

"'She's Alive!'

"I never heard such a sound of comprehension and terror in a man's voice. The very horrified assurance of it, made actual to me the thing that, before, had only lurked in my subconscious mind. I knew he was right; I knew that the explanation, my reason and my training, both repelled and reached towards, was the true one. . . . . . . I wonder whether anyone can possibly understand our feelings in that moment. . . . The unmitigable horror of it, and the incredibleness.

"As the light of the match burned up fully, I saw that the mass of living matter, coming towards us, was streaked and veined with purple, the veins standing out, enormously distended. The whole thing quivered continuously to each ponderous Thud! Thud! Thud! Thud! of that gargantuan organ that pulsed within the huge grey-white bulk. The flame of the match reached the Captain's fingers, and there came to me a little sickly whiff of burned flesh; but he seemed unconscious of any pain. Then the flame went out, in a brief sizzle; yet at the last moment, I had seen an extraordinary raw look, become visible upon the end of that monstrous, protruding lappet. It had become dewed with a hideous, purplish sweat. And with the darkness, there came a sudden charnel-like stench.

"I heard the match-box split in Captain Gannington's hands, as he wrenched it open. Then he swore, in a queer frightened voice; for he had come to the end of his matches. He turned clumsily in the darkness, and tumbled over the nearest thwart, in his eagerness to get to the stern of the boat; and I after him; for we knew that thing was coming towards us through the darkness; reaching over that piteous mingled heap of human bones, all jumbled together in the bows. We shouted madly to the men, and for answer saw the bows of the boat emerge dimly into view, round the starboard counter of the derelict.

"'Thank God!' I gasped out; but Captain Gannington yelled to them to show a light. Yet this they could not do; for the lamp had just been stepped on, in their desperate efforts to force the boat round to us.

"'Quick! Quick!' I shouted.

"'For God's sake be smart, men!' roared the Captain; and both of us faced the darkness under the port counter, out of which we knew (but could not see) the thing was coming towards us.

"'An oar! Smart now; pass me an oar!' shouted the Captain; and reached out his hands through the gloom towards the oncoming boat. I saw a figure stand up in the bows, and hold something out to us, across the intervening yards of scum. Captain Gannington swept his hands through the darkness, and encountered it.

"'I've got it. Let go there!' he said, in a quick, tense voice.

"In the same instant, the boat we were in, was pressed over suddenly to starboard by some tremendous weight. Then I heard the Captain shout:—'Duck y'r head, Doctor;' and directly afterwards he swung the heavy, fourteen-foot ash oar round his head, and struck into the darkness. There came a sudden squelch, and he struck again, with a savage grunt of fierce energy. At the second blow, the boat righted, with a slow movement, and directly afterwards the other boat bumped gently into ours.

"Captain Gannington dropped the oar, and springing across to the Second Mate, hove him up off the thwart, and pitched him with knee and arms clear in over the bows among the men; then he shouted to me to follow, which I did, and he came after me, bringing the oar with him. We carried the Second Mate aft, and the Captain shouted to the men to back the boat a little; then they got her bows clear of the boat we had just left, and so headed out through the scum for the open sea.

"'Where's Tom 'Arrison?' gasped one of the men, in the midst of his exertions. He happened to be Tom Harrison's particular chum; and Captain Gannington answered him briefly enough:—

"'Dead! Pull! Don't talk!'

"Now, difficult as it had been to force the boat through the scum to our rescue, the difficulty to get clear seemed tenfold. After some five minutes pulling, the boat seemed hardly to have moved a fathom, if so much; and a quite dreadful fear took me afresh; which one of the panting men put suddenly into words:—

"'It's got us!' he gasped out; 'same as poor Tom!' It was the man who had inquired where Harrison was.

"'Shut y'r mouth an' pull!' roared the Captain. And so another few minutes passed. Abruptly, it seemed to me that the dull, ponderous Thud ! Thud! Thud! Thud! came more plainly through the dark, and I stared intently over the stern. I sickened a little; for I could almost swear that the dark mass of the monster was actually nearer ... that it was coming nearer to us through the darkness.

Captain Gannington must have had the same thought; for after a brief look into the darkness, he made one jump to the stroke-oar, and began to double-bank it.

"'Get forrid under the thwarts, Doctor!' he said to me, rather breathlessly. 'Get in the bows, an' see if you can't free the stuff a bit round the bows.'

"I did as he told me, and a minute later I was in the bows of the boat, puddling the scum from side to side with the boathook, and trying to break up the viscid, clinging muck. A heavy, almost animal-like odour rose off it, and all the air seemed full of the deadening smell. I shall never find words to tell any one the whole horror of it all—the threat that seemed to hang in the very air around us; and, but a little astern, that incredible thing, coming, as I firmly believe, nearer, and the scum holding us like half melted glue.

'The minutes passed in a deadly, eternal fashion, and I kept staring back astern into the darkness; but never ceasing to puddle that filthy scum, striking at it and switching it from side to side, until I sweated.

"Abruptly, Captain Gannington sang out:—

"'We're gaining, lads. Pull! 'And I felt the boat forge ahead perceptibly, as they gave way, with renewed hope and energy. There was soon no doubt of it; for presently that hideous Thud! Thud! Thud! Thud! had grown quite dim and vague somewhere astern, and I could no longer see the derelict; for the night had come down tremendously dark, and all the sky was thick overset with heavy clouds. As we drew nearer and nearer to the edge of the scum, the boat moved more and more freely, until suddenly we emerged with a clean, sweet, fresh sound, into the open sea.

"'Thank God!' I said aloud, and drew in the boathook, and made my way aft again to where Captain Gannington now sat once more at the tiller. I saw him looking anxiously up at the sky, and across to where the lights of our vessel burned, and again he would seem to listen intently; so that I found myself listening also.

"'What's that, Captain?' I said sharply; for it seemed to me that I heard a sound far astern, something between a queer whine and a low whistling. 'What's that?'

"'It's wind, Doctor,' he said, in a low voice. 'I wish to God we were aboard.'

"Then, to the men:—'Pull! Put y'r backs into it, or ye'll never put y'r teeth through good bread again!'

"The men obeyed nobly, and we reached the vessel safely, and had the boat safely stowed, before the storm came, which it did in a furious white smother out of the West. I could see it for some minutes beforehand, tearing the sea, in the gloom, into a wall of phosphorescent foam; and as it came nearer, that peculiar whining, piping sound, grew louder and louder, until it was like a vast steam whistle, rushing towards us across the sea.

"And when it did come, we got it very heavy indeed; so that the morning showed us nothing but a welter of white seas; and that grim derelict was many a score of miles away in the smother, lost as utterly as our hearts could wish to lose her.

"When I came to examine the Second Mate's feet, I found them in a very extraordinary condition. The soles of them had the appearance of having been partly digested. I know of no other word that so exactly describes their condition; and the agony the man suffered, must have been dreadful.

"Now," concluded the Doctor, "that is what I call a case in point. If we could know exactly what that old vessel had originally been loaded with, and the juxtaposition of the various articles of her cargo, plus the heat and time she had endured, plus one or two other only guessable quantities, we should have solved the chemistry of the Life-Force, gentlemen. Not necessarily the origin, mind you; but, at least, we should have taken a big step on the way. I've often regretted that gale, you know—in a way, that is, in a way! It was a most amazing discovery; but, at the time, I had nothing but thankfulness to be rid of it. . . . A most amazing chance. I often think of the way the monster woke out of its torpor.... And that scum.... The dead pigs caught in it.... I fancy that was a grim kind of net, gentlemen.... It caught many things.... It ..."

The old Doctor sighed and nodded.

"If I could have had her bill of lading," he said, his eyes full of regret. "If—— It might have told me something to help. But, anyway...." He began to fill his pipe again.... "I suppose," he ended, looking round at us gravely, "I s'pose we humans are an ungrateful lot of beggars, at the best! ... But ... but what a chance! What a chance—eh?"

MY HOUSE SHALL BE CALLED THE HOUSE OF PRAYER

(An incident in the life of Father Johnson, Roman Catholic Priest.)

"And the Great Deep of Life."

Father Johnson's Irish village is not Irish. For some unknown reason it is polyglot. They are, as one might say, a most extraordinary family.

I took my friend, James Pelple, down with me for an afternoon's jaunt, to give the priest a call in his new house; for he had moved since last I saw him. Pelple knew of Father Johnson, by hearsay, and disapproved strongly. There is no other word to describe his feelings.

"A good man, yes," he would remark. "But if all you tell me, and half of what I hear from others, is true, he is much too lax. His ritual—"

"I've never been to his place," I interrupted. "I know him only as the man. As a man, I love him, as you know; as a priest, I admire him. Concerning his ritual, I know nothing. I don't believe he is the man to be unduly lax on vital points."

"Just so! Just so!" said Pelple. "I know nothing; but I've heard some very peculiar things."

I smiled to myself. Certainly, Father Johnson has some unusual ways. I have seen him, for instance, when we have been alone, forget to say his grace, until, maybe, he had eaten one dish. Then, remembering, he would touch his fingers together, and say:—"Bless this food to me" (glancing at the empty dish), "an' I thank Thee for it" (looking at the full one in front). Then, remembering the dish yet on the stove:—"An' that too, Lord," and direct the Lord's attention to the same, by a backward nod of his head. Afterwards, resuming his eating and talking, in the most natural fashion.

"I've heard that he allows his church to be used for some very extraordinary purposes," continued Pelple. "I cannot, of course, credit some of the things I hear; but I have been assured that the women take their knitting into the church on weekday evenings, whilst the men assemble there, as to a kind of rendezvous, where village topics are allowed. I consider it most improper, most improper! Don't you?"

But I found it difficult to criticise Father Johnson. I was frankly an admirer, as I am to-day. So I held my peace, assisted by an elusive movement of the head, that might have been either a nod or a negative.

When we reached the village, and asked for the priest's new house, three men of the place escorted us there in state, as to the house of a chieftain. Reaching it, two of them pointed to him through the window, where he sat at table, smoking, after his early tea. The third man would have accompanied us in; but I told him that I wanted to see the priest alone; whereupon they all went happily. To have need to see the priest alone, was a need that each and all understood, as a part of their daily lives.

I lifted the latch, and we passed in, as all are welcome to do at any hour of the day or night. The door of his house opened into a short half-passage, and I could see direct into his little room, out of which went the small scullery-kitchen. As we entered, I heard Sally, his servant-wench, washing dishes in the little scullery; and just then Father Johnson called out to her:—"Sally, I'll make a bet with ye."

In the scullery, I heard a swift rustling and a subdued clatter, and knew that Sally (having heard that preliminary often before) was stealthily removing the handles of the knives from the boiling water. Then her reply:—

"Did y'r riv'rence sphake?"

"I did, Sally, colleen," said the priest's voice. "I'll make a bet with ye, Sally, you've the handles av thim knives over hilt in the hot water—eh, Sally!"

And then Sally's voice, triumphant:—

"Ye're wrong, y'r riv'rence, thim knives is on the dhresser!"

"Aye, Sally," said Father Johnson; "but were they not in the hot water whin I sphoke firrst?"

"They was, y'r riv'rence," said Sally, in a shamed voice; just as she had been making the same confession for the past seven years. And then the priest had a little fit of happy, almost silent laughter, puffing out great clouds of smoke; in the midst of which we walked in on him.

After our greetings, which the priest had met with that strange magnetism of heartiness, that had left even the critical Pelple less disapproving, we were set down to a tea, which we simply had to eat, the priest waiting on us himself, and making the little meal "go," as you might say, with the abundance of his energy and humour—telling a hundred quaint tales and jests of the country-side, with his brogue making points of laughter where more formal speech would have left us dull and untouched.

The meal over, the priest suggested that we might like to accompany him down to his chapel, and see whether things were "kapin' happy," as he phrased it. As you may suppose, we were quite eager to accept his invitation; for, as I have made clear already, I had never been down to his place before, and I had heard many things—even as had Pelple—about his chapel and his methods.

We had not far to go. On the way, Father Johnson pointed with his thumb to a little stone-built cabin, very small and crude, which I learned was rented by a certain old Thomas Cardallon, who was not an Irishman.

"Tom's wife died last week," said the priest, quietly. "He's to be evicted to-morrow as iver is, if he cannot fhind the rint."

I put my hand into my pocket, with a half involuntary movement; but he shook his head, as much as to say no good could be done that way. This was all, and we were past the small hovel in a minute; but I found myself looking back with a sudden, new curiosity at the little rough-built living-place, that, before, had been only one poor hut among many; yet was now instinct to me with a history of its own, so that it stood out, in my memory, from the others, that were here and there about, as something indicative of the life-hope and striving of two poor humans. I put it badly. I know; but it was just such a jumble of vague thoughts and emotions as these, that stirred in my mind. I had reason afterwards to have further memory of the cottage and its one-time occupants.

We reached the chapel very soon; but when we entered, I stood for a moment, in astonishment, looking up the single aisle of the long whitewashed room. There was not much noise; for, as I discovered, reverence and the sense of the Place, held power all the time; moreover, they were Father Johnson's people. I looked at my friend, smiling, I fear.

"Even worse than Rumour foretold," I suggested in a low voice; but he made no reply; for he appeared to me to be stifled by the excess of his astounded disapproval. The priest was a few paces before us, where we had made our involuntary pause in the doorway; and he, too, came to a stand, and looked at the scene, unobserved.

You will understand that there was cause for my astonishment, and even—as many will agree—with the strong disapprobation which my friend was feeling, when I tell you that there was an auction in progress within the House; for within the doorway to the left, was a pile of household goods, evidently from the cottage of one of the very poor. In front of the little heap was an old man, and round him, in a semicircle, stood a number of the villagers, listening intently to the old man's extolling of each article of his household gear, which he was putting up for sale.

"'My House shall be called—'" I quoted softly and involuntarily; but less with any blame in my heart, than a great wonder, salted by a vague shockedness. The priest, still standing a little before me, caught my half unconscious quotation; but he only said "Hush!" so gently that I felt suddenly ashamed, as if I were a child fumbling with the Garments of Life, which the priest had worn upon his shoulders all the long years.

For maybe the half of a minute longer, we stood staring at the scene, Father Johnson still a few paces before us into the chapel.

"Tom Cardallon," he explained presently, over his shoulder. "If he sold outside, the officers would confiscate. I showed ye the house av him, as we passed."

He beckoned us to join the group of villagers round the pitiful pile of household goods, which we did, whilst he went on up the chapel, speaking a word here and there to the many who were gathered together in companionship for the quiet hour that preceded the evening Rosary. Some were praying; a few were sitting quietly in restful isolation from the world of reality; many of the women, I noticed, were knitting, or sitting making butter in small glass jars, which they shook constantly in their hands.

The whole scene, in the soft evening light that came in through the long narrow windows, giving me an extraordinary sense of restfulness and natural humanity.

I turned presently from my viewing of the general chapel, to the particular corner where I stood upon the skirt of the little group around the old man. I began to catch the drift of his remarks, uttered in a low tone, and found myself edging nearer, to hear more plainly. I gathered—as the priest had told us—that he had just lost his wife, after a long illness which had run them hopelessly into debt. Indeed, as you know, the eviction from the little hovel was arranged for the morrow, if the old man could not find the small sum which would make it possible for him to stay on in the old cottage, where he had evidently spent many very happy years.

"This 'ere," the old man was saying, holding up a worn saucepan, "wer' one as my missus 'as cooked a pow'r o' spuds in."

He stopped, and turned half from us a moment, with a queer little awkward gesture, as if looking round for something that he knew subconsciously he was not in search of. I believe, in reality, the movement was prompted by an unrealised desire to avert his face momentarily, which had begun to work, as memory stirred in him. He faced round again.

"Eh," he continued, "she wer' great on chips in batter, she wer'. Me 'n 'er used ter 'ave 'em every Sunday night as ever was. Like as they was good to sleep on, so she said. An' I guess they was all cooked in this 'ere ole pan."

He finished his curious eulogy, rather lamely, and pulled out his old red handkerchief. After he had blown his nose, and furtively wiped his eyes, he used the handkerchief to polish the interior and exterior of the pan; after which he held it up once more to the view of the silent and sympathetic crowd.

"What'll ye give for it?" he asked, looking round anxiously at the many faces.

"Sixpence," said a low voice, and the old man, after a quick glance round the crowd, said: "It's yours, Mrs. Mike Callan," and handed it across to a woman in the front of the crowd. The money was paid into his hand in coppers, as I could tell by the chink.

I looked towards the purchaser, feeling that I should like to buy back the saucepan, and return it to the old man. This way, I saw Father Johnson moving here and there through the little crowd, with a calico bag in his hand. From this, in a surreptitious manner, he drew something constantly—which I conceived, by the faint chinking, to be money—and distributed it to a man here and a woman there among the onlookers, accompanying each act with a few whispered words.

I understood much and guessed the rest. It was obvious that the people had little money to spare; for both their clothes and their little huts, all told of an utter poverty. This poverty, Father Johnson was remedying for the occasion, and his whispered words were probably hints concerning the articles for which to bid, and the amount to be bid for each. This, of course, is only a guess; but I believe that I am correct, in the main.

Once, I bid for a little old crock, offering double or treble its original value; but the old man took not the slightest notice, and continued to offer the article to bids that counted pence to the shillings of my offer. I was astonished, and began to see newly, if I may put it in that way. The man next to me, bid fivepence; then turned and put up his finger, shaking his head in a friendly fashion, but warningly. Evidently, I was to be allowed no part in this function of neighbourly help, which was obviously ordered by rules of which I lacked a fundamental knowledge. A woman, near to me, made things somewhat clearer. She bent my-wards, and whispered:

"'E'd not take it back from you, Sir, nor the price you offered, neither. 'E's got a inderpendent 'eart, 'e 'as, Sir. Poor old man."

So the things were going to be given back, after all. I wondered how they would arrange the returning. It was evident that he had no conceiving of the intentions of his neighbours; for the emotion of distress was too plainly writ in his face, with each familiar article that he auctioned. I learned afterwards that he was detained in chapel by Father Johnson for a few "worrds," during which the household gear was replaced in his cottage.

When everything else had been sold, there remained only a poor bundle of something, done up in a faded shawl. It was as if the old man had put off, to the very end, the selling of this. Now, he got down clumsily on to his knees, and began to undo the knots, fumbling stupidly, and bending his head low over the bundle. He got the knots undone at last, and presently, after a little turning over of the few things, in a way that I perceived to be more a dumb caressing, than because he sought any particular article, he rose to his feet, holding an old worn skirt.

"This 'ere," he said, slowly, "wer' my missus's best, an' she wer' very spechul 'bout it, these 'ere thirty year. I mind w'en she first wor' it." (His face lined a moment with emotion, grotesquely.) "She wer' that slim 's she hed ter put a tuck in ther waistban'; not that it 'armed it; she tuk pertickler care, an—"

I lost the old man's low-voiced explanation at this point; for I was aware suddenly that Father Johnson was almost at my side. I glanced an instant at him; but he was staring at the old man, with the oddest expression on his face. I noticed, subconsciously, that he was clenching and unclenching his hands rapidly. Then the old man's quaver caught my ear again:—

"It's fine an' good cloth, an' them stain-marks couldn't be 'elped. As she said, it wer' ther Lord's will, an' she mustn't complain. This 'ere one on the 'em wer' done fifteen year back—" Again my attention was distracted. I caught the sharp flip of a finger and thumb, and a man looked round and sidled out of the crowd, up to Father Johnson, in obedience to his signal.

"Sthop ut, Mike! Sthop ut this instant!" I heard the priest whisper, his brogue coming out strong, because he was stirred. "Offer tin bob for the lot, an' sthop ut; 'tis breakin' the hearts av us."

He handed the man some money, and Mike bid for the shawl-full. But, even then, it was horrible to see old Cardallon's fight, before he could relinquish the garments to the buyer.

The sale was over. The latter part of it had been attended by an ever increasing audience, from those who at first had been content to sit and talk and rest quietly on the benches; and who— coming from the outlying districts—were not intimate neighbours of old Tom. As they broke up to return to their seats, I saw one or two women crying openly.

James Pelple and I stayed for the service of the Rosary, in all reverence, though of another persuasion. Afterwards, as we stood in the doorway, waiting for Father Johnson, I looked across at him.

"Well?" I queried, "a den of thieves?"

But Pelple, "the Stickler," shook his head.

"A wonderful man," he said, "a wonderful man. I should like to know him better."

I laughed outright.

"So you've come under the banner too," I said. "I wondered whether you would." And just then, Father Johnson joined us in his cassock, and we began our return journey to his house.

On the way, we passed the door of Cardallon's cottage, the upper half of which was open. The priest looked in, with a cheery word, and we joined him. The old man was standing in the centre of his hard-beaten mud floor, staring round in a stunned, incredulous fashion at all his restored household goods. He looked half-vacantly at Father Johnson, the tears running slowly down his wrinkled face. In his right hand, he held the little bundle, knotted round with the faded shawl.

The priest stretched a hand over the half-door, and blessed old Tom Cardallon in the loveliest, homeliest way, that stirred me, I admit frankly, to the very depths.

Then he turned away, and we resumed our walk, leaving the old man to his tears, which I am convinced were signs, in part at least, of a gentle happiness.

"He would not take the money from us," said the priest, later. "But do ye think the heart av him would let him sind back the gear!"

I looked across at Pelple, and smiled to his nod; for I knew that his last vague questioning was answered.

FROM THE TIDELESS SEA

The Captain of the schooner leant over the rail, and stared for a moment, intently.

"Pass us them glasses, Jock," he said, reaching a hand behind him.

Jock left the wheel for an instant, and ran into the little companionway. He emerged immediately with a pair of marine-glasses, which he pushed into the waiting hand.

For a little, the Captain inspected the object through the binoculars. Then he lowered them, and polished the object glasses.

"Seems like er water-logged barr'l as sumone's been doin' fancy paintin' on," he remarked after a further stare. "Shove ther 'elm down er bit, Jock, an' we'll 'ave er closer look at it."

Jock obeyed, and soon the schooner bore almost straight for the object which held the Captain's attention. Presently, it was within some fifty feet, and the Captain sung out to the boy in the caboose to pass along the boathook.

Very slowly, the schooner drew nearer, for the wind was no more than breathing gently. At last the cask was within reach, and the Captain grappled at it with the boathook. It bobbed in the calm water, under his ministrations; and, for a moment, the thing seemed likely to elude him. Then he had the hook fast in a bit of rotten-looking rope which was attached to it. He did not attempt to lift it by the rope; but sung out to the boy to get a bowline round it. This was done, and the two of them hove it up on to the deck.

The Captain could see now, that the thing was a small water-breaker, the upper part of which was ornamented with the remains of a painted name.

"H—M—E—B—" spelt out the Captain with difficulty, and scratched his head. "'ave er look at this 'ere, Jock. See wot you makes of it."

Jock bent over from the wheel, expectorated, and then stared at the breaker. For nearly a minute he looked at it in silence.

"I'm thinkin' some of the letterin's washed awa'," he said at last, with considerable deliberation. "I have ma doots if he'll be able to read it.

"Hadn't ye no better knock in the end?" he suggested, after a further period of pondering. "I'm thinkin' ye'll be lang comin' at them contents otherwise."

"It's been in ther water er thunderin' long time," remarked the Captain, turning the bottom side upwards. "Look at them barnacles!"

Then, to the boy:—

"Pass erlong ther 'atchet outer ther locker."

Whilst the boy was away, the Captain stood the little barrel on end, and kicked away some of the barnacles from the underside. With them, came away a great shell of pitch. He bent, and inspected it.

"Blest if ther thing ain't been pitched!" he said. "This 'ere's been put afloat er purpose, an' they've been, mighty anxious as ther stuff in it shouldn't be 'armed.

He kicked away another mass of the barnacle-studded pitch. Then, with a sudden impulse, he picked up the whole thing and shook it violently. It gave out a light, dull, thudding sound, as though something soft and small were within. Then the boy came with the hatchet.

"Stan' clear!" said the Captain, and raised the implement. The next instant, he had driven in one end of the barrel. Eagerly, he stooped forward. He dived his hand down and brought out a little bundle stitched up in oilskin.

"I don' spect as it's anythin' of valley," he remarked. "But I guess as there's sumthin' 'ere as 'll be worth tellin' 'bout w'en we gets 'ome."

He slit up the oilskin as he spoke. Underneath, there was another covering of the same material, and under that a third. Then a longish bundle done up in tarred canvas. This was removed, and a black, cylindrical shaped case disclosed to view. It proved to be a tin canister, pitched over. Inside of it, neatly wrapped within a last strip of oilskin, was a roll of papers, which, on opening, the Captain found to be covered with writing. The Captain shook out the various wrappings; but found nothing further. He handed the MS. across to Jock.

"More 'n your line 'n mine, I guess," he remarked. "Jest you read it up, an' I'll listen."

He turned to the boy.

"Fetch thef dinner erlong 'ere. Me an' ther Mate 'll 'ave it comfortable up 'ere, an' you can take ther wheel.... Now then, Jock!"

And, presently, Jock began to read.

"The Losing of the Homebird"

"The 'Omebird!" exclaimed the Captain. "Why, she were lost w'en I wer' quite a young feller. Let me see—seventy-three. That were it. Tail end er seventy-three w'en she left 'ome, an' never 'eard of since; not as I knows. Go a'ead with ther yarn, Jock."

"It is Christmas eve. Two years ago to-day, we became lost to the world. Two years! It seems like twenty since I had my last Christmas in England. Now, I suppose, we are already forgotten—and this ship is but one more among the missing! My God! to think upon our loneliness gives me a choking feeling, a tightness across the chest!

"I am writing this in the saloon of the sailing ship, Homebird, and writing with but little hope of human eye ever seeing that which I write; for we are in the heart of the dread Sargasso Sea—the Tideless Sea of the North Atlantic. From the stump of our mizzen mast, one may see, spread out to the far horizon, an interminable waste of weed—a treacherous, silent vastitude of slime and hideousness!

"On our port side, distant some seven or eight miles, there is a great, shapeless, discoloured mass. No one, seeing it for the first time, would suppose it to be the hull of a long lost vessel. It bears but little resemblance to a sea-going craft, because of a strange superstructure which has been built upon it. An examination of the vessel herself, through a telescope, tells one that she is unmistakably ancient. Probably a hundred, possibly two hundred, years. Think of it! Two hundred years in the midst of this desolation! It is an eternity.

"At first we wondered at that extraordinary superstructure. Later, we were to learn its use—and profit by the teaching of hands long withered. It is inordinately strange that we should have come upon this sight for the dead! Yet, thought suggests, that there may be many such, which have lain here through the centuries in this World of Desolation. I had not imagined that the earth contained so much loneliness, as is held within the circle, seen from the stump of our shattered mast. Then comes the thought that I might wander a hundred miles in any direction—and still be lost.

"And that craft yonder, that one break in the monotony, that monument of a few men's misery, serves only to make the solitude the more atrocious; for she is a very effigy of terror, telling of tragedies in the past, and to come!

"And now to get back to the beginnings of it. I joined the Homebird, as a passenger, in the early part of November. My health was not quite the thing, and I hoped the voyage would help to set me up. We had a lot of dirty weather for the first couple of weeks out, the wind dead ahead. Then we got a Southerly slant, that carried us down through the forties; but a good deal more to the Westward than we desired. Here we ran right into a tremendous cyclonic storm. All hands were called to shorten sail, and so urgent seemed our need, that the very officers went aloft to help make up the sails, leaving only the Captain (who had taken the wheel) and myself upon the poop. On the maindeck; the cook was busy letting go such ropes as the Mates desired.

"Abruptly, some distance ahead, through the vague sea-mist, but rather on the port bow, I saw loom up a great black wall of cloud.

"'Look, Captain!' I exclaimed; but it had vanished before I had finished speaking. A minute later it came again, and this time the Captain saw it.

"'O, my God!' he cried, and dropped his hands from the wheel. He leapt into the companionway, and seized a speaking trumpet. Then out on deck. He put it to his lips.

"'Come down from aloft! Come down! Come down!' he shouted. And suddenly I lost his voice in a terrific mutter of sound from somewhere to port. It was the voice of the storm—shouting. My God! I had never heard anything like it! It ceased as suddenly as it had begun, and, in the succeeding quietness, I heard the whining of the kicking-tackles through the blocks. Then came a quick clang of brass upon the deck, and I turned quickly. The Captain had thrown down the trumpet, and sprung back to the wheel. I glanced aloft, and saw that many of the men were already in the rigging, and racing down like cats.

"I heard the Captain draw his breath with a quick gasp.

"'Hold on for your lives!' he shouted, in a hoarse, unnatural voice.

"I looked at him. He was staring to windward with a fixed stare of painful intentness, and my gaze followed his. I saw, not four hundred yards distant, an enormous mass of foam and water coming down upon us. In the same instant, I caught the hiss of it, and immediately it was a shriek, so intense and awful, that I cringed impotently with sheer terror.

"The smother of water and foam took the ship a little fore-side of the beam, and the wind was with it. Immediately, the vessel rolled over on to her side, the sea-froth flying over her in tremendous cataracts.

"It seemed as though nothing could save us. Over, over we went, until I was swinging against the deck, almost as against the side of a house; for I had grasped the weather rail at the Captain's warning. As I swung there, I saw a strange thing. Before me was the port quarter boat. Abruptly, the canvas cover was flipped clean off it, as though by a vast, invisible hand.

"The next instant, a flurry of oars, boats' masts and odd gear flittered up into the air, like so many feathers, and blew to leeward and was lost in the roaring chaos of foam. The boat, herself, lifted in her chocks, and suddenly was blown clean down on to the maindeck, where she lay all in a ruin of white-painted timbers.

"A minute of the most intense suspense passed; then, suddenly, the ship righted, and I saw that the three masts had carried away. Yet, so hugely loud was the crying of the storm, that no sound of their breaking had reached me.

"I looked towards the wheel; but no one was there. Then I made out something crumpled up against the lee rail. I struggled across to it, and found that it was the Captain. He was insensible, and queerly limp in his right arm and leg. I looked round. Several of the men were crawling aft along the poop. I beckoned to them, and pointed to the wheel, and then to the Captain. A couple of them came towards me, and one went to the wheel. Then I made out through the spray the form of the Second Mate. He had several more of the men with him, and they had a coil of rope, which they took forrard. I learnt afterwards that they were hastening to get out a sea-anchor, so as to keep the ship's head towards the wind.

"We got the Captain below, and into his bunk. There, I left him in the hands of his daughter and the steward, and returned on deck.

"Presently, the Second Mate came back, and with him the remainder of the men. I found then that only seven had been saved in all. The rest had gone.

"The day passed terribly—the wind getting stronger hourly; though, at its worst, it was nothing like so tremendous as that first burst.

"The night came—a night of terror, with the thunder and hiss of the giant seas in the air above us, and the wind bellowing like some vast Elemental beast.

"Then, just before the dawn, the wind lulled, almost in a moment; the ship rolling and wallowing fearfully, and the water coming aboard—hundreds of tons at a time. Immediately afterwards it caught us again; but more on the beam, and bearing the vessel over on to her side, and this only by the pressure of the element upon the stark hull. As we came head to wind again, we righted, and rode, as we had for hours, amid a thousand fantastic hills of phosphorescent flame.

"Again the wind died—coming again after a longer pause, and then, all at once, leaving us. And so, for the space of a terrible half hour, the ship lived through the most awful, windless sea that can be imagined. There was no doubting but that we had driven right into the calm centre of the cyclone—calm only so far as lack of wind, and yet more dangerous a thousand times than the most furious hurricane that ever blew.

"For now we were beset by the stupendous Pyramidal Sea; a sea once witnessed, never forgotten; a sea in which the whole bosom of the ocean is projected towards heaven in monstrous hills of water; not leaping forward, as would be the case if there were wind; but hurling upwards in jets and peaks of living brine, and falling back in a continuous thunder of foam.

"Imagine this, if you can, and then have the clouds break away suddenly overhead, and the moon shine down upon that hellish turmoil, and you will have such a sight as has been given to mortals but seldom, save with death. And this is what we saw, and to my mind there is nothing within the knowledge of man to which I can liken it.

"Yet we lived through it, and through the wind that came later. But two more complete days and nights had passed, before the storm ceased to be a terror to us, and then, only because it had carried us into the seaweed laden waters of the vast Sargasso Sea.

"Here, the great billows first became foamless; and dwindled gradually in size as we drifted further among the floating masses of weed. Yet the wind was still furious, so that the ship drove on steadily, sometimes between banks, and other times over them.

"For a day and a night we drifted thus; and then astern I made out a great bank of weed, vastly greater than any which hitherto we had encountered. Upon this, the wind drove us stern foremost, so that we over-rode it. We had been forced some distance across it, when it occurred to me that our speed was slackening. I guessed presently that the sea-anchor, ahead, had caught in the weed, and was holding. Even as I surmised this, I heard from beyond the bows a faint, droning, twanging sound, blending with the roar of the wind. There came an indistinct report, and the ship lurched backwards through the weed. The hawser, connecting us with the sea-anchor, had parted.

"I saw the Second Mate run forrard with several men. They hauled in upon the hawser, until the broken end was aboard. In the meantime, the ship, having nothing ahead to keep her "bows on," began to slew broadside towards the wind. I saw the men attach a chain to the end of the broken hawser; then they paid it out again, and the ship's head came back to the gale.

"When the Second Mate came aft, I asked him why this had been done, and he explained that so long as the vessel was end-on, she would travel over the weed. I inquired why he wished her to go over the weed, and he told me that one of the men had made out what appeared to be clear water astern, and that—could we gain it—we might win free.

"Through the whole of that day, we moved rearwards across the great bank; yet, so far from the weed appearing to show signs of thinning, it grew steadily thicker, and, as it became denser, so did our speed slacken, until the ship was barely moving. And so the night found us.

"The following morning discovered to us that we were within a quarter of a mile of a great expanse of clear water—apparently the open sea; but unfortunately the wind had dropped to a moderate breeze, and the vessel was motionless, deep sunk in the weed; great tufts of which rose up on all sides, to within a few feet of the level of our maindeck.

"A man was sent up the stump of the mizzen, to take a look round. From there, he reported that he could see something, that might be weed, across the water; but it was too far distant for him to be in any way certain. Immediately afterwards, he called out that there was something, away on our port beam; but what it was, he could not say, and it was not until a telescope was brought to bear, that we made it out to be the hull of the ancient vessel I have previously mentioned.

"And now, the Second Mate began to cast about for some means by which he could bring the ship to the clear water astern. The first thing which he did, was to bend a sail to a spare yard, and hoist it to the top of the mizzen stump. By this means, he was able to dispense with the cable towing over the bows, which, of course, helped to prevent the ship from moving. In addition, the sail would prove helpful to force the vessel across the weed. Then he routed out a couple of kedges. These, he bent on to the ends of a short piece of cable, and, to the bight of this, the end of a long coil of strong rope.

"After that, he had the starboard quarter boat lowered into the weed, and in it he placed the two kedge anchors. The end of another length of rope, he made fast to the boat's painter. This done, he took four of the men with him, telling them to bring chain-hooks, in addition to the oars—his intention being to force the boat through the weed, until he reached the clear water. There, in the marge of the weed, he would plant the two anchors in the thickest clumps of the growth; after which we were to haul the boat back to the ship, by means of the rope attached to the painter.

"'Then,' as he put it, 'we'll take the kedge-rope to the capstan, and heave her out of this blessed cabbage heap!'

"The weed proved a greater obstacle to the progress of the boat, than, I think, he had anticipated. After half an hour's work, they had gone scarcely more than some two hundred feet from the vessel; yet, so thick was the stuff, that no sign could we see of them, save the movement they made among the weed, as they forced the boat along.

"Another quarter of an hour passed away, during which the three men left upon the poop, paid out the ropes as the boat forged slowly ahead. All at once, I heard my name called. Turning, I saw the Captain's daughter in the companionway, beckoning to me. I walked across to her.

"'My father has sent me up to know, Mr. Philips, how they are getting on?'

"'Very slowly, Miss Knowles,' I replied. 'Very slowly indeed. The weed is so extraordinarily thick.'

"She nodded intelligently, and turned to descend; but I detained her a moment.

"'Your father, how is he?' I asked.

"She drew her breath swiftly.

"'Quite himself,' she said; 'but so dreadfully weak. He—'

"An outcry from one of the men, broke across her speech:—

"'Lord 'elp us, mates! wot were that!'

"I turned sharply. The three of them were staring over the taffrail. I ran towards them, and Miss Knowles followed.

"'Hush!' she said, abruptly. 'Listen!'

"I stared astern to where I knew the boat to be. The weed all about it was quaking queerly—the movement extending far beyond the radius of their hooks and oars. Suddenly, I heard the Second Mate's voice:

"'Look out, lads! My God, look out!'

"And close upon this, blending almost with it, came the hoarse scream of a man in sudden agony.

"I saw an oar come up into view, and descend violently, as though someone struck at something with it. Then the Second Mate's voice, shouting:—

"'Aboard there! Aboard there! Haul in on the rope! Haul in on the rope!' It broke off into a sharp cry.

"As we seized hold of the rope, I saw the weed hurled in all directions, and a great crying and choking swept to us over the brown hideousness around.

"'Pull!' I yelled, and we pulled. The rope tautened; but the boat never moved.

"'Tek it ter ther capsting!' gasped one of the men.

"Even as he spoke, the rope slackened. "'It's coming!' cried Miss Knowles. 'Pull! Oh! Pull!'

"She had hold of the rope along with us, and together we hauled, the boat yielding to our strength with surprising ease.

"'There it is!' I shouted, and then I let go of the rope. There was no one in the boat.

"'For the half of a minute, we stared, dumfoundered. Then my gaze wandered astern to the place from which we had plucked it. There was a heaving movement among the great weed masses. I saw something waver up aimlessly against the sky; it was sinuous, and it flickered once or twice from side to side; then sank back among the growth, before I could concentrate my attention upon it.

"I was recalled to myself by a sound of dry sobbing. Miss Knowles was kneeling upon the deck, her hands clasped round one of the iron uprights of the rail. She seemed momentarily all to pieces.

"'Come! Miss Knowles,' I said, gently. 'You must be brave. We cannot let your father know of this in his present state.'

"She allowed me to help her to her feet. I could feel that she was trembling badly. Then, even as I sought for words with which to reassure her, there came a dull thud from the direction of the companionway. We looked round. On the deck, face downward, lying half in and half out of the scuttle, was the Captain. Evidently, he had witnessed everything. Miss Knowles gave out a wild cry, and ran to her father. I beckoned to one of the men to help me, and, together, we carried him back to his bunk. An hour later, he recovered from his swoon. He was quite calm, though very weak, and evidently in considerable pain.

"Through his daughter, he made known to me that he wished me to take the reins of authority in his place. This, after a slight demur, I decided to do; for, as I reassured myself, there were no duties required of me, needing any special knowledge of shipcraft. The vessel was fast; so far as I could see, irrevocably fast. It would be time to talk of freeing her, when the Captain was well enough to take charge once more.

"I returned on deck, and made known to the men the Captain's wishes. Then I chose one to act as a sort of bo'sun over the other two, and to him I gave orders that everything should be put to rights before the night came. I had sufficient sense to leave him to manage matters in his own way; for, whereas my knowledge of what was needful, was fragmentary, his was complete.

"By this time, it was near to sunsetting, and it was with melancholy feelings that I watched the great hull of the sun plunge lower. For awhile, I paced the poop, stopping ever and anon to stare over the dreary waste by which we were surrounded. The more I looked about, the more a sense of lonesomeness and depression and fear assailed me. I had pondered much upon the dread happening of the day, and all my ponderings led to a vital questioning:—What was there among all that quiet weed, which had come upon the crew of the boat, and destroyed them? And I could not make answer, and the weed was silent—dreadly silent!

"The sun had drawn very near to the dim horizon, and I watched it, moodily, as it splashed great clots of red fire across the water that lay stretched into the distance across our stern. Abruptly, as I gazed, its perfect lower edge was marred by an irregular shape. For a moment, I stared, puzzled. Then I fetched a pair of glasses from the holdfast in the companion. A glance through these, and I knew the extent of our fate. That line, blotching the round of the sun, was the conformation of another enormous weed bank.

"I remembered that the man had reported something as showing across the water, when he was sent up to the top of the mizzen stump in the morning; but, what it was, he had been unable to say. The thought flashed into my mind that it had been only just visible from aloft in the morning, and now it was in sight from the deck. It occurred to me that the wind might be compacting the weed, and driving the bank which surrounded the ship, down upon a larger portion. Possibly, the clear stretch of water had been but a temporary rift within the heart of the Sargasso Sea. It seemed only too probable.

"Thus it was that I meditated, and so, presently, the night found me. For some hours further, I paced the deck in the darkness, striving to understand the incomprehensible; yet with no better result than to weary myself to death. Then, somewhere about midnight, I went below to sleep.

"The following morning, on going on deck, I found that the stretch of clear water had disappeared entirely, during the night, and now, so far as the eye could reach, there was nothing but a stupendous desolation of weed.

"The wind had dropped completely, and no sound came from all that weed-ridden immensity. We had, in truth, reached the Cemetery of the Ocean!

"The day passed uneventfully enough. It was only when I served out some food to the men, and one of them asked whether they could have a few raisins, that I remembered, with a pang of sudden misery, that it was Christmas day. I gave them the fruit, as they desired, and they spent the morning in the galley, cooking their dinner. Their stolid indifference to the late terrible happenings, appalled me somewhat, until I remembered what their lives were, and had been. Poor fellows! One of them ventured aft at dinner time, and offered me a slice of what he called 'plum duff.' He brought it on a plate which he had found in the galley and scoured thoroughly with sand and water. He tendered it shyly enough, and I took it, so graciously as I could, for I would not hurt his feelings; though the very smell of the stuff was an abomination.

"During the afternoon, I brought out the Captain's telescope, and made a thorough examination of the ancient hulk on our port beam. Particularly did I study the extraordinary superstructure around her sides; but could not, as I have said before, conceive of its use.

"The evening, I spent upon the poop, my eyes searching wearily across that vile quietness, and so, in a little, the night came—Christmas night, sacred to a thousand happy memories. I found myself dreaming of the night a year previous, and, for a little while, I forgot what was before me. I was recalled suddenly—terribly. A voice rose out of the dark which hid the maindeck. For the fraction of an instant, it expressed surprise; then pain and terror leapt into it. Abruptly, it seemed to come from above, and then from somewhere beyond the ship, and so in a moment there was silence, save for a rush of feet and the bang of a door forrard.

"I leapt down the poop ladder, and ran along the maindeck, towards the fo'cas'le. As I ran, something knocked off my cap. I scarcely noticed it then. I reached the fo'cas'le, and caught at the latch of the port door. I lifted it and pushed; but the door was fastened.

"'Inside there!' I cried, and banged upon the panels with my clenched fist.

"A man's voice came, incoherently.

"'Open the door!' I shouted. 'Open the door!'

"'Yes, Sir—I'm com—ming, Sir,' said one of them, jerkily.

"I heard footsteps stumble across the planking. Then a hand fumbled at the fastening, and the door flew open under my weight.

"The man who had opened to me, started back. He held a flaring slush-lamp above his head, and, as I entered, he thrust it forward. His hand was trembling visibly, and, behind him, I made out the face of one of his mates, the brow and dirty, clean-shaven upper lip drenched with sweat. The man who held the lamp, opened his mouth, and gabbered at me; but, for a moment, no sound came.

"'Wot—wot were it? Wot we-ere it?' he brought out at last, with a gasp.

"The man behind, came to his side, and gesticulated.

"'What was what?' I asked sharply, and looking from one to the other. 'Where's the other man? What was that screaming?'

"The second man drew the palm of his hand across his brow; then flirted his fingers deckwards.

"'We don't know, Sir! We don't know! It were Jessop! Somethin's took 'im just as we was comin' forrid! We—we—He-he-HARK!'

"His head came forward with a jerk as he spoke, and then, for a space, no one stirred. A minute passed, and I was about to speak, when, suddenly, from somewhere out upon the deserted maindeck, there came a queer, subdued noise, as though something moved stealthily hither and thither. The man with the lamp caught me by the sleeve, and then, with an abrupt movement, slammed the door and fastened it.

"'That's IT, Sir!' he exclaimed, with a note of terror and conviction in his voice.

"I bade him be silent, while I listened; but no sound came to us through the door, and so I turned to the men and told them to let me have all they knew.

"It was little enough. They had been sitting in the galley, yarning, until, feeling tired, they had decided to go forrard and turn-in. They extinguished the light, and came out upon the deck, closing the door behind them. Then, just as they turned to go forrard, Jessop gave out a yell. The next instant they heard him screaming in the air above their heads, and, realising that some terrible thing was upon them, they took forthwith to their heels, and ran for the security of the fo'cas'le.

"Then I had come.

"As the men made an end of telling me, I thought I heard something outside, and held up my hand for silence. I caught the sound again. Someone was calling my name. It was Miss Knowles. Likely enough she was calling me to supper—and she had no knowledge of the dread thing which had happened. I sprang to the door. She might be coming along the maindeck in search of me. And there was Something out there, of which I had no conception—something unseen, but deadly tangible!

"'Stop, Sir!' shouted the men, together; but I had the door open.

"'Mr. Philips!' came the girl's voice at no great distance. 'Mr. Philips!'

"'Coming, Miss Knowles!' I shouted, and snatched the lamp from the man's hand.

"'The next instant, I was running aft, holding the lamp high, and glancing fearfully from side to side. I reached the place where the mainmast had been, and spied the girl coming towards me.

"'Go back!' I shouted. 'Go back!'

"She turned at my shout, and ran for the poop ladder. I came up with her, and followed close at her heels. On the poop, she turned and faced me.

"'What is it, Mr. Philips?'

"I hesitated. Then:—

"'I don't know!' I said.

"'My father heard something,' she began. 'He sent me. He—'

"I put up my hand. It seemed to me that I had caught again the sound of something stirring on the maindeck.

"'Quick!' I said sharply. 'Down into the cabin!.' And she, being a sensible girl, turned and ran down without waste of time. I followed, closing and fastening the companion-doors behind me.

"In the saloon, we had a whispered talk, and I told her everything. She bore up bravely, and said nothing; though her eyes were very wide, and her face pale. Then the Captain's voice came to us from the adjoining cabin.

"'Is Mr. Philips there, Mary?'

"'Yes, father.'

"'Bring him in.'

"I went in.

"'What was it, Mr. Philips?' he asked, collectedly.

"I hesitated; for I was willing to spare him the ill news; but he looked at me with calm eyes for a moment, and I knew that it was useless attempting to deceive him.

"'Something has happened, Mr. Philips,' he said, quietly. 'You need not be afraid to tell me.'

"At that, I told him so much as I knew, he listening, and nodding his comprehension of the story.

"'It must be something big,' he remarked, when I had made an end. 'And yet you saw nothing when you came aft?'

"'No,' I replied.

"'It is something in the weed,' he went on. 'You will have to keep off the deck at night.'

"After a little further talk, in which he displayed a calmness that amazed me, I left him, and went presently to my berth.

"The following day, I took the two men, and, together, we made a thorough search through the ship; but found nothing. It was evident to me that the Captain was right. There was some dread Thing hidden within the weed. I went to the side and looked down. The two men followed me. Suddenly, one of them pointed.

"'Look, Sir!' he exclaimed. 'Right below you, Sir! Two eyes like blessed great saucers! Look!'

"I stared; but could see nothing. The man left my side, and ran into the galley. In a moment, he was back with a great lump of coal.

"'Just there, Sir,' he said, and hove it down into the weed immediately beneath where we stood.

"Too late, I saw the thing at which he aimed—two immense eyes, some little distance below the surface of the weed. I knew instantly to what they belonged; for I had seen large specimens of the octopus some years previously, during a cruise in Australasian waters.

"'Look out, man!' I shouted, and caught him by the arm. 'It's an octopus! Jump back!' I sprang down on to the deck. In the same instant, huge masses of weed were hurled in all directions, and half a dozen immense tentacles whirled up into the air. One lapped itself about his neck. I caught his leg; but he was torn from my grasp, and I tumbled backwards on to the deck. I heard a scream from the other man as I scrambled to my feet. I looked to where he had been; but of him there was no sign. Regardless of the danger, in my great agitation, I leapt upon the rail, and gazed down with frightened eyes. Yet, neither of him nor his mate, nor the monster, could I perceive a vestige.

"How long I stood there staring down bewilderedly, I cannot say; certainly some minutes. I was so bemazed that I seemed incapable of movement. Then, all at once, I became aware that a light quiver ran across the weed, and the next instant, something stole up out of the depths with a deadly celerity. Well it was for me that I had seen it in time, else should I have shared the fate of those two—and the others. As it was, I saved myself only by leaping backwards on to the deck. For a moment, I saw the feeler wave above the rail with a certain apparent aimlessness; then it sank out of sight, and I was alone.

"An hour passed before I could summon a sufficiency of courage to break the news of this last tragedy to the Captain and his daughter, and when I had made an end, I returned to the solitude of the poop; there to brood upon the hopelessness of our position.

"As I paced up and down, I caught myself glancing continuously at the nearer weed tufts. The happenings of the past two days had shattered my nerves, and I feared every moment to see some slender death-grapple searching over the rail for me. Yet, the poop, being very much higher out of the weed than the maindeck, was comparatively safe; though only comparatively.

"Presently, as I meandered up and down, my gaze fell upon the hulk of the ancient ship, and, in a flash, the reason for that great superstructure was borne upon me. It was intended as a protection against the dread creatures which inhabited the weed. The thought came to me that I would attempt some similar means of protection; for the feeling that, at any moment, I might be caught and lifted out into that slimy wilderness, was not to be borne. In addition, the work would serve to occupy my mind, and help me to bear up against the intolerable sense of loneliness which assailed me.

"I resolved that I would lose no time, and so, after some thought as to the manner in which I should proceed, I routed out some coils of rope and several sails. Then I went down on to the maindeck and brought up an armful of capstan bars. These I lashed vertically to the rail all round the poop. Then I knotted the rope to each, stretching it tightly between them, and over this framework stretched the sails, sewing the stout canvas to the rope, by means of twine and some great needles which I found in the Mate's room.

"It is not to be supposed that this piece of work was accomplished immediately. Indeed, it was only after three days of hard labour that I got the poop completed. Then I commenced work upon the maindeck. This was a tremendous undertaking, and a whole fortnight passed before I had the entire length of it enclosed; for I had to be continually on the watch against the hidden enemy. Once, I was very nearly surprised, and saved myself only by a quick leap. Thereafter, for the rest of that day, I did no more work; being too greatly shaken in spirit. Yet, on the following morning, I recommenced, and from thence, until the end, I was not molested.

"Once the work was roughly completed, I felt at ease to begin and perfect it. This I did, by tarring the whole of the sails with Stockholm tar ; thereby making them stiff, and capable of resisting the weather. After that, I added many fresh uprights, and much strengthening ropework, and finally doubled the sailcloth with additional sails, liberally smeared with the tar.

"In this manner, the whole of January passed away, and a part of February. Then, it would be on the last day of the month, the Captain sent for me, and told me, without any preliminary talk, that he was dying. I looked at him; but said nothing; for I had known long that it was so. In return, he stared back with a strange intentness, as though he would read my inmost thoughts, and this for the space of perhaps two minutes.

"'Mr. Philips,' he said at last, 'I may be dead by this time to-morrow. Has it ever occurred to you that my daughter will be alone with you ?'

"'Yes, Captain Knowles,' I replied, quietly, and waited.

"For a few seconds, he remained silent; though, from the changing expressions of his face, I knew that he was pondering how best to bring forward the thing which it was in his mind to say.

"'You are a gentleman—' he began, at last.

"'I will marry her,' I said, ending the sentence for him.

"A slight flush of surprise crept into his face.

"'You—you have thought seriously about it?'

"'I have thought very seriously,' I explained.

"'Ah!' he said, as one who comprehends. And then, for a little, he lay there quietly. It was plain to me that memories of past days were with him. Presently, he came out of his dreams, and spoke, evidently referring to my marriage with his daughter.

"'It is the only thing,' he said, in a level voice.

"I bowed, and after that, he was silent again for a space. In a little, however, he turned once more to me:—

"'Do you—do you love her?'

"His tone was keenly wistful, and a sense of trouble lurked in his eyes.

"'She will be my wife,' I said, simply; and he nodded.

"'God has dealt strangely with us,' he murmured presently, as though to himself.

"Abruptly, he bade me tell her to come in.

"And then he married us.]

"Three days later, he was dead, and we were alone.

"For a while, my wife was a sad woman; but gradually time eased her of the bitterness of her grief.

"Then, some eight months after our marriage, a new interest stole into her life. She whispered it to me, and we, who had borne our loneliness uncomplainingly, had now this new thing to which to look forward. It became a bond between us, and bore promise of some companionship as we grew old. Old! At the idea of age, a sudden flash of thought darted like lightning across the sky of my mind:— FOOD! Hitherto, I had thought of myself, almost as of one already dead, and had cared naught for anything beyond the immediate troubles which each day forced upon me. The loneliness of the vast Weed World had become an assurance of doom to me, which had clouded and dulled my faculties, so that I had grown apathetic. Yet, immediately, as it seemed, at the shy whispering of my wife, was all this changed.

"That very hour, I began a systematic search through the ship. Among the cargo, which was of a 'general' nature, I discovered large quantities of preserved and tinned provisions, all of which I put carefully on one side. I continued my examination until I had ransacked the whole vessel. The business took me near upon six months to complete, and when it was finished, I seized paper, and made calculations, which led me to the conclusion that we had sufficient food in the ship to preserve life in three people for some fifteen to seventeen years. I could not come nearer to it than this; for I had no means of computing the quantity the child would need year by year. Yet it is sufficient to show me that seventeen years must be the limit. Seventeen years! And then—

"Concerning water, I am not troubled; for I have rigged a great sailcloth tun-dish, with a canvas pipe into the tanks; and from every rain, I draw a supply, which has never run short.

"The child was born nearly five months ago. She is a fine little girl, and her mother seems perfectly happy. I believe I could be quietly happy with them, were it not that I have ever in mind the end of those seventeen years. True! we may be dead long before then; but, if not, our little girl will be in her teens—and it is a hungry age.

"If one of us died—but no! Much may happen in seventeen years. I will wait.

"My method of sending this clear of the weed is likely to succeed. I have constructed a small fire-balloon, and this missive, safely enclosed in a little barrel, will be attached. The wind will carry it swiftly hence.

"Should this ever reach civilised beings, will they see that it is forwarded to:—"

(Here followed an address, which, for some reason, had been roughly obliterated. Then came the signature of the writer)

"Arthur Samuel Philips."

The captain of the schooner looked over at Jock, as the man made an end of his reading.

"Seventeen years pervisions," he muttered thoughtfully. "An' this 'ere were written sumthin' like twenty-nine years ago!" He nodded his head several times. "Poor creatures!" he exclaimed. "It'd be er long while, Jock—a long while!"

FROM THE TIDELESS SEA

(Further News of the "Homebird")

In the August of 1902, Captain Bateman, of the schooner Agnes, picked up a small barrel, upon which was painted a half obliterated word; which, finally, he succeeded in deciphering as "Homebird," the name of a full-rigged ship, which left London in the November of 1873, and from thenceforth was heard of no more by any man.

Captain Bateman opened the barrel, and discovered a packet of Manuscript, wrapped in oilskin. This, on examination, proved to be an account of the losing of the Homebird amid the desolate wastes of the Sargasso Sea. The papers were written by one, Arthur Samuel Philips, a passenger in the ship; and, from them, Captain Bateman was enabled to gather that the ship, mastless, lay in the very heart of the dreaded Sargasso; and that all of the crew had been lost—some in the storm which drove them thither, and some in attempts to free the ship from the weed, which locked them in on all sides.

Only Mr. Philips and the Captain's daughter had been left alive, and they two, the dying Captain had married. To them had been born a daughter, and the papers ended with a brief but touching allusion to their fear that, eventually, they must run short of food.

There is need to say but little more. The account was copied into most of the papers of the day, and caused widespread comment. There was even some talk of fitting out a rescue expedition; but this fell through, owing chiefly to lack of knowledge of the whereabouts of the ship in all the vastness of the immense Sargasso Sea. And so, gradually, the matter has slipped into the background of the Public's memory.

Now, however, interest will be once more excited in the lonesome fate of this lost trio; for a second barrel, identical, it would seem, with that found by Captain Bateman, has been picked up by a Mr. Bolton, of Baltimore, master of a small brig, engaged in the South American coast-trade. In this barrel was enclosed a further message from Mr. Philips—the fifth that he has sent abroad to the world; but the second, third and fourth, up to this time, have not been discovered.

This "fifth message" contains a vital and striking account of their lives during the year 1879, and stands unique as a document informed with human lonesomeness and longing. I have seen it, and read it through, with the most intense and painful interest. The writing, though faint, is very legible; and the whole manuscript bears the impress of the same hand and mind that wrote the piteous account of the losing of the Homebird, of which I have already made mention, and with which, no doubt, many are well acquainted.

In closing this little explanatory note, I am stimulated to wonder whether, somewhere, at some time, those three missing messages ever shall be found. And then there may be others. What stories of human, strenuous fighting with Fate may they not contain.

We can but wait and wonder. Nothing more may we ever learn; for what is this one little tragedy among the uncounted millions that the silence of the sea holds so remorselessly. And yet, again, news may come to us out of the Unknown—out of the lonesome silences of the dread Sargasso Sea—the loneliest and the most inaccessible place of all the lonesome and inaccessible places of this earth.

And so I say, let us wait. W. H. H.

THE FIFTH MESSAGE

"This is the fifth message that I have sent abroad over the loathsome surface of this vast Weed-World, praying that it may come to the open sea, ere the lifting power of my fire-balloon be gone, and yet, if it come there—the which I could now doubt—how shall I be the better for it! Yet write I must, or go mad, and so I choose to write, though feeling as I write that no living creature, save it be the giant octopi that live in the weed about me, will ever see the thing I write.

"My first message I sent out on Christmas Eve, 1875, and since then, each eve of the birth of Christ has seen a message go skywards upon the winds, towards the open sea. It is as though this approaching time, of festivity and the meeting of parted loved ones, overwhelms me, and drives away the half apathetic peace that has been mine through spaces of these years of lonesomeness; so that I seclude myself from my wife and the little one, and with ink, pen, and paper, try to ease my heart of the pent emotions that seem at times to threaten to burst it.

"It is now six completed years since the Weed-World claimed us from the World of the Living—six years away from our brothers and sisters of the human and living world—It has been six years of living in a grave! And there are all the years ahead! Oh! My God! My God! I dare not think upon them! I must control myself—

"And then there is the little one, she is nearly four and a half now, and growing wonderfully, out among these wilds. Four and a half years, and the little woman has never seen a human face besides ours—think of it! And yet, if she lives four and forty years, she will never see another.... Four and forty years! It is foolishness to trouble about such a space of time; for the future, for us, ends in ten years—eleven at the utmost. Our food will last no longer than that.... My wife does not know; for it seems to me a wicked thing to add unnecessarily to her punishment. She does but know that we must waste no ounce of food-stuff, and for the rest she imagines that the most of the cargo is of an edible nature. Perhaps, I have nurtured this belief. If anything happened to me, the food would last a few extra years; but my wife would have to imagine it an accident, else would each bite she took sicken her.

"I have thought often and long upon this matter, yet I fear to leave them; for who knows but that their very lives might at any time depend upon my strength, more pitifully, perhaps, than upon the food which they must come at last to lack. No, I must not bring upon them, and myself, a near and certain calamity, to defer one that, though it seems to have but little less certainty, is yet at a further distance.

"Until lately, nothing has happened to us in the past four years, if I except the adventures that attended my mad attempt to cut a way through the surrounding weed to freedom, and from which it pleased God that I and those with me should be preserved. [1] Yet, in the latter part of this year, an adventure, much touched with grimness, came to us most unexpectedly, in a fashion quite unthought of—an adventure that has brought into our lives a fresh and more active peril; for now I have learned that the weed holds other terrors besides that of the giant octopi.

"Indeed, I have grown to believe this world of desolation capable of holding any horror, as well it might. Think of it—an interminable stretch of dank, brown loneliness in all directions, to the distant horizon; a place where monsters of the deep and the weed have undisputed reign; where never an enemy may fall upon them; but from which they may strike with sudden deadliness! No human can ever bring an engine of destruction to bear upon them, and the humans whose fate it is to have sight of them, do so only from the decks of lonesome derelicts, whence they stare lonely with fear, and without ability to harm.

"I cannot describe it, nor can any hope ever to imagine it! When the wind falls, a vast silence holds us girt, from horizon to horizon, yet it is a silence through which one seems to feel the pulse of hidden things all about us, watching and waiting—waiting and watching; waiting but for the chance to reach forth a huge and sudden death-grapple.... It is no use! I cannot bring it home to any; nor shall I be better able to convey the frightening sound of the wind, sweeping across these vast, quaking plains—the shrill whispering of the weed-fronds, under the stirring of the winds. To hear it from beyond our canvas screen, is like listening to the uncounted dead of the mighty Sargasso wailing their own requiems. Or again, my fancy, diseased with much loneliness and brooding, likens it to the advancing rustle of armies of the great monsters that are always about us—waiting.

"And so to the coming of this new terror:—

"It was in the latter end of October that we first had knowledge of it—a tapping in the night time against the side of the vessel, below the water-line; a noise that came distinct, yet with a ghostly strangeness in the quietness of the night. It was on a Monday night when first I heard it. I was down in the lazarette, overhauling our stores, and suddenly I heard it—tap—tap—tap—against the outside of the vessel upon the starboard side, and below the water line. I stood for awhile listening; but could not discover what it was that should come a-tapping against our side, away out here in this lonesome world of weed and slime. And then, as I stood there listening, the tapping ceased, and so I waited, wondering, and with a hateful sense of fear, weakening my manhood, and taking the courage out of my heart....

"Abruptly, it recommenced; but now upon the opposite side of the vessel, and as it continued, I fell into a little sweat; for it seemed to me that some foul thing out in the night was tapping for admittance. Tap—tap—tap—it went, and continued, and there I stood listening, and so gripped about with frightened thoughts, that I seemed without power to stir myself; for the spell of the Weed-World, and the fear bred of its hidden terrors and the weight and dreeness of its loneliness have entered into my marrow, so that I could, then and now, believe in the likelihood of matters which, ashore and in the midst of my fellows, I might laugh at in contempt. It is the dire lonesomeness of this strange world into which I have entered, that serves so to take the heart out of a man.

"And so, as I have said, I stood there listening, and full of frightened, but undefined, thoughts; and all the while the tapping continued, sometimes with a regular insistence, and anon with a quick spasmodic tap, tap, tap-a-tap, as though some Thing, having Intelligence, signalled to me.

"Presently, however, I shook off something of the foolish fright that had taken me, and moved over to the place from which the tapping seemed to sound. Coming near to it, I bent my head down, close to the side of the vessel, and listened. Thus, I heard the noises with greater plainness, and could distinguish easily, now, that something knocked with a hard object upon the outside of the ship, as though someone had been striking her iron side with a small hammer.

"Then, even as I listened, came a thunderous blow close to my ear, so loud and astonishing, that I leaped sideways in sheer fright. Directly afterwards there came a second heavy blow, and then a third, as though someone had struck the ship's side with a heavy sledge-hammer, and after that, a space of silence, in which I heard my wife's voice at the trap of the lazarette, calling down to me to know what had happened to cause so great a noise.

"'Hush, My Dear!' I whispered; for it seemed to me that the thing outside might hear her; though this could not have been possible, and I do but mention it as showing how the noises had set me off my natural balance.

"At my whispered command, my wife turned her about and came down the ladder into the semi-darkness of the place.

"'What is it, Arthur?' she asked, coming across to me, and slipping her hand between my arm and side.

"As though in reply to her query, there came against the outside of the ship, a fourth tremendous blow, filling the whole of the lazarette with a dull thunder.

"My wife gave out a frightened cry, and sprang away from me; but the next instant, she was back, and gripping hard at my arm.

"'What is it, Arthur? What is it?' she asked me; her voice, though no more than a frightened whisper, easily heard in the succeeding silence.

"'I don't know, Mary,' I replied, trying to speak in a level tone. 'It's—'

"'There's something again,' she interrupted, as the minor tapping noises recommenced.

"For about a minute, we stood silent, listening to those eerie taps. Then my wife turned to me:—

"'Is it anything dangerous, Arthur—tell me? I promise you I shall be brave.'

"'I can't possibly say, Mary,' I answered. 'I can't say; but I'm going up on deck to listen.... Perhaps,' I paused a moment to think; but a fifth tremendous blow against the ship's side, drove whatever I was going to say, clean from me, and I could do no more than stand there, frightened and bewildered, listening for further sounds. After a short pause, there came a sixth blow. Then my wife caught me by the arm, and commenced to drag me towards the ladder.

"'Come up out of this dark place, Arthur,' she said. 'I shall be ill if we stay here any longer. Perhaps the—the thing outside can hear us, and it may stop if we go upstairs.'

"By this, my wife was all of a shake, and I but little better, so that I was glad to follow her up the ladder. At the top, we paused for a while to listen, bending down over the open hatchway. A space of, maybe, some five minutes passed away in silence; then there commenced again the tapping noises, the sounds coming clearly up to us where we crouched. Presently, they ceased once more, and after that, though we listened for a further space of some ten minutes, they were not repeated. Neither were there any more of the great bangs.

"In a little, I led my wife away from the hatch, to a seat in the saloon; for the hatch is situated under the saloon table. After that, I returned to the opening, and replaced the cover. Then I went into our cabin—the one which had been the Captain's, her father,—and brought from there a revolver, of which we have several. This, I loaded with care, and afterwards placed in my side pocket.

"Having done this, I fetched from the pantry, where I have made it my use to keep such things at hand, a bull's-eye lantern, the same having been used on dark nights when clearing up the ropes from the decks. This, I lit, and afterwards turned the dark-slide to cover the light. Next, I slipped off my boots; and then, as an afterthought, I reached down one of the long-handled American axes from the rack about the mizzenmast—these being keen and very formidable weapons.

"After that, I had to calm my wife and assure her that I would run no unnecessary risks, if, indeed, there were any risks to run; though, as may be imagined, I could not say what new peril might not be upon us. And then, picking up the lantern, I made my way silently on stockinged feet, up the companionway. I had reached the top, and was just stepping out on to the deck, when something caught my arm. I turned swiftly, and perceived that my wife had followed me up the steps, and from the shaking of her hand upon my arm, I gathered that she was very much agitated.

"'Oh, My Dear, My Dear, don't go! don't go!' she whispered, eagerly. 'Wait until it is daylight. Stay below to-night. You don't know what may be about in this horrible place.'

"I put the lantern and the axe upon the deck beside the companion; then bent towards the opening, and took her into my arms, soothing her, and stroking her hair; yet with ever an alert glance to and fro along the indistinct decks. Presently, she was more like her usual self, and listened to my reasoning, that she would do better to stay below, and so, in a little, left me, having made me promise afresh that I would be very wary of danger.

"When she had gone, I picked up the lantern and the axe, and made my way cautiously to the side of the vessel. Here, I paused and listened very carefully, being just above that spot upon the port side where I had heard the greater part of the tapping, and all of the heavy bangs; yet, though I listened, as I have said, with much attention, there was no repetition of the sounds.

"Presently, I rose and made my way forrard to the break of the poop. Here, bending over the rail which ran across, I listened, peering along the dim maindecks; but could neither see nor hear anything; not that, indeed, I had any reason for expecting to see or hear ought unusual aboard of the vessel; for all of the noises had come from over the side, and, more than that, from beneath the water-line. Yet in the state of mind in which I was, I had less use for reason than fancy; for that strange thudding and tapping, out here in the midst of this world of loneliness, had set me vaguely imagining unknowable terrors, stealing upon me from every shadow that lay upon the dimly-seen decks.

"Then, as still I listened, hesitating to go down on to the maindeck, yet too dissatisfied with the result of my peerings, to cease from my search, I heard, faint yet clear in the stillness of the night, the tapping noises recommence.

"I took my weight from off the rail, and listened; but I could no longer hear them, and at that, I leant forward again over the rail, and peered down on to the maindeck. Immediately, the sounds came once more to me, and I knew now, that they were borne to me by the medium of the rail, which conducted them to me through the iron stanchions by which it is fixed to the vessel.

"At that, I turned and went aft along the poop deck, moving very warily and with quietness. I stopped over the place where first I had heard the louder noises, and stooped, putting my ear against the rail. Here, the sounds came to me with great distinctness.

"For a little, I listened; then stood up, and slid away that part of the tarred canvas-screen which covers the port opening through which we dump our refuse; they being made here for convenience, one upon each side of the vessel. This, I did very silently; then, leaning forward through the opening, I peered down into the dimness of the weed. Even as I did so, I heard plainly below me a heavy thud, muffled and dull by reason of the intervening water, against the iron side of the ship. It seemed to me that there was some disturbance amid the dark, shadowy masses of the weed. Then I had opened the dark-slide of my lantern, and sent a clear beam of light down into the blackness. For a brief instant, I thought I perceived a multitude of things moving. Yet, beyond that they were oval in shape, and showed white through the weed fronds, I had no clear conception of anything; for with the flash of the light, they vanished, and there lay beneath me only the dark, brown masses of the weed—demurely quiet.

"But an impression they did leave upon my over excited imagination—an impression that might have been due to morbidity, bred of too much loneliness; but nevertheless it seemed to me that I had seen momentarily a multitude of dead white faces, upturned towards me among the meshes of the weed.

"For a little, I leant there, staring down at the circle of illumined weed; yet with my thoughts in such a turmoil of frightened doubts and conjectures, that my physical eyes did but poor work, compared with the orb that looks inward. And through all the chaos of my mind there rose up weird and creepy memories—ghouls, the un-dead. There seemed nothing improbable, in that moment, in associating the terms with the fears that were besetting me. For no man may dare to say what terrors this world holds, until he has become lost to his brother men, amid the unspeakable desolation of the vast and slimy weed-plains of the Sargasso Sea.

"And then, as I leaned there, so foolishly exposing myself to those dangers which I had learnt did truly exist, my eyes caught and subconsciously noted the strange and subtle undulation which always foretells the approach of one of the giant octopi. Instantly, I leapt back, and whipped the tarred canvas-cover across the opening, and so stood alone there in the night, glancing frightenedly before and behind me, the beam from my lamp casting wavering splashes of light to and fro about the decks. And all the time, I was listening—listening; for it seemed to me that some Terror was brooding in the night, that might come upon us at any moment and in some unimagined form.

"Then, across the silence, stole a whisper, and I turned swiftly towards the companionway. My wife was there, and she reached out her arms to me, begging me to come below into safety. As the light from my lantern flashed upon her, I saw that she had a revolver in her right hand, and at that, I asked her what she had it for; whereupon she informed me that she had been watching over me, through the whole of the time that I had been on deck, save for the little while that it had taken her to get and load the weapon.

"At that, as may be imagined, I went and embraced her very heartily, kissing her for the love that had prompted her actions; and then, after that, we spoke a little together in low tones—she asking that I should come down and fasten up the companion-doors, and I demurring, telling her that I felt too unsettled to sleep; but would rather keep watch about the poop for a while longer.

"Then, even as we discussed the matter, I motioned to her for quietness. In the succeeding silence, she heard it, as well as I, a slow—tap! tap! tap! coming steadily along the dark maindecks. I felt a swift vile fear, and my wife's hold upon me became very tense, despite that she trembled a little. I released her grip from my arm, and made to go towards the break of the poop; but she was after me instantly, praying me at least to stay where I was, if I would not go below.

"Upon that, I bade her very sternly to release me, and go down into the cabin; though all the while I loved her for her very solicitude. But she disobeyed me, asserting very stoutly, though in a whisper, that if I went into danger, she would go with me; and at that I hesitated; but decided, after a moment, to go no further than the break of the poop, and not to venture on to the maindeck.

"I went very silently to the break, and my wife followed me. From the rail across the break, I shone the light of the lantern; but could neither see nor hear anything; for the tapping noise had ceased. Then it recommenced, seeming to have come near to the port side of the stump of the mainmast. I turned the lantern towards it, and, for one brief instant, it seemed to me that I saw something pale, just beyond the brightness of my light. At that, I raised my pistol and fired, and my wife did the same, though without any telling on my part. The noise of the double explosion went very loud and hollow sounding along the decks, and after the echoes had died away, we both of us thought we heard the tapping going away forrard again.

"After that, we stayed awhile, listening and watching; but all was quiet, and, presently, I consented to go below and bar up the companion, as my wife desired; for, indeed, there was much sense in her plea of the futility of my staying up upon the decks.

"The night passed quietly enough, and on the following morning, I made a very careful inspection of the vessel, examining the decks, the weed outside of the ship, and the sides of her. After that, I removed the hatches, and went down into the holds; but could nowhere find anything of an unusual nature.

"That night, just as we were making an end of our supper, we heard three tremendous blows given against the starboard side of the ship, whereat, I sprang to my feet, seized and lit the dark-lantern, which I had kept handy, and ran quickly and silently up on to the deck. My pistol, I had already in my pocket, and as I had soft slippers upon my feet, I needed not to pause to remove my footgear. In the companionway, I had left the axe, and this I seized as I went up the steps.

"Reaching the deck, I moved over quietly to the side, and slid back the canvas door; then I leant out and opened the slide of the lantern, letting its light play upon the weed in the direction from which the bangs had seemed to proceed; but nowhere could I perceive anything out of the ordinary, the weed seeming undisturbed. And so, after a little, I drew in my head, and slid-to the door in the canvas screen; for it was but wanton folly to stand long exposed to any of the giant octopi that might chance to be prowling near, beneath the curtain of the weed.

"From then, until midnight, I stayed upon the poop, talking much in a quiet voice to my wife, who had followed me up into the companion. At times, we could hear the knocking, sometimes against one side of the ship, and again upon the other. And, between the louder knocks, and accompanying them, would sound the minor tap, tap, tap-a-tap, that I had first heard.

"About midnight, feeling that I could do nothing, and no harm appearing to result to us from the unseen things that seemed to be encircling us my wife and I made our way below to rest, securely barring the companion-doors behind us.

"It would be, I should imagine, about two o'clock in the morning, that I was aroused from a somewhat troubled sleep, by the agonised screaming of our great boar, away forrard. I leant up upon my elbow, and listened, and so grew speedily wide awake. I sat up, and slid from my bunk to the floor. My wife, as I could tell from her breathing, was sleeping peacefully, so that I was able to draw on a few clothes without disturbing her.

"Then, having lit the dark-lantern, and turned the slide over the light, I took the axe in my other hand, and hastened towards the door that gives out of the forrard end of the saloon, on to the maindeck, beneath the shelter of the break of the poop. This door, I had locked before turning-in, and now, very noiselessly, I unlocked it, and turned the handle, opening the door with much caution. I peered out along the dim stretch of the maindeck; but could see nothing; then I turned on the slide of the lamp, and let the light play along the decks; but still nothing unusual was revealed to me.

"Away forrard, the shrieking of the pig had been succeeded by an absolute silence, and there was nowhere any noise, if I except an occasional odd tap-a-tap, which seemed to come from the side of the ship. And so, taking hold of my courage, I stepped out on to the maindeck, and proceeded slowly forrard, throwing the beam of light to and fro continuously, as I walked.

"Abruptly, I heard away in the bows of the ship a sudden multitudinous tapping and scraping and slithering; and so loud and near did it sound, that I was brought up all of a round-turn, as the saying is. For, perhaps, a whole minute, I stood there hesitating, and playing the light all about me, not knowing but that some hateful thing might leap upon me from out of the shadows.

"And then, suddenly, I remembered that I had left the door open behind me, that led into the saloon, so that, were there any deadly thing about the decks, it might chance to get in upon my wife and child as they slept. At the thought, I turned and ran swiftly aft again, and in through the door to my cabin. Here, I made sure that all was right with the two sleepers, and after that, I returned to the deck, shutting the door, and locking it behind me.

"And now, feeling very lonesome out there upon the dark decks, and cut off in a way from a retreat, I had need of all my manhood to aid me forrard to learn the wherefore of the pig's crying, and the cause of that manifold tapping. Yet go I did, and have some right to be proud of the act; for the dreeness and lonesomeness and the cold fear of the Weed-World, squeeze the pluck out of one in a very woeful manner.

"As I approached the empty fo'cas'le, I moved with all wariness, swinging the light to and fro, and holding my axe very handily, and the heart within my breast like a shape of water, so in fear was I. Yet, I came at last to the pigsty, and so discovered a dreadful sight. The pig, a huge boar of twenty-score pounds, had been dragged out on to the deck, and lay before the sty with all his belly ripped up, and stone dead. The iron bars of the sty—great bars they are too—had been torn apart, as though they had been so many straws; and, for the rest, there was a deal of blood both within the sty and upon the decks.

"Yet, I did not stay then to see more; for, all of a sudden, the realisation was borne upon me that this was the work of some monstrous thing, which even at that moment might be stealing upon me; and, with the thought, an overwhelming fear leapt upon me, overbearing my courage; so that I turned and ran for the shelter of the saloon, and never stopped until the stout door was locked between me and that which had wrought such destruction upon the pig. And as I stood there, quivering a little with very fright, I kept questioning dumbly as to what manner of wild-beast thing it was that could burst asunder iron bars, and rip the life out of a great boar, as though it were of no more account than a kitten. And then more vital questions:—How did it get aboard, and where had it hidden? And again:—What was it? And so in this fashion for a good while, until I had grown something more calmed.

"But through all the remainder of that night, I slept not so much as a wink.

"Then in the morning when my wife awoke, I told her of the happenings of the night; whereat she turned very white, and fell to reproaching me for going out at all on to the deck, declaring that I had run needlessly into danger, and that, at least, I should not have left her alone, sleeping in ignorance of what was towards. And after that, she fell into a fit of crying, so that I had some to-do comforting her. Yet, when she had come back to calmness, she was all for accompanying me about the decks, to see by daylight what had indeed befallen in the night-time. And from this decision, I could not turn her; though I assured her I should have told her nothing, had it not been that I wished to warn her from going to and fro between the saloon and the galley, until I had made a thorough search about the decks. Yet, as I have remarked, I could not turn her from her purpose of accompanying me, and so was forced to let her come, though against my desire.

"We made our way on deck through the door that opens under the break of the poop, my wife carrying her loaded revolver half-clumsily in both hands, whilst I had mine held in my left, and the long-handled axe in my right—holding it very readily.

"On stepping out on to the deck, we closed the door behind us, locking it and removing the key; for we had in mind our sleeping child. Then we went slowly forrard along the decks, glancing about warily. As we came fore-side of the pigsty, and my wife saw that which lay beyond it, she let out a little exclamation of horror, shuddering at the sight of the mutilated pig, as, indeed, well she might.

"For my part, I said nothing; but glanced with much apprehension about us; feeling a fresh access of fright; for it was very plain to me that the boar had been molested since I had seen it—the head having been torn, with awful might, from the body; and there were, besides, other new and ferocious wounds, one of which had come nigh to severing the poor brute's body in half. All of which was so much additional evidence of the formidable character of the monster, or Monstrosity, that had attacked the animal.

"I did not delay by the pig, nor attempt to touch it; but beckoned my wife to follow me up on to the fo'cas'le head. Here, I removed the canvas cover from the small skylight which lights the fo'cas'le beneath; and, after that, I lifted off the heavy top, letting a flood of light down into the gloomy place. Then I leant down into the opening, and peered about; but could discover no signs of any lurking thing, and so returned to the maindeck, and made an entrance into the fo'cas'le through the starboard doorway. And now I made a more minute search; but discovered nothing, beyond the mournful array of sea-chests that had belonged to our dead crew.

"My search concluded, I hastened out from the doleful place, into the daylight, and after that made fast the door again, and saw to it that the one upon the port side was also securely locked. Then I went up again on to the fo'cas'le head, and replaced the skylight-top and the canvas cover, battening the whole down very thoroughly.

"And in this wise, and with an incredible care, did I make my search through the ship, fastening up each place behind me, so that I should be certain that no Thing was playing some dread game of hide and seek with me.

"Yet I found nothing, and had it not been for the grim evidence of the dead and mutilated boar, I had been like to have thought nothing more dreadful than an over vivid Imagination had roamed the decks in the darkness of the past night.

"That I had reason to feel puzzled, may be the better understood, when I explain that I had examined the whole of the great, tarred-canvas screen, which I have built about the ship as a protection against the sudden tentacles of any of the roaming giant octopi, without discovering any torn place such as must have been made if any conceivable monster had climbed aboard out of the weed. Also, it must be borne in mind that the ship stands many feet out of the weed, presenting only her smooth iron sides to anything that desires to climb aboard.

"And yet there was the dead pig, lying brutally torn before its empty sty! An undeniable proof that, to go out upon the decks after dark, was to run the risk of meeting a horrible and mysterious death!

"Through all that day, I pondered over this new fear that had come upon us, and particularly upon the monstrous and unearthly power that had torn apart the stout iron bars of the sty, and so ferociously wrenched off the head of the boar. The result of my pondering was that I removed our sleeping belongings that evening from the cabin to the iron half-deck—a little, four-bunked house, standing fore-side of the stump of the main mast, and built entirely of iron, even to the single door, which opens out of the after end.

"Along with our sleeping matters, I carried forrard to our new lodgings, a lamp, and oil, also the dark-lantern, a couple of the axes, two rifles, and all of the revolvers, as well as a good supply of ammunition. Then I bade my wife forage out sufficient provisions to last us for a week, if need be, and whilst she was so busied, I cleaned out and filled the water breaker which belonged to the half-deck.

"At half-past six, I sent my wife forrard to the little iron house, with the baby, and then I locked up the saloon and all of the cabin doors, finally locking after me the heavy, teak door that opened out under the break of the poop.

"Then I went forrard to my wife and child, and shut and bolted the iron door of the half-deck for the night. After that, I went round and saw to it that all of the iron storm-doors, that shut over the eight ports of the house, were in good working order, and so we sat down, as it were, to await the night.

"By eight o'clock, the dusk was upon us, and before half-past, the night hid the decks from my sight. Then I shut down all the iron port-flaps, and screwed them up securely, and after that, I lit the lamp.

"And so a space of waiting ensued, during which I whispered reassuringly to my wife, from time to time, as she looked across at me from her seat beside the sleeping child, with frightened eyes, and a very white face; for somehow there had come upon us within the last hour, a sense of chilly fright, that went straight to one's heart, robbing one vilely of pluck.

"A little later, a sudden sound broke the impressive silence—a sudden dull thud against the side of the ship; and, after that, there came a succession of heavy blows, seeming to be struck all at once upon every side of the vessel; after which there was quietness for maybe a quarter of an hour.

"Then, suddenly, I heard, away forrard, a tap, tap, tap, and then a loud rattling, slurring noise, and a loud crash. After that, I heard many other sounds, and always that tap, tap, tap, repeated a hundred times, as though an army of wooden-legged men were busied all about the decks at the fore end of the ship.

"Presently, there came to me the sound of something coming down the deck, tap, tap, tap, it came. It drew near to the house, paused for nigh a minute; then continued away aft towards the saloon:—tap, tap, tap. I shivered a little, and then, fell half consciously to thanking God that I had been given wisdom to bring my wife and child forrard to the security of the iron deck-house.

"About a minute later, I heard the sound of a heavy blow struck somewhere away aft; and after that a second, and then a third, and seeming by the sounds to have been against iron—the iron of the bulkshead that runs across the break of the poop. There came the noise of a fourth blow, and it blended into the crash of broken woodwork. And therewith, I had a little tense quivering inside me; for the little one and my wife might have been sleeping aft there at that very moment, had it not been for the Providential thought which had sent us forrard to the half-deck.

"With the crash of the broken door, away aft, there came, from forrard of us, a great tumult of noises; and, directly, it sounded as though a multitude of wooden-legged men were coming down the decks from forrard. Tap, tap, tap; tap-a-tap, the noises came, and drew abreast of where we sat in the house, crouched and holding our breaths, for fear that we should make some noise to attract THAT which was without. The sounds passed us, and went tapping away aft, and I let out a little breath of sheer easement. Then, as a sudden thought came to me, I rose and turned down the lamp, fearing that some ray from it might be seen from beneath the door. And so, for the space of an hour, we sat wordless, listening to the sounds which came from away aft, the thud of heavy blows, the occasional crash of wood, and, presently, the tap, tap, tap, again, coming forrard towards us.

"The sounds came to a stop, opposite the starboard side of the house, and, for a full minute, there was quietness. Then suddenly, 'Boom!' a tremendous blow had been struck against the side of the house. My wife gave out a little gasping cry, and there came a second blow; and, at that, the child awoke and began to wail, and my wife was put to it, with trying to soothe her into immediate silence.

"A third blow was struck, filling the little house with a dull thunder of sound, and then I heard the tap, tap, tap, move round to the after end of the house. There came a pause, and then a great blow right upon the door. I grasped the rifle, which I had leant against my chair, and stood up; for I did not know but that the thing might be upon us in a moment, so prodigious was the force of the blows it struck. Once again it struck the door, and after that went tap, tap, tap, round to the port side of the house, and there struck the house again; but now I had more ease of mind; for it was its direct attack upon the door, that had put such horrid dread into my heart.

"After the blows upon the port side of the house, there came a long spell of silence, as though the thing outside were listening; but, by the mercy of God, my wife had been able to soothe the child, so that no sound from us, told of our presence.

"Then, at last, there came again the sounds:—tap, tap, tap, as the voiceless thing moved away forrard. Presently, I heard the noises cease aft; and, after that, there came a multitudinous tap-a-tapping, coming along the decks. It passed the house without so much as a pause, and receded away forrard.

"For a space of over two hours, there was an absolute silence; so that I judged that we were now no longer in danger of being molested. An hour later, I whispered to my wife; but, getting no reply, knew that she had fallen into a doze, and so I sat on, listening tensely; yet making no sort of noise that might attract attention.

"Presently, by the thin line of light from beneath the door, I saw that the day was breaking; and, at that, I rose stiffly, and commenced to unscrew the iron port-covers. I unscrewed the forrard ones first, and looked out into the wan dawn; but could discover nothing unusual about so much of the decks as I could see from there.

"After that, I went round and opened each, as I came to it, in its turn; but it was not until I had uncovered the port which gave me a view of the port side of the after maindeck, that I discovered anything extraordinary. Then I saw, at first dimly, but more clearly as the day brightened, that the door, leading from beneath the break of the poop into the saloon, had been broken to flinders, some of which lay scattered upon the deck, and some of which still hung from the bent hinges; whilst more, no doubt, were strewed in the passage beyond my sight.

"Turning from the port, I glanced towards my wife, and saw that she lay half in and half out of the baby's bunk, sleeping with her head beside the child's, both upon one pillow. At the sight, a great wave of holy thankfulness took me, that we had been so wonderfully spared from the terrible and mysterious danger that had stalked the decks in the darkness of the preceding night. Feeling thus, I stole across the floor of the house, and kissed them both very gently, being full of tenderness, yet not minded to waken them. And, after that, I lay down in one of the bunks, and slept until the sun was high in the heaven.

"When I awoke, my wife was about and had tended to the child and prepared our breakfast, so that I had naught to do but tumble out and set to, the which I did with a certain keenness of appetite, induced, I doubt not, by the stress of the night. Whilst we ate, we discussed the peril through which we had just passed; but without coming any the nearer to a solution of the weird mystery of the Terror.

"Breakfast over, we took a long and final survey of the decks, from the various ports, and then prepared to sally out. This we did with instinctive caution and quietness, both of us armed as on the previous day. The door of the half-deck we closed and locked behind us, thereby ensuring that the child was open to no danger whilst we were in other parts of the ship.

"After a quick look about us, we proceeded aft towards the shattered door beneath the break of the poop. At the doorway, we stopped, not so much with the intent to examine the broken door, as because of an instinctive and natural hesitation to go forward into the saloon, which but a few hours previous had been visited by some incredible monster or monsters. Finally, we decided to go up upon the poop and peer down through the skylight. This we did, lifting the sides of the dome for that purpose; yet though we peered long and earnestly, we could perceive no signs of any lurking thing. But broken woodwork there appeared to be in plenty, to judge by the scattered pieces.

"After that, I unlocked the companion, and pushed back the big, over-arching slide. Then, silently, we stole down the steps and into the saloon. Here, being now able to see the big cabin through all its length, we discovered a most extraordinary scene; the whole place appeared to be wrecked from end to end; the six cabins that line each side had their bulksheading driven into shards and slivers of broken wood in places. Here, a door would be standing untouched, whilst the bulkshead beside it was in a mass of flinders—There a door would be driven completely from its hinges, whilst the surrounding woodwork was untouched. And so it was, wherever we looked.

"My wife made to go towards our cabin; but I pulled her back, and went forward myself. Here the desolation was almost as great. My wife's bunk-board had been ripped out, whilst the supporting side-batten of mine had been plucked forth, so that all the bottom-boards of the bunk had descended to the floor in a cascade.

"But it was neither of these things that touched us so sharply, as the fact that the child's little swing cot had been wrenched from its standards, and flung in a tangled mass of white-painted iron-work across the cabin. At the sight of that, I glanced across at my wife, and she at me, her face grown very white. Then down she slid to her knees, and fell to crying and thanking God together, so that I found myself beside her in a moment, with a very humble and thankful heart.

"Presently, when we were more controlled, we left the cabin, and finished our search. The pantry, we discovered to be entirely untouched, which, somehow, I do not think was then a matter of great surprise to me; for I had ever a feeling that the things which had broken a way into our sleeping cabin, had been looking for us.

"In a little while, we left the wrecked saloon and cabins, and made our way forrard to the pigsty; for I was anxious to see whether the carcass of the pig had been touched. As we came round the corner of the sty, I uttered a great cry; for there, lying upon the deck, on its back, was a gigantic crab, so vast in size that I had not conceived so huge a monster existed. Brown it was in colour, save for the belly part, which was of a light yellow.

"One of its pincer-claws, or mandibles, had been torn off in the fight in which it must have been slain (for it was all disembowelled). And this one claw weighed so heavy that I had some to-do to lift it from the deck; and by this you may have some idea of the size and formidableness of the creature itself.

"Around the great crab, lay half a dozen smaller ones, no more than from seven or eight to twenty inches across, and all white in colour, save for an occasional mottling of brown. These had all been killed by a single nip of an enormous mandible, which had in every case smashed them almost into two halves. Of the carcass of the great boar, not a fragment remained.

"And so was the mystery solved; and, with the solution, departed the superstitious terror which had suffocated me through those three nights, since the tapping had commenced. We had been attacked by a wandering shoal of giant crabs, which, it is quite possible, roam across the weed from place to place, devouring aught that comes in their path.

"Whether they had ever boarded a ship before, and so, perhaps, developed a monstrous lust for human flesh, or whether their attack had been prompted by curiosity, I cannot possibly say. It may be that, at first, they mistook the hull of the vessel for the body of some dead marine monster, and hence their blows upon her sides, by which, possibly, they were endeavouring to pierce through our somewhat unusually tough hide!

"Or, again, it may be that they have some power of scent, by means of which they were able to smell our presence aboard the ship; but this (as they made no general attack upon us in the deck-house) I feel disinclined to regard as probable. And yet—I do not know. Why their attack upon the saloon, and our sleeping-cabin? As I say, I cannot tell, and so must leave it there.

"The way in which they came aboard, I discovered that same day; for, having learned what manner of creature it was that had attacked us, I made a more intelligent survey of the sides of the ship; but it was not until I came to the extreme bows, that I saw how they had managed. Here, I found that some of the gear of the broken bowsprit and jibboom, trailed down on to the weed, and as I had not extended the canvas-screen across the heel of the bowsprit, the monsters had been able to climb up the gear, and thence aboard, without the least obstruction being opposed to their progress.

"This state of affairs, I very speedily remedied; for, with a few strokes of my axe, I cut through the gear, allowing it to drop down among the weed; and after that, I built a temporary breastwork of wood across the gap, between the two ends of the screen; later on making it more permanent.

"Since that time, we have been no more molested by the giant crabs; though for several nights afterwards, we heard them knocking strangely against our sides. Maybe, they are attracted by such refuse as we are forced to dump overboard, and this would explain their first tappings being aft, opposite to the lazarette; for it is from the openings in this part of the canvas-screen that we cast our rubbish.

"Yet, it is weeks now since we heard aught of them, so that I have reason to believe that they have betaken themselves elsewhere, maybe to attack some other lonely humans, living out their short span of life aboard some lone derelict, lost even to memory in the depth of this vast sea of weed and deadly creatures.

"I shall send this message forth on its journey, as I have sent the other four, within a well-pitched barrel, attached to a small fire balloon. The shell of the severed claw of the monster crab, I shall enclose, [2] as evidence of the terrors that beset us in this dreadful place. Should this message, and the claw, ever fall into human hands, let them, contemplating this vast mandible, try to imagine the size of the other crab or crabs that could destroy so formidable a creature as the one to which this claw belonged.

"What other terrors does this hideous world hold for us?

"I had thought of inclosing, along with the claw, the shell of one of the white smaller crabs. It must have been some of these moving in the weed that night, that set my disordered fancy to imagining of ghouls and the Un-Dead. But, on thinking it over, I shall not; for to do so would be to illustrate nothing that needs illustration, and it would but increase needlessly the weight which the balloon will have to lift.

"And so I grow wearied of writing. The night is drawing near, and I have little more to tell. I am writing this in the saloon, and, though I have mended and carpentered so well as I am able, nothing I can do will hide the traces of that night when the vast crabs raided through these cabins, searching for—WHAT?

"There is nothing more to say. In health, I am well, and so is my wife and the little one, but....

"I must have myself under control, and be patient. We are beyond all help, and must bear that which is before us, with such bravery as we are able. And with this, I end; for my last word shall not be one of complaint.

"Arthur Samuel Philips."

"Christmas Eve, 1879."

Big John Carlos, captain of the Santa, stood looking up at the long tapered window in the otherwise great, grey blank of the convent wall, a dozen yards away.

The wall formed the background of the quay, and between it and the side of the vessel was a litter of unloaded gear and cargo. The Captain's face, as he stared upward at that one lonesome window, had an extraordinarily set expression; and his Mate, a little lop-shouldered man, very brown and lean, watched him over the coaming of the main hatchway, with a curious grimace of half-sympathy and half-curiosity.

"Old Man's got it bad as ever," he muttered, in an accent and language that spoke of the larger English. He transferred his gaze from the silent form of the skipper, standing, in the stern, to the long taper of the one window that broke the towering side of the convent.

Presently, the thing for which the two men watched, came into view, as it did twice daily, at morning and evening—a long line of half-veiled nuns, who were obviously ascending some stairway within the convent, on to which this solitary window threw light.

Most of the women went by the window quietly, with faces composed, and looking before them; but here and there a young nun would take this opportunity to glance out into the Carnal World which they had renounced forever. Young, beautiful faces they were, that looked out momentarily, showing doubly human, because of the cold ascetic garb of renunciation which framed them; then were gone on from sight, in the long, steadily moving procession of silent figures.

It was about the middle of the procession, after a weary line of seeming mutes had gone past, that the mate saw that for which he waited. For, suddenly, the great body of the Captain stiffened and became rigid, as the head of one of the moving figures turned and stared out on to the quay. The Mate saw her face clearly. It was still young and lovely, but seemed very white and hopeless. He noted the eager, hungry look in the eyes; and then the wonderful way in which they lit up, as with a strange inward fire, at the sight of the big man standing there; and the whole face seemed to quiver into living emotion. Immediately afterwards, she was gone past, and more mutes were making the grey, ascending line.

"Gord! that's 'er!" said the Mate, and glanced towards his master. The face of the big skipper was still upturned and set with a fixed, intense stare, as though even now he saw her face at the long window. His body was yet rigid with intensity, and his great hands gripped tightly the front of his slack jumper, straining it, unconsciously down upon his hips. For some moments longer he stood like this, lost to all knowledge except the tellings of his memory, and stunned with his emotions. Then he relaxed abruptly, as if some string within him had been loosed, and turned towards the open hatchway, where the Mate bent once more to his work.

"W'y don't 'e get 'er out," the Mate remarked to himself. "They've bin doin' that years 'n years, from wot I can see an' 'ear, an' breakin' their blessed 'earts. W'y the 'ell don't 'e get 'er out! It's easy ter see she's a woman, a sight more'n a bloomin' nun!" In all of which the little crooked shouldered Mate showed a fund of common sense; but likewise an insufficient ability to realise how thoroughly a religious belief may sometimes prove a stumbling-block in the pathway to mere human happiness.

How a man of the stamp of Big John Carlos came to be running an onion boat, must be conjectured. His name is explained by his father having been a Spaniard and his mother an Englishwoman. Originally, Big John had been a merchant, of a kind, going to sea in his own ship, and trading abroad.

As a youth, he had become engaged to Marvonna Della, whose father had owned much property, farther up the coast. Her father had died, and she had been an heiress, sought by all the youths about; but he—Big John Carlos—had won her.

They were to have been married on his return from his next trading voyage; but the report went home to his sweetheart that he had been drowned at sea; and indeed he had truly fallen overboard; but had been picked up by a China-bound sailing-ship, and had been a little over a year lost to his friends, before he had managed to reach home, to carry the news that he still lived. For this was before the days of the telegraph, and his one letter had gone astray.

When, at last, he reached home, it was to find sad changes. His sweetheart, broken-hearted, had become a nun at the great convent of St. Sebastian's, and had endowed it with all her wealth and lands. What attempts he made to have speech with her, I do not know; but if his religious scruples had allowed him to beg her to renounce her vows and retirement, and return to the world to be his wife, they had certainly been unsuccessful; though it is quite conceivable that no word had ever passed between them, since she had put the world behind her.

From then onward, through nine long years, Big John Carlos had traded along the coast. His former business, he had dropped, and now he wandered from port to port in his small craft. And twice in every year, he would come alongside of the little wharf opposite to the great, grey wall of the convent, and there lie for a week, watching year by year that long narrow window for the two brief glimpses daily of his lost sweetheart.

After a week, he would go. It was always a week that he stayed there by the old wharf. Then, as if that had exhausted his strength—as if the pain of the thing had grown in that time to be too dreadful to continue, he would haul out, and away, whatever the weather or the state of trade. All of this the little twisted Mate knew, more or less clearly in detail, having learned it in the previous visits, which he had made with Big John Carlos to the insignificant port where the convent stood.

And she—what can the young nun have thought and felt? How she must have fought to endure the grey weary months between the far-apart visits; and day by day glanced out of the tall stair-window, as she passed in the long, mute procession, for a sight of the little onion boat and the big man standing in the stern, watching—tense and silent—for that one brief glimpse of her, as she passed in the remorseless line of figures. And something of this also, the little crooked-shouldered Mate had realised, vaguely, and had achieved an instant though angry sympathy. But his point of view was limited and definite:—"Why the 'ell don't 'e get 'er out!" was his brief formula. And that marked the limit of his imagination, and therefore of his understanding.

His own religious beliefs were of the kind that are bred in the docks (London docks, in his case), and fostered in dirty fo'cas'les; and now he was "come down to this onion shuntin'," as he would have worded it. Yet, whatever his religious lack, or even his carelessness on a point of ethics, he was thoroughly and masculinely human.

"W'y the 'ell—" he began again, in his continual grumble to himself; and had no power to conceive that the woman, having taken a certain step, might believe that step to be unretraceable—that usage, belief, and finally (bred of these two) Conscience might forbid even the thought, stamping it as a crime that would shut her out from the Joy of the Everlasting.

The Joy of the Everlasting! The little twisted man would have grinned at you, had you mentioned it. "W'y the 'ell don't 'e get 'er out!" would have been his reply, accompanied by a profuseness of tobacco-juice.

And yet, it is conceivable that the heart of the woman was, even this long while, grown strong to do battle for dear Happiness—her heart that had known, silently and secretly and dumbly, all along, the unnatural wickedness of her outrage of her Womanhood. Visit by visit, through the long years, her heart must have grown fiercely strong to end this torture which her brain (darkened with the Clouds of Belief) had put upon her, to endure through all her life.

And so, all unknowingly, because of the loyal brain that would not be aware of the growing victory of her heart, she was come to a condition in which her beliefs held her no more than if they had been cords that had rotted upon her, as indeed they might be said to have done. That she was free to come, the little Mate had seen, using his eyes and his heart and his wit. To him, it was merely a matter of ways and means—physical. "W'y the 'ell—!" that was his puzzle.

Why? With an angry impatience, that came near to verging upon the borderland of scorn, the little Mate would question inwardly. Was Big John Carlos bit wiv them religious notions, same as the other dagoes! He did not understand the complaint, or how it was achieved; but he knew, as an outside fact, that there was something of that kind which infected the peoples along the coasts he travelled. If Big John were not troubled in this way, "why the 'ell—" And so he would return to his accustomed formula, working furiously, in sheer irritation of mind:—"If 'e ain't religious, wot is it? Carn't 'e see the way 'er eyes blessed well looks at 'im! Carn't 'e see she's mad an' double mad to be out wiv 'im!"

Why did not John Carlos attempt to win back for himself the one thing that he desired in all the world? Maybe (and I think that it is very possible) in the early years of his return, he had so striven; but the young nun, shaken with the enormousness of the thought, hopelessly weighted with her vows, had not dared to think upon it—had retreated with horror from the suggestion; had turned with an intention of double ardour to seek in her religious duties, the calm and sweetness, the peace and joy, which she felt to be lost to her forever in any more earthly way.

And then had followed the long years, with her heart fighting silently and secretly—secretly almost from herself—unto victory. And the man (having lost the force of that first fierce unpenting of his intention to win her—and mayhap having been repulsed, as it would seem to his masculine mind, hopelessly) had fallen back under the sway of the religious beliefs, which ruled him in his more normal hours; and so, year by year, had withheld from any further attempt to win her; striving to content his soul with those two brief visits each year to the old wharf; each time to endure a mad week of those futile watchings for his beloved.

Yet, in him, as in the woman, there had been going forward, without his knowledge, that steady disruption of religious belief—the rotting and decaying of all arbitrary things, before the primal need of the human heart; so that the olden barriers of "Impossibility," were now but as shadows, that would be gone in a moment, when next the Force of his Need should urge him to take his heart's desire.

His first attempt—if there had ever been such—had been the outcome of his natural want—his Love—; but lacking the foundations of Sureness of Himself and of his Power to withstand the Future. Indeed, it is conceivable that had he succeeded at the first, and gained his desire, the two of them would have wilted in the afterblast of thought and fear-of-the-hereafter, and in the Fires of Scruples which would have burned in their path through all the years.

But now, whatever they might do, they would do—if it ever came to pass—with a calm and determined Intention; having done their thinking first, and weighed all known costs, and proved their strength, and learned the utterness of their need to be truly greater than all else that might be set as balance against it. And because of this, they were ripe—wanting only the final stimulus to set into action the ready Force that had concentrated through the years.

Yet, strangely, neither the man nor the woman knew, as I have shown, that they had developed to this. Their brains refused to know; their Consciences looked, each with its blind eye, at their hearts, and saw nothing to give cause of offence to the ethical in them; or, did Conscience catch an odd glimpse, with its seeing eye, of impossible wickedness, there followed hours of imagined repentance, deep and painful, resulting in a double assuredness, within the brain (and "Manufactured" Parts) of a conquered and chastened heart, and of fiercer resolutions for the future Torture of Salvation. But always, deep within, the unconquerable heart fought for victory that was each year more assured.

And so, as you have already seen, these two, the man and the woman, were but waiting—the man for some outward stimulus, to put into action all the long-pent force in him, revealing to him his actual nature, developed and changed in the course of the long years of pain, until he should be scarcely likely to recognise himself in the first moments of his awakening to this reality. And the woman, waiting, subconsciously, for the action of the man to bring her to knowledge of the realities—to an awareness of the woman she had become, of the woman into which she had developed, unable any more to endure the bondage of aught save her heart that leaped to the ordering of Mother Nature. Nay, more, fiercely and steadfastly eager to take with both hands the forbidden joy of her Natural Birthright, and calm and resolute and unblinking to face the future, with its unsolvable problem of the Joy of the Everlasting.

And thus were these two standing, as it might be said, on the brink of their destinies; waiting, with blinded eyes, and as that they listened unknowingly for the coming of the unknown one who should give the little push forward, and so cause them to step over the borderland into all natural and long craved for happiness.

Who would be That One?

"W'y the 'ell don't 'e get 'er out?" the Mate had asked the First Hand, who knew all the story, having sailed years with big John Carlos. But the First Hand had raised his arms in horror, and made plain in broken English his opinion of the sacrilege, though that was not how he had pronounced it.

"Sacrilege be jiggered!" the Mate had replied, humping his twisted shoulders. "I s'pose though there'd be a 'oly rumpus, hey?"

The First Hand had intimated very definitely that there would be a "rumpus," which, the Mate ferreted out, might involve some very unpleasant issues both for the man and the woman guilty of such a thing. The First Hand spoke (in broken English) as if he were the Religious Conscience of his nation. Such things could not be tolerated. His phraseology did not include such words; but he was sufficiently definite.

"Nice 'ealthy lot o' savages, you!" the Mate had explained, after listening to much intolerant jabbering. "Strike me! If you ain't canniballs!" And straightway saddled on to the unfortunate

Catholic Faith the sins peculiar to a hot-blooded and emotional People, whose enthusiasms and prejudices would have been just as apparent, had they been called forth by some other force than their Faith, or by a Faith differently shaped and Denominated.

It was the little crooked Mate who was speaking to Big John Carlos, in the evening of the sixth day of their stay beside the old wharf. And the big man was listening, in a stunned kind of silence. Through those six days the little man had watched the morning and evening tragedy, and the sanity of his free thoughts had been as a yeast in him. Now he was speaking, unlading all the things that he had to say.

"W'y the 'ell don't you take 'er out?" he had asked in so many words. And to him it had seemed, that very evening, that the woman's eyes had been saying the same thing to the Captain, as she looked her brief, dumb agony of longing across the little space that had lain between; yet which, as it were, was in verity the whole width of Eternity. And now the little Mate was putting it all into definite words—standing there, an implement of Fate or Providence or the Devil, according to the way that you may look at it, his twisted shoulder heaving with the vehemence of his speech:—

"You didn't orter do it, Capting," he said. "You're breakin' 'er up, an' you're breakin' you up; an' no good to it. W'y the 'ell don't you do somefink! Rescue 'er, or keep away. If it's 'ell for you, it's just 's much 'ell for 'er! She'll come like a little bloomin' bird. See 'ow she looks at you. She's fair askin' you to come an' take 'er out of it all—an' you just standin' there! My Gord!"

"What can I do," said the Captain, hoarsely; and put his hands suddenly to his head. He did not ask a question, or voice any hopelessness; but just gave out the words, as so many sounds, mechanically; for he was choked, suffocating during those first few moments, with the vast surge of hope that rose and beat upward in him, as the little twisted Mate's words crashed ruthlessly through the shrouding films of Belief.

And suddenly he knew. He knew that he could do this thing; that all scruples, all bonds of belief, of usage, of blind fears for the future, and of the Hereafter, were all fallen from him, as so much futile dust. Until that moment, as I have shown to you before, he had not known that he could do it—had not known of his steady and silent development. But now, suddenly, all his soul and being, lighted with Hope, he looked inward, and saw himself, as the man he was—the man to which he had grown and come to be. He knew. He knew.

"Would she ... would she?" The question came unconsciously from his lips; but the little twisted man took it up.

"Arsk 'er! Arsk 'er!" he said, vehemently. "I knows she'll come. I seen it in 'er eyes to-night w'en she looked out at you. She was sayin' as plain as your 'at, 'W'y the 'ell don't you take me out? W'y the 'ell don't you?' You arsk 'er, an' she'll come like a bird."

The little Mate spoke with the eagerness of conviction, and indulged in no depressing knowledge of incongruities. "Arsk 'er!" was his refrain. "You arsk 'er!"

"How?" said the Captain, coming suddenly to realities.

The little man halted, and stumbled over his unreadiness. He had no plan; nothing but his feelings. He sought around in his mind, and grasped at an idea.

"Write it on an 'atch cover, wiv chalk," he said, triumphant. "Lean the 'atch cover by you. W'en she comes, point to it, 'n she'll read it."

"Ha!" said the Captain, in a strange voice, as if he both approved, and, at the same time, had remembered something.

"Then she'll nod," continued the little man. "No one else ever looks outer that winder, scarcely, not to think to read writin', anyway. An' you can cover it, till she's due to show. Then we'll plan 'ow to get 'er out."

All that night, Big John Carlos paced the deck of his little craft, alone, thinking, and thrilling with great surges of hope and maddened determination.

In the morning, he put the plan to the test; only that he wrote the question on the hatch-cover in peculiar words, that he had not used all those long grey years; for he made use of a quaint but simple transposition of letters, which had been a kind of love-language between them, in the olden days. This was why he had called "Ha!" so strangely, being minded suddenly of it, and to have the sweetness of using it to that one particular purpose.

Slowly, the line of grey moving figures came into view, descending. Big John Carlos kept the hatch-cover turned to him, and counted; for well he knew just when she would appear. The one hundred and ninth mute would pass, and the one hundred and tenth would show the face of his Beloved. The order never changed through the years, in that changeless world within.

As the hundred and seventh figure passed the narrow window, he turned the hatch-cover, so that the writing was exposed, and pointed down to it, so that his whole attitude should direct her glance instantly to his question, that she might have some small chance to read it, in the brief moment that was hers as she went slowly past the narrow panes. The hundred and ninth figure passed down from sight, and then he was looking dumbly into her face, as she moved into view, her eyes already strained to meet his. His heart was beating with a dull, sickening thudding, and there seemed just the faintest of mists before his vision; but he knew that her glance had flown eagerly to the message, and that her white face had flashed suddenly to a greater whiteness, disturbed by the battle of scores of emotions loosed in one second of time. Then she was gone downward out of his sight, and he let the hatch-cover fall, gripping the shrouds with his left hand.

The little twisted man stole up to him.

"She saw, Capting! She 'adn't time to answer. Not to know if she was on 'er 'ead or 'er 'eels. Look out to-night. She'll nod then." He brought it all out in little whispered jerks, and the big man, wiping his forehead, nodded.

Within the convent, a woman (outwardly a nun) was even then descending the stairs, with shaking knees, and a brain that had become in a few brief instants a raging gulf of hope. Before she had descended three steps below the level of the window, even whilst her sight-memory still held the message out for her brain to read and comprehend, she had realised that spiritually she was clothed only with the ashes of Belief and Fear and Faith. The original garment had become charred to nothing in the Fire of Love and Pain, with which the years had enveloped her. No bond held her; no fear held her; nothing in all the world mattered, except to be his for all the rest of her life. She took and realised the change in her character, in a moment of time. Eight long years had the yeast of love been working in her, which had bred the chemistry of pain; but only in that instant did she know and comprehend that she was developed so extensively, as to be changed utterly from the maid of eight years gone. Yet, in the next few steps she took, she had adapted herself to the new standpoint of her fresh knowledge of herself. She had no pause or doubt; but acknowledged with an utter startled joyfulness that she would go—that all was as nothing to her, now, except that she go to him. Willing, beyond all words that might express her willingness, to risk (aye, even to exchange) the unknown Joy of the Everlasting for this certain "mess of pottage" that was so desired of her hungry heart. And having acknowledged to herself that she was utterly willing, she had no thought of anything but to pass on the knowledge of her altered state to the man who would be waiting there in the little onion boat at sunset.

That evening, just before the dusk, Big John Carlos saw the hundred and tenth grey figure nod swiftly to him, in passing; and he held tightly to the shroud, until the suffocation of his emotion passed from him.

After all, the Rescue—if it can be named by a term so heroic—proved a ridiculously easy matter. It was the spiritual prison that had held the woman so long—the Physical expression of the same, was easily made to give up its occupant.

In the morning, expectant, she read in her fleeting glance at the onion boat, a message written on the hatch-cover. She was to be at the window at midnight. That evening, as she ascended in the long grey line of mutes for the last weary time, she nodded her utter agreement and assent.

After night had fallen thickly on the small, deserted wharf, the little twisted Mate and the Captain reared a ladder against the convent side. By midnight, they had cut out entirely the lead framing of all the lower part of the window.

A few minutes later, the woman came. The Captain held out his big hands, in an absolute silence, and lifted the trembling figure gently down on to the ladder. He steadied her firmly, and they climbed down to the wharf, and were presently aboard the vessel, with no word yet between them to break the ten years of loneliness and silence; for it was ten years, as you will remember, since Big John Carlos had sailed on that voyage of dismay.

And now, full grown man and woman, they stood near to each other, in a dream-quietness, who had lived on the two sides of Eternity so long. And still they had no word. Youth and Maiden they had parted with tears; Man and Woman they met in a great silence—too grown and developed to have words over-easily at such a moment-of-life. Yet their very quiet, held a speech too full and subtle, aye and subtile, for made-words of sound. It came from them, almost as it were a soul-fragrance, diffused around them, and made visible only in the quiet trembling of hands—that reached unknowing unto the hands of the other. For the two were full-grown, as I have said, and had come nigh to the complete awareness of life, and the taste of the brine of sorrow was yet in them. They had been ripened in the strange twin Suns of Love and Pain—that ripen the unseen fruit of the soul. Their hands met, trembling, and gripped a long, long while, till the little twisted Mate came stumbling aft, uneasy to be gone. Then the big man and the fragile woman stood apart, the woman dreaming, while the big man went to give the little Mate a hand.

Together, the two men worked to get the sail upon the small vessel, and the ropes cast off. They left the First and Second Hands sleeping. Presently, with light airs from the land, they moved outward to the sea.

There was no pursuit. All the remainder of that night, the small onion boat went outward into the mystery of the dark, the big man steering, and the woman close beside him; and for a long while the constant silence of communion.

As I have said, there was no pursuit, and at dawn the little twisted man wandered. He searched the empty sea, and found only their own shadow upon the almost calm waters. Perhaps the First Hand had held a wrong impression. The Peoples of the Coast may have been shocked, when they learned. Maybe they never learned. Convents, like other institutions, can keep their secrets, odd whiles. Possibly this was one of those times. Perhaps they remembered, with something of worldly wisdom, that they held the Substance; wherefore trouble overmuch concerning the shadow—of a lost nun. Certainly, not to the bringing of an ill-name upon their long holiness. Surely, Satan can be trusted, etc. We can all finish the well-hackneyed thought. Or, maybe, there were natural human hearts in diverse places, that—knowing something of the history of this love-tale—held sympathy in silence, and silence in sympathy. Is this too much to hope?

That evening, the man and the woman stood in the stern, looking into the wake, whilst the Second-Hand steered. Forrard, in the growing dusk, there was a noise of scuffling. The little humped Mate was having a slight difference of opinion with the First Hand, who had incautiously made use of a parallel word for "Sacrilege," for the second time. The scuffling continued; for the little twisted man was emphatic:—

"Sacrilege be jiggered! Wot the 'ell——"

The physical sounds of his opinion, drowned the monotonous accompaniment of his speech. The small craft sailed on into the sunset, and the two in the stern stared blindly into distances, holding hands like two little children.

THE VOICE IN THE NIGHT

It was a dark, starless night. We were becalmed in the Northern Pacific. Our exact position I do not know; for the sun had been hidden during the course of a weary, breathless week, by a thin haze which had seemed to float above us, about the height of our mastheads, at whiles descending and shrouding the surrounding sea.

With there being no wind, we had steadied the tiller, and I was the only man on deck. The crew, consisting of two men and a boy, were sleeping forrard in their den; while Will—my friend, and the master of our little craft—was aft in his bunk on the port side of the little cabin.

Suddenly, from out of the surrounding darkness, there came a hail:—

"Schooner, ahoy!"

The cry was so unexpected that I gave no immediate answer, because of my surprise.

It came again—a voice curiously throaty and inhuman, calling from somewhere upon the dark sea away on our port broadside:—

"Schooner, ahoy!"

"Hullo!" I sung out, having gathered my wits somewhat. "What are you? What do you want?"

"You need not be afraid," answered the queer voice, having probably noticed some trace of confusion in my tone. "I am only an old—man."

The pause sounded oddly; but it was only afterwards that it came back to me with any significance.

"Why don't you come alongside, then?" I queried somewhat snappishly; for I liked not his hinting at my having been a trifle shaken.

"I—I—can't. It wouldn't be safe. I—" The voice broke off, and there was silence.

"What do you mean?" I asked, growing more and more astonished. "Why not safe? Where are you?"

I listened for a moment; but there came no answer. And then, a sudden indefinite suspicion, of I knew not what, coming to me, I stepped swiftly to the binnacle, and took out the lighted lamp. At the same time, I knocked on the deck with my heel to waken Will. Then I was back at the side, throwing the yellow funnel of light out into the silent immensity beyond our rail. As I did so, I heard a slight, muffled cry, and then the sound of a splash, as though some one had dipped oars abruptly. Yet I cannot say that I saw anything with certainty; save, it seemed to me, that with the first flash of the light, there had been something upon the waters, where now there was nothing.

"Hullo, there!" I called. "What foolery is this!"

But there came only the indistinct sounds of a boat being pulled away into the night.

Then I heard Will's voice, from the direction of the after scuttle:—

"What's up, George?"

"Come here, Will!" I said.

"What is it?" he asked, coming across the deck.

I told him the queer thing which had happened. He put several questions; then, after a moment's silence, he raised his hands to his lips, and hailed: —

"Boat, ahoy!"

From a long distance away, there came back to us a faint reply, and my companion repeated his call. Presently, after a short period of silence, there grew on our hearing the muffled sound of oars; at which Will hailed again.

This time there was a reply:—

"Put away the light."

"I'm damned if I will," I muttered; but Will told me to do as the voice bade, and I shoved it down under the bulwarks.

"Come nearer," he said, and the oar-strokes continued. Then, when apparently some half-dozen fathoms distant, they again ceased.

"Come alongside," exclaimed Will. "There's nothing to be frightened of aboard here!"

"Promise that you will not show the light?"

"What's to do with you," I burst out, "that you're so infernally afraid of the light?"

"Because—" began the voice, and stopped short.

"Because what?" I asked, quickly.

Will put his hand on my shoulder.

"Shut up a minute, old man," he said, in a low voice. "Let me tackle him."

He leant more over the rail.

"See here, Mister," he said, "this is a pretty queer business, you coming upon us like this, right out in the middle of the blessed Pacific. How are we to know what sort of a hanky-panky trick you're up to? You say there's only one of you. How are we to know, unless we get a squint at you—eh? What's your objection to the light, anyway?"

As he finished, I heard the noise of the oars again, and then the voice came; but now from a greater distance, and sounding extremely hopeless and pathetic.

"I am sorry—sorry! I would not have troubled you, only I am hungry, and—so is she."

The voice died away, and the sound of the oars, dipping irregularly, was borne to us.

"Stop!" sung out Will. "I don't want to drive you away. Come back! We'll keep the light hidden, if you don't like it."

He turned to me:—

"It's a damned queer rig, this; but I think there's nothing to be afraid of?"

There was a question in his tone, and I replied.

"No, I think the poor devil's been wrecked around here, and gone crazy."

The sound of the oars drew nearer.

"Shove that lamp back in the binnacle," said Will; then he leaned over the rail, and listened. I replaced the lamp, and came back to his side. The dipping of the oars ceased some dozen yards distant.

"Won't you come alongside now?" asked Will in an even voice. "I have had the lamp put back in the binnacle."

"I—I cannot," replied the voice. "I dare not come nearer. I dare not even pay you for the—the provisions."

"That's all right," said Will, and hesitated. "You're welcome to as much grub as you can take—" Again he hesitated.

"You are very good," exclaimed the voice. "May God, Who understands everything, reward you—" It broke off huskily.

"The—the lady?" said Will, abruptly. "Is she—"

"I have left her behind upon the island," came the voice.

"What island?" I cut in.

"I know not its name," returned the voice. "I would to God——!" it began, and checked itself as suddenly.

"Could we not send a boat for her?" asked Will at this point.

"No!" said the voice, with extraordinary emphasis. "My God! No!" There was a moment's pause; then it added, in a tone which seemed a merited reproach:—

"It was because of our want I ventured—Because her agony tortured me."

"I am a forgetful brute," exclaimed Will. "Just wait a minute, whoever you are, and I will bring you up something at once."

In a couple of minutes he was back again, and his arms were full of various edibles. He paused at the rail.

"Can't you come alongside for them?" he asked.

"No—I dare not," replied the voice, and it seemed to me that in its tones I detected a note of stifled craving—as though the owner hushed a mortal desire. It came to me then in a flash, that the poor old creature out there in the darkness, was suffering for actual need of that which Will held in his arms; and yet, because of some unintelligible dread, refraining from dashing to the side of our little schooner, and receiving it. And with the lightning-like conviction, there came the knowledge that the Invisible was not mad; but sanely facing some intolerable horror.

"Damn it, Will!" I said, full of many feelings, over which predominated a vast sympathy. "Get a box. We must float off the stuff to him in it."

This we did—propelling it away from the vessel, out into the darkness, by means of a boathook. In a minute, a slight cry from the Invisible came to us, and we knew that he had secured the box.

A little later, he called out a farewell to us, and so heartful a blessing, that I am sure we were the better for it. Then, without more ado, we heard the ply of oars across the darkness.

"Pretty soon off," remarked Will, with perhaps just a little sense of injury.

"Wait," I replied. "I think somehow he'll come back. He must have been badly needing that food."

"And the lady," said Will. For a moment he was silent; then he continued:—

"It's the queerest thing ever I've tumbled across, since I've been fishing."

"Yes," I said, and fell to pondering.

And so the time slipped away—an hour, another, and still Will stayed with me; for the queer adventure had knocked all desire for sleep out of him.

The third hour was three parts through, when we heard again the sound of oars across the silent ocean.

"Listen!" said Will, a low note of excitement in his voice.

"He's coming, just as I thought," I muttered.

The dipping of the oars grew nearer, and I noted that the strokes were firmer and longer. The food had been needed.

They came to a stop a little distance off the broadside, and the queer voice came again to us through the darkness:—

"Schooner, ahoy!"

"That you?" asked Will.

"Yes," replied the voice. "I left you suddenly; but—but there was great need."

"The lady?" questioned Will.

"The—lady is grateful now on earth. She will be more grateful soon in—in heaven."

Will began to make some reply, in a puzzled voice; but became confused, and broke off short. I said nothing. I was wondering at the curious pauses, and, apart from my wonder, I was full of a great sympathy.

The voice continued:—

"We—she and I, have talked, as we shared the result of God's tenderness and yours—"

Will interposed; but without coherence.

"I beg of you not to—to belittle your deed of Christian charity this night," said the voice. "Be sure that it has not escaped His notice."

It stopped, and there was a full minute's silence. Then it came again:—

"We have spoken together upon that which—which has befallen us. We had thought to go out, without telling any, of the terror which has come into our—lives. She is with me in believing that to-night's happenings are under a special ruling, and that it is God's wish that we should tell to you all that we have suffered since—since—"

"Yes?" said Will, softly.

"Since the sinking of the 'Albatross.'"

"Ah!" I exclaimed, involuntarily. "She left Newcastle for 'Frisco some six months ago, and hasn't been heard of since."

"Yes," answered the voice. "But some few degrees to the North of the line she was caught in a terrible storm, and dismasted. When the day came, it was found that she was leaking badly, and, presently, it falling to a calm, the sailors took to the boats, leaving—leaving a young lady—my fiancée—and myself upon the wreck.

"We were below, gathering together a few of our belongings, when they left. They were entirely callous, through fear, and when we came up upon the decks, we saw them only as small shapes afar off upon the horizon. Yet we did not despair, but set to work and constructed a small raft. Upon this we put such few matters as it would hold, including a quantity of water and some ship's biscuit. Then, the vessel being very deep in the water, we got ourselves on to the raft, and pushed off.

"It was later, when I observed that we seemed to be in the way of some tide or current, which bore us from the ship at an angle; so that in the course of three hours, by my watch, her hull became invisible to our sight, her broken masts remaining in view for a somewhat longer period. Then, towards evening, it grew misty, and so through the night. The next day we were still encompassed by the mist, the weather remaining quiet.

"For four days, we drifted through this strange haze, until, on the evening of the fourth day, there grew upon our ears the murmur of breakers at a distance. Gradually it became plainer, and, somewhat after midnight, it appeared to sound upon either hand at no very great space. The raft was raised upon a swell several times, and then we were in smooth water, and the noise of the breakers was behind.

"When the morning came, we found that we were in a sort of great lagoon; but of this we noticed little at the time; for close before us, through the enshrouding mist, loomed the hull of a large sailing-vessel. With one accord, we fell upon our knees and thanked God; for we thought that here was an end to our perils. We had much to learn.

"The raft drew near to the ship, and we shouted on them, to take us aboard; but none answered. Presently, the raft touched against the side of the vessel, and, seeing a rope hanging downwards, I seized it and began to climb. Yet I had much ado to make my way up, because of a kind of grey, lichenous fungus, which had seized upon the rope, and which blotched the side of the ship, lividly.

"I reached the rail, and clambered over it, on to the deck. Here, I saw that the decks were covered, in great patches, with the grey masses, some of them rising into nodules several feet in height; but at the time, I thought less of this matter than of the possibility of there being people aboard the ship. I shouted; but none answered. Then I went to the door below the poop deck. I opened it, and peered in. There was a great smell of staleness, so that I knew in a moment that nothing living was within, and with the knowledge, I shut the door quickly; for I felt suddenly lonely.

"I went back to the side, where I had scrambled up. My—my sweetheart was still sitting quietly upon the raft. Seeing me look down, she called up to know whether there were any aboard of the ship. I replied that the vessel had the appearance of having been long deserted; but that if she would wait a little, I would see whether there was anything in the shape of a ladder, by which she could ascend to the deck. Then we would make a search through the vessel together. A little later, on the opposite side of the decks, I found a rope side-ladder. This I carried across, and a minute afterwards, she was beside me.

"Together, we explored the cabins and apartments in the after-part of the ship; but nowhere was there any sign of life. Here and there, within the cabins themselves, we came across odd patches of that queer fungus; but this, as my sweetheart said, could be cleansed away.

"In the end, having assured ourselves that the after portion of the vessel was empty, we picked our ways to the bows, between the ugly grey nodules of that strange growth; and here we made a further search, which told us that there was indeed none aboard but ourselves.

"This being now beyond any doubt, we returned to the stern of the ship, and proceeded to make ourselves as comfortable as possible. Together, we cleared out and cleaned two of the cabins; and, after that, I made examination whether there was anything eatable in the ship. This I soon found was so, and thanked God in my heart for His goodness. In addition to this, I discovered the whereabouts of the freshwater pump, and having fixed it, I found the water drinkable, though somewhat unpleasant to the taste.

"For several days, we stayed aboard the ship, without attempting to get to the shore. We were busily engaged in making the place habitable. Yet even thus early, we became aware that our lot was even less to be desired than might have been imagined; for though, as a first step, we scraped away the odd patches of growth that studded the floors and walls of the cabins and saloon, yet they returned almost to their original size within the space of twenty-four hours, which not only discouraged us, but gave us a feeling of vague unease.

"Still, we would not admit ourselves beaten, so set to work afresh, and not only scraped away the fungus, but soaked the places where it had been, with carbolic, a can-full of which I had found in the pantry. Yet, by the end of the week, the growth had returned in full strength, and, in addition, it had spread to other places, as though our touching it had allowed germs from it to travel elsewhere.

"On the seventh morning, my sweetheart woke to find a small patch of it growing on her pillow, close to her face. At that, she came to me, so soon as she could get her garments upon her. I was in the galley at the time, lighting the fire for breakfast.

"'Come here, John,' she said, and led me aft. When I saw the thing upon her pillow, I shuddered, and then and there we agreed to go right out of the ship, and see whether we could not fare to make ourselves more comfortable ashore.

"Hurriedly, we gathered together our few belongings, and even among these, I found that the fungus had been at work; for one of her shawls had a little lump of it growing near one edge. I threw the whole thing over the side, without saying anything to her.

"The raft was still alongside; but it was too clumsy to guide, and I lowered down a small boat that hung across the stern, and in this we made our way to the shore. Yet, as we drew near to it, I became gradually aware that here the vile fungus, which had driven us from the ship, was growing riot. In places it rose into horrible, fantastic mounds, which seemed almost to quiver, as with a quiet life, when the wind blew across them. Here and there, it took on the forms of vast fingers, and in others it just spread out flat and smooth and treacherous. Odd places, it appeared as grotesque stunted trees, seeming extraordinarily kinked and gnarled—The whole quaking vilely at times.

"At first, it seemed to us that there was no single portion of the surrounding shore which was not hidden beneath the masses of the hideous lichen; yet, in this, I found we were mistaken; for somewhat later, coasting along the shore at a little distance, we descried a smooth white patch of what appeared to be find sand, and there we landed. It was not sand. What it was, I do not know. All that I have observed, is that upon it, the fungus will not grow; while everywhere else, save where the sand-like earth wanders oddly, path-wise, amid the grey desolation of the lichen, there is nothing but that loathsome greyness.

"It is difficult to make you understand how cheered we were to find one place that was absolutely free from the growth, and here we deposited our belongings. Then we went back to the ship for such things as it seemed to us we should need. Among other matters, I managed to bring ashore with me one of the ship's sails, with which I constructed two small tents, which, though exceedingly rough-shaped, served the purposes for which they were intended. In these, we lived and stored our various necessities, and thus for a matter of some four weeks, all went smoothly and without particular unhappiness. Indeed, I may say with much of happiness—for—for we were together.

"It was on the thumb of her right hand, that the growth first showed. It was only a small circular spot, much like a little grey mole. My God! how the fear leapt to my heart when she showed me the place. We cleansed it, between us, washing it with carbolic and water. In the morning of the following day, she showed her hand to me again. The grey warty thing had returned. For a little while, we looked at one another in silence. Then, still wordless, we started again to remove it. In the midst of the operation, she spoke suddenly.

"What's that on the side of your face, Dear!" Her voice was sharp with anxiety. I put my hand up to feel.

"'There! Under the hair by your ear. A little to the front a bit.' My finger rested upon the place, and then I knew.

"'Let us get your thumb done first,' I said. And she submitted, only because she was afraid to touch me until it was cleansed. I finished washing and disinfecting her thumb, and then she turned to my face. After it was finished, we sat together and talked awhile of many things; for there had come into our lives sudden, very terrible thoughts. We were, all at once, afraid of something worse than death. We spoke of loading the boat with provisions and water, and making our way out on to the sea; yet we were helpless, for many causes, and—and the growth had attacked us already. We decided to stay. God would do with us what was His will. We would wait.

"A month, two months, three months passed, and the places grew somewhat, and there had come others. Yet we fought so strenuously with the fear, that its headway was but slow, comparatively speaking.

"Occasionally, we ventured off to the ship for such stores as we needed. There, we found that the fungus grew persistently. One of the nodules on the main deck became soon as high as my head.

"We had now given up all thought or hope of leaving the island. We had realised that it would be unallowable to go among healthy humans, with the thing from which we were suffering.

"With this determination and knowledge in our minds, we knew that we should have to husband our food and water; for we did not know, at that time, but that we should possibly live for many years.

"This reminds me that I have told you that I am an old man. Judged by years this is not so. But—but—"

He broke off; then continued somewhat abruptly:—

"As I was saying, we knew that we should have to use care in the matter of food. But we had no idea then how little food there was left, of which to take care. It was a week later, that I made the discovery that all the other bread tanks—which I had supposed full—were empty, and that (beyond odd tins of vegetables and meat, and some other matters) we had nothing on which to depend, but the bread in the tank which I had already opened.

"After learning this, I bestirred myself to do what I could, and set to work at fishing in the lagoon; but with no success. At this, I was somewhat inclined to feel desperate, until the thought came to me to try outside the lagoon, in the open sea.

"Here, at times, I caught odd fish; but, so infrequently, that they proved of but little help in keeping us from the hunger which threatened. It seemed to me that our deaths were likely to come by hunger, and not by the growth of the thing which had seized upon our bodies.

"We were in this state of mind when the fourth month wore out. Then I made a very horrible discovery. One morning, a little before midday, I came off from the ship, with a portion of the biscuits which were left. In the mouth of her tent, I saw my sweetheart sitting, eating something.

"'What is it, my Dear?' I called out as I leapt ashore. Yet, on hearing my voice, she seemed confused, and, turning, slyly threw something towards the edge of the little clearing. It fell short, and, a vague suspicion having arisen within me, I walked across and picked it up. It was a piece of the grey fungus.

"As I went to her, with it in my hand, she turned deadly pale; then a rose red.

"I felt strangely dazed and frightened.

"'My Dear! My Dear!' I said, and could say no more. Yet, at my words, she broke down and cried bitterly. Gradually, as she calmed, I got from her the news that she had tried it the preceding day, and—and liked it. I got her to promise on her knees not to touch it again, however great our hunger. After she had promised, she told me that the desire for it had come suddenly, and that, until the moment of desire, she had experienced nothing towards it, but the most extreme repulsion.

"Later in the day, feeling strangely restless, and much shaken with the thing which I had discovered, I made my way along one of the twisted paths—formed by the white, sand-like substance—which led among the fungoid growth. I had, once before, ventured along there; but not to any great distance. This time, being involved in perplexing thought, I went much further than hitherto.

"Suddenly, I was called to myself, by a queer hoarse sound on my left. Turning quickly, I saw that there was movement among an extraordinarily shaped mass of fungus, close to my elbow. It was swaying uneasily, as though it possessed life of its own. Abruptly, as I stared, the thought came to me that the thing had a grotesque resemblance to the figure of a distorted human creature. Even as the fancy flashed into my brain, there was a slight, sickening noise of tearing, and I saw that one of the branch-like arms was detaching itself from the surrounding grey masses, and coming towards me. The head of the thing—a shapeless grey ball, inclined in my direction. I stood stupidly, and the vile arm brushed across my face. I gave out a frightened cry, and ran back a few paces. There was a sweetish taste upon my lips, where the thing had touched me. I licked them, and was immediately filled with an inhuman desire. I turned and seized a mass of the fungus. Then more, and—more. I was insatiable. In the midst of devouring, the remembrance of the morning's discovery swept into my mazed brain. It was sent by God. I dashed the fragment I held, to the ground. Then, utterly wretched and feeling a dreadful guiltiness, I made my way back to the little encampment.

"I think she knew, by some marvellous intuition which love must have given, so soon as she set eyes on me. Her quiet sympathy made it easier for me, and I told her of my sudden weakness; yet omitted to mention the extraordinary thing which had gone before. I desired to spare her all unnecessary terror.

"But, for myself, I had added an intolerable knowledge, to breed an incessant terror in my brain; for I doubted not but that I had seen the end of one of those men who had come to the island in the ship in the lagoon; and in that monstrous ending, I had seen our own.

"Thereafter, we kept from the abominable food, though the desire for it had entered into our blood. Yet, our drear punishment was upon us; for, day by day, with monstrous rapidity, the fungoid growth took hold of our poor bodies. Nothing we could do would check it materially, and so—and so—we who had been human, became—Well, it matters less each day. Only—only we had been man and maid!

"And day by day, the fight is more dreadful, to withstand the hunger-lust for the terrible lichen.

"A week ago we ate the last of the biscuit, and since that time I have caught three fish. I was out here fishing to-night, when your schooner drifted upon me out of the mist. I hailed you. You know the rest, and may God, out of His great heart, bless you for your goodness to a—a couple of poor outcast souls."

There was the dip of an oar—another. Then the voice came again, and for the last time, sounding through the slight surrounding mist, ghostly and mournful.

"God bless you! Good-bye!"

"Good-bye," we shouted together, hoarsely, our hearts full of many emotions.

I glanced about me. I became aware that the dawn was upon us.

The sun flung a stray beam across the hidden sea; pierced the mist dully, and lit up the receding boat with a gloomy fire. Indistinctly, I saw something nodding between the oars. I thought of a sponge—a great, grey nodding sponge—The oars continued to ply. They were grey—as was the boat—and my eyes searched a moment vainly for the conjunction of hand and oar. My gaze flashed back to the—head. It nodded forward as the oars went backward for the stroke. Then the oars were dipped, the boat shot out of the patch of light, and the—the thing went nodding into the mist.

THROUGH THE VORTEX OF A CYCLONE

(The Cyclone—"The most fearful enemy which the mariner's perilous calling obliges him to encounter.")

It was in the middle of November that the four-masted barque, Golconda, came down from Crockett and anchored off Telegraph Hill, San Francisco. She was loaded with grain, and was homeward bound round Cape Horn. Five days later she was towed out through the Golden Gates, and cast loose off the Heads, and so set sail upon the voyage that was to come so near to being her last.

For a fortnight we had baffling winds; but after that time, got a good slant that carried us down to within a couple of degrees of the Line. Here it left us, and over a week passed before we managed to tack and drift our way into the Southern Hemisphere.

About five degrees South of the Line, we met with a fair wind that helped us Southward another ten or twelve degrees, and there, early one morning, it dropped us, ending with a short, but violent, thunder storm, in which, so frequent were the lightning flashes, that I managed to secure a picture of one, whilst in the act of snapshotting the sea and clouds upon our port side.

During the day, the wind, as I have remarked, left us entirely, and we lay becalmed under a blazing hot sun. We hauled up the lower sails to prevent them from chafing as the vessel rolled lazily on the scarce perceptible swells, and busied ourselves, as is customary on such occasions, with much swabbing and cleaning of paint-work.

As the day proceeded, so did the heat seem to increase; the atmosphere lost its clear look, and a low haze seemed to lie about the ship at a great distance. At times, the air seemed to have about it a queer, unbreathable quality; so that one caught oneself breathing with a sense of distress.

And, hour by hour, as the day moved steadily onward, the sense of oppression grew ever more acute.

Then, it was, I should think, about three-thirty in the afternoon, I became conscious of the fact that a strange, unnatural, dull, brick-red glare was in the sky. Very subtle it was, and I could not say that it came from any particular place; but rather it seemed to shine in the atmosphere. As I stood looking at it, the Mate came up beside me. After about half a minute, he gave out a sudden exclamation:—

"Hark!" he said. "Did you hear that?"

"No, Mr. Jackson," I replied. "What was it like?"

"Listen!" was all his reply, and I obeyed; and so perhaps for a couple of minutes we stood there in silence.

"There!—--There it is again!" he exclaimed, suddenly; and in the same instant I heard it ... a sound like low, strange growling far away in the North-East. It lasted for about fifteen seconds, and then died away in a low, hollow, moaning noise, that sounded indescribably dree.

After that, for a space longer, we stood listening; and so, at last, it came again ... a far, faint, wild beast growling, away over the North-Eastern horizon. As it died away, with that strange hollow note, the Mate touched my arm:—

"Go and call the Old Man," he said, meaning the Captain. "And while you're down, have a look at the barometer."

In both of these matters I obeyed him, and in a few moments the Captain was on deck, standing beside the Mate—listening.

"How's the glass?" asked the Mate, as I came up.

"Steady," I answered, and at that, he nodded his head, and resumed his expectant attitude. Yet, though we stood silent, maybe for the better part of half an hour, there came no further repetition of that weird, far-off growling, and so, as the glass was steady, no serious notice was taken of the matter.

That evening, we experienced a sunset of quite indescribable gorgeousness, which had, to me, an unnatural glow about it, especially in the way in which it lit up the surface of the sea, which was, at this time, stirred by a slight evening breeze. Evidently, the Mate was of the opinion that it foreboded something in the way of ill weather; for he gave orders for the watch on deck to take the three royals off her.

By the time the men had got down from aloft, the sun had set, and the evening was fading into dusk; yet, despite that, all the sky to the North-East was full of the most vivid red and orange; this being, it will be remembered, the direction from which we had heard earlier that sullen growling.

It was somewhat later, I remember, that I heard the Mate remark to the Captain that we were in for bad weather, and that it was his belief a Cyclone was coming down upon us; but this, the Captain— who was quite a young fellow—poo-poohed; telling him that he pinned his faith to the barometer, which was perfectly steady. Yet, I could see that the Mate was by no means so sure; but forebore to press further his opinion against his superior's.

Presently, as the night came down upon the world, the orange tints went out of the sky, and only a sombre, threatening red was left, with a strangely bright rift of white light running horizontally across it, about twenty degrees above the North-Eastern horizon.

This lasted for nigh on to half an hour, and so did it impress the crew with a sense of something impending, that many of them crouched, staring over the port rail, until long after it had faded into the general greyness.

That night, I recollect, it was my watch on deck from midnight until four in the morning. When the boy came down to wake me, he told me that it had been lightning during the past watch. Even as he spoke, a bright, bluish glare lit up the port-hole; but there was no succeeding thunder.

I sprang hastily from my bunk, and dressed; then, seizing my camera, ran out on deck. I opened the shutter, and the next instant—flash! a great stream of electricity sprang out of the zenith.

Directly afterwards, the Mate called to me from the break of the poop to know whether I had managed to secure that one. I replied, Yes, I thought I had, and he told me to come up on to the poop, beside him, and have a further try from there; for he, the Captain and the Second Mate were much interested in my photographic hobby, and did all in their power to aid me in the securing of successful snaps.

That the Mate was uneasy, I very soon perceived; for, presently, a little while after he had relieved the Second Mate, he ceased his pacing of the poop deck, and came and leant over the rail, alongside of me.

"I wish to goodness the Old Man would have her shortened right down to lower topsails," he said, a moment later, in a low voice. "There's some rotten, dirty weather knocking around. I can smell it." And he raised his head, and sniffed at the air.

"Why not shorten her down, on your own?" I asked him.

"Can't!" he replied. "The Old Man's left orders not to touch anything; but to call him if any change occurs. He goes too damn much by the barometer, to suit me, and won't budge a rope's end, because it's steady."

All this time, the lightning had been playing at frequent intervals across the sky; but now there came several gigantic flashes, seeming extraordinarily near to the vessel, pouring down out of a great rift in the clouds—veritable torrents of electric fluid. I switched open the shutter of my camera, and pointed the lens upward; and the following instant, I secured a magnificent photograph of a great flash, which, bursting down from the same rift, divided to the East and West in a sort of vast electric arch.

For perhaps a minute afterwards, we waited, thinking that such a flash must be followed by thunder; but none came. Instead, from the darkness to the North-East, there sounded a faint, far-drawn-out wailing noise, that seemed to echo queerly across the quiet sea. And after that, silence.

The Mate stood upright, and faced round at me.

"Do you know," he said, "only once before in my life have I heard anything like that, and that was before the Cyclone in which the Lancing, and the Eurasian were lost, in the Indian Ocean."

"Do you think then there's really any danger of a Cyclone now?" I asked him, with something of a little thrill of excitement.

"I think—" he began, and then stopped, and swore suddenly. "Look!" he said, in a loud voice. "Look! 'Stalk' lightning, as I'm a living man!" And he pointed to the North-East. "Photograph that, while you've got the chance; you'll never have another as long as you live!"

I looked in the direction which he indicated, and there, sure enough, were great, pale, flickering streaks and tongues of flame rising apparently out of the sea. They remained steady for some ten or fifteen seconds, and in that time I was able to take a snap of them.

This photograph, as I discovered when I came to develop the negative, has not, I regret to say, taken regard of a strange, indefinable dull-red glare that lit up the horizon at the same time; but, as it is, it remains to me a treasured record of a form of electrical phenomenon but seldom seen, even by those whose good, or ill, fortune has allowed them to come face to face with a Cyclonic Storm. Before leaving this incident, I would once more impress upon the reader that this strange lightning was not descending from the atmosphere; but rising from the sea.

It was after I had secured this last snap, that the Mate declared it to be his conviction that a great Cyclonic Storm was coming down upon us from the North-East, and, with that—for about the twentieth time that watch—he went below to consult the barometer.

He came back in about ten minutes, to say that it was still steady; but that he had called the Old Man, and told him about the upward "Stalk" lightning; yet the Captain, upon hearing from him that the glass was still steady, had refused to be alarmed, but had promised to come up and take a look round. This, in a while, he did; but, as Fate would have it, there was no further display of the "Stalk" lightning, and, as the other kind had now become no more than an occasional dull glare behind the clouds to the North-East, he retired once more, leaving orders to be called if there were any change either in the glass or the weather.

With the sunrise there came a change, a low, slow-moving scud driving down from the North-East, and drifting across the face of the newly-risen sun, which was shining with a queer, unnatural glare. Indeed, so stormy and be-burred looked the sun, that I could have applied to it with truth the line:—

"And the red Sun all bearded with the Storm,"
to describe its threatening aspect.

The glass also showed a change at last, rising a little for a short while, and then dropping about a tenth, and, at that, the Mate hurried down to inform the Skipper, who was speedily up on deck.

He had the fore and mizzen t'gallants taken off her; but nothing more; for he declared that he wasn't going to throw away a fine fair wind for any Old Woman's fancies.

Presently, the wind began to freshen; but the orange-red burr about the sun remained, and also it seemed to me that the tint of the water had a "bad weather" look about it. I mentioned this to the Mate, and he nodded agreement; but said nothing in so many words, for the Captain was standing near.

By eight bells (4 a.m.) the wind had freshened so much that we were lying over to it, with a big cant of the decks, and making a good twelve knots, under nothing higher than the main t'gallant.

We were relieved by the other watch, and went below for a short sleep. At eight o'clock, when again I came on deck, I found that the sea had begun to rise somewhat; but that otherwise the weather was much as it had been when I left the decks; save that the sun was hidden by a heavy squall to windward, which was coming down upon us.

Some fifteen minutes later, it struck the ship, making the foam fly, and carrying away the main topsail sheet. Immediately upon this, the heavy iron ring in the clew of the sail began to thrash and beat about, as the sail flapped in the wind, striking great blows against the steel yard; but the clewline was manned, and some of the men went aloft to repair the damage, after which the sail was once more sheeted home, and we continued to carry on.

About this time, the Mate sent me down into the saloon to take another look at the glass, and I found that it had fallen a further tenth. When I reported this to him, he had the main t'gallant taken in; but hung on to the mainsail, waiting for eight bells, when the whole crowd would be on deck to give a hand.

By that time, we had begun to ship water, and most of us were speedily very thoroughly soused; yet, we got the sail off her, and she rode the easier for the relief.

A little after one o'clock in the afternoon, I went out on deck to have a final "squint" at the weather, before turning-in for a short sleep, and found that the wind had freshened considerably, the seas striking the counter of the vessel at times, and flying to a considerable height in foam.

At four o'clock, when once more I appeared on deck, I discovered the spray flying over us with a good deal of freedom, and the solid water coming aboard occasionally in odd tons.

Yet, so far there was, to a sailorman, nothing worthy of note, in the severity of the weather. It was merely blowing a moderately heavy gale, before which, under our six topsails and foresail, we were making a good twelve knots an hour to the Southward. Indeed, it seemed to me, at this time, that the Captain was right in his belief that we were not in for any very dirty weather, and I said as much to the Mate; whereat he laughed somewhat bitterly.

"Don't you make any sort of mistake!" he said, and pointed to leeward, where continual flashes of lightning darted down from a dark bank of cloud. "We're already within the borders of the Cyclone. We are travelling, so I take it, about a knot slower an hour to the South than the bodily forward movement of the Storm; so that you may reckon it's overtaking us at the rate of something like a mile an hour. Later on, I expect, it'll get a move on it, and then a torpedo boat wouldn't catch it! This bit of a breeze that we're having now"—and he gestured to windward with his elbow—"is only fluff—nothing more than the outer fringe of the advancing Cyclone! Keep your eye lifting to the North-East, and keep your ears open. Wait until you hear the thing yelling at you as loud as a million mad tigers!"

He came to a pause, and knocked the ashes out of his pipe; then he slid the empty "weapon" into the side pocket of his long oilskin coat. And all the time, I could see that he was ruminating.

"Mark my words," he said, at last, and speaking with great deliberation. "Within twelve hours it'll be upon us!"

He shook his head at me. Then he added:—

"Within twelve hours, my boy, you and I and every other soul in this blessed packet may be down there in the cold!" And the brute pointed downward into the sea, and grinned cheerfully at me.

It was our watch that night from eight to twelve; but, except that the wind freshened a trifle, hourly, nothing of note occurred during our watch. The wind was just blowing a good fresh gale, and giving us all we wanted, to keep the ship doing her best under topsails and foresail.

At midnight, I went below for a sleep. When I was called at four o'clock, I found a very different state of affairs. The day had broken, and showed the sea in a very confused state, with a tendency to run up into heaps, and there was a good deal less wind; but what struck me as most remarkable, and brought home with uncomfortable force the Mate's warning of the previous day, was the colour of the sky, which seemed to be everywhere one great glare of gloomy, orange-coloured light, streaked here and there with red. So intense was this glare that the seas, as they rose clumsily into heaps, caught and reflected the light in an extraordinary manner, shining and glittering gloomily, like vast moving mounds of liquid flame. The whole presenting an effect of astounding and uncanny grandeur.

I made my way up on to the poop, carrying my camera. There, I met the Mate.

"You'll not want that pretty little box of yours," he remarked, and tapped my camera. "I guess you'll find a coffin more useful."

"Then it's coming?" I said.

"Look!" was all his reply, and he pointed into the North-East.

I saw in an instant what it was at which he pointed. It was a great black wall of cloud that seemed to cover about seven points of the horizon, extending almost from North to East, and reaching upward some fifteen degrees towards the zenith. The intense, solid blackness of this cloud was astonishing, and threatening to the beholder, seeming, indeed, to be more like a line of great black cliffs standing out of the sea, than a mass of thick vapour.

I glanced aloft, and saw that the other watch were securing the mizzen upper topsail. At the same moment, the Captain appeared on deck, and walked over to the Mate.

"Glass has dropped another tenth, Mr. Jackson," he remarked, and glanced to windward. "I think we'd better have the fore and main upper topsails off her."

Scarcely had he given the order, before the Mate was down on the main deck, shouting:—"Fore and main topsail hal'yards! Lower away! Man clewlines and spillinglines!" So eager was he to have the sail off her.

By the time that the upper topsails were furled, I noted that the red glare had gone out of the greater part of the sky to windward, and a stiffish looking squall was bearing down upon us. Away more to the North, I saw that the black rampart of cloud had disappeared, and, in place thereof, it seemed to me that the clouds in that quarter were assuming a hard, tufted appearance, and changing their shapes with surprising rapidity.

The sea also at this time was remarkable, acting uneasily, and hurling up queer little mounds of foam, which the passing squall caught and spread.

All these points, the Mate noted; for I heard him urging the Captain to take in the foresail and mizzen lower topsail. Yet, this, the Skipper seemed unwilling to do; but finally agreed to have the mizzen topsail off her. Whilst the men were up at this, the wind dropped abruptly in the tail of the squall, the vessel rolling heavily, and taking water and spray with every roll.

Now, I want the Reader to try and understand exactly how matters were at this particular and crucial moment. The wind had dropped entirely, and, with the dropping of the wind, a thousand different sounds broke harshly upon the ear, sounding almost unnatural in their distinctness, and impressing the ear with a sense of discomfort. With each roll of the ship, there came a chorus of creaks and groans from the swaying masts and gear, and the sails slatted with a damp, disagreeable sound. Beyond the ship, there was the constant, harsh murmur of the seas, occasionally changing to a low roar, as one broke near us. One other sound there was that punctuated all these, and that was the loud, slapping blows of the seas, as they hove themselves clumsily against the ship; and, for the rest, there was a strange sense of silence.

Then, as sudden as the report of a heavy gun, a great bellowing came out of the North and East, and died away into a series of monstrous grumbles of sound. It was not thunder. It was the Voice of the approaching Cyclone.

In the same instant, the Mate nudged my shoulder, and pointed, and I saw, with an enormous feeling of surprise, that a large waterspout had formed about four hundred yards astern, and was coming towards us. All about the base of it, the sea was foaming in a strange manner, and the whole thing seemed to have a curious luminous quality.

Thinking about it now, I cannot say that I perceived it to be in rotation; but nevertheless, I had the impression that it was revolving swiftly. Its general onward motion seemed to be about as fast as would be attained by a well-manned gig.

I remember, in the first moments of astonishment, as I watched it, hearing the Mate shout something to the Skipper about the foresail, then I realised suddenly that the spout was coming straight for the ship. I ran hastily to the taffrail, raised my camera, and snapped it, and then, as it seemed to tower right up above me, gigantic, I ran backwards in sudden fright. In the same instant, there came a blinding flash of lightning, almost in my face, followed instantaneously by a tremendous roar of thunder, and I saw that the thing had burst within about fifty yards of the ship. The sea, immediately beneath where it had been, leapt up in a great hummock of solid water, and foam, as though something as great as a house had been cast into the ocean. Then, rushing towards us, it struck the stern of the vessel, flying as high as our topsail yards in spray, and knocking me backwards on to the deck.

As I stood up, and wiped the water hurriedly from my camera, I heard the Mate shout out to know if I were hurt, and then, in the same moment, and before I could reply, he cried out:—

"It's coming! Up hellum! Up hellum! Look out everybody! Hold on for your lives!"

Directly afterwards, a shrill, yelling noise seemed to fill the whole sky with a deafening, piercing sound. I glanced hastily over the port quarter. In that direction the whole surface of the ocean seemed to be torn up into the air in monstrous clouds of spray. The yelling sound passed into a vast scream, and the next instant the Cyclone was upon us.

Immediately, the air was so full of flying spray that I could not see a yard before me, and the wind slapped me back against the teak companion, pinning me there for a few moments, helpless. The ship heeled over to a terrible angle, so that, for some seconds, I thought we were going to capsize. Then, with a sudden lurch, she hove herself upright, and I became able to see about me a little, by switching the water from my face, and shielding my eyes. Near to me, the helmsman—a little Dago—was clinging to the wheel, looking like nothing so much as a drowned monkey, and palpably frightened to such an extent that he could hardly stand upright.

From him, I looked round at so much of the vessel as I could see, and up at the spars, and so, presently, I discovered how it was that she had righted. The mizzen topmast was gone just below the heel of the t'gallantmast, and the fore topmast a little above the cap. The main topmast alone stood. It was the losing of these spars which had eased her, and allowed her to right so suddenly. Marvellously enough, the foresail—a small, new, No. 1 canvas stormsail—had stood the strain, and was now bellying out, with a high foot, the sheets evidently having surged under the wind pressure. What was more extraordinary, was that the fore and main lower topsails were standing, [3] and this, despite the fact that the bare upper spars on both the fore and mizzen masts, had been carried away.

And now, the first awful burst of the Cyclone having passed with the righting of the vessel, the three sails stood, though tested to their utmost, and the ship, under the tremendous urging force of the Storm, was tearing forward at a high speed through the seas.

I glanced down now at myself and camera. Both were soaked; yet, as I discovered later, the latter would still take photographs. I struggled forward to the break of the poop, and stared down on to the maindeck. The seas were breaking aboard every moment, and the spray flying over us continually in huge white clouds. And in my ears was the incessant, wild, roaring-scream of the monster Whirl-Storm.

Then I saw the Mate. He was up against the lee rail, chopping at something with a hatchet. At times the water left him visible to his knees; anon he was completely submerged; but ever there was the whirl of his weapon amid the chaos of water, as he hacked and cut at the gear that held the mizzen t'gallant mast crashing against the side.

I saw him glance round once, and he beckoned with the hatchet to a couple of his watch who were fighting their way aft along the streaming decks. He did not attempt to shout, for no shout could have been heard in the incredible roaring of the wind. Indeed, so vastly loud was the noise made by this element, that I had not heard even the topmasts carry away; though the sound of a large spar breaking will make as great a noise as the report of a big gun. The next instant, I had thrust my camera into one of the hencoops upon the poop, and turned to struggle aft to the companionway; for I knew it was no use going to the Mate's aid without axes.

Presently, I was at the companion, and had the fastenings undone; then I opened the door, and sprang in on to the stairs. I slammed-to the door, bolted it, and made my way below, and so, in a minute, had possessed myself of a couple of axes. With these, I returned to the poop, fastening the companion doors carefully behind me, and, in a little, was up to my neck in water on the maindeck, helping to clear away the wreckage. The second axe, I had pushed into the hands of one of the men.

Presently, we had the gear cleared away.

Then we scrambled away forrard along the decks, through the boiling swirls of water and foam that swept the vessel, as the seas thundered aboard; and so we came to the assistance of the Second Mate, who was desperately busied, along with some of his watch, in clearing away the broken fore-topmast and yards that were held by their gear, thundering against the side of the ship.

Yet, it must not be supposed that we were to manage this piece of work, without coming to some harm; for, just as we made an end of it, an enormous sea swept aboard, and dashed one of the men against the spare topmast that was lashed along, inside the bulwarks, below the pin-rail. When we managed to pull the poor senseless fellow out from underneath the spar, where the sea had jammed him, we found that his left arm and collar-bone were broken. We took him forrard to the fo'cas'le, and there, with rough surgery, made him so comfortable as we could; after which we left him, but half conscious, in his bunk.

After that, several wet, weary hours were spent in rigging rough preventer-stays. Then the rest of us, men as well as officers, made our way aft to the poop; there to wait, desperately ready to cope with any emergency where our poor, futile human strength might aid to our salvation.

With great difficulty, the Carpenter had managed to sound the well, and, to our delight, had found that we were not making any water; so that the blows of the broken spars had done us no vital harm.

By midday, the following seas had risen to a truly formidable height, and two hands were working half naked at the wheel; for any carelessness in steering would, most certainly, have had horrible consequences.

In the course of the afternoon, the Mate and I went down into the saloon to get something to eat, and here, out of the deafening roar of the wind, I managed to get a short chat with my senior officer.

Talking about the waterspout which had so immediately preceded the first rush of the Cyclone, I made mention of its luminous appearance; to which he replied that it was due probably to a vast electric action going on between the clouds and the sea.

After that, I asked him why the Captain did not heave to, and ride the Storm out, instead of running before it, and risking being pooped, or broaching to.

To this, the Mate made reply that we were right in the line of translation; in other words, that we were directly in the track of the vortex, or centre, of the Cyclone, and that the Skipper was doing his best to edge the ship to leeward, before the centre, with the awful Pyramidal Sea, should overtake us.

"If we can't manage to get out of the way," he concluded, grimly, "you'll probably have a chance to photograph something that you'll never have time to develop!"

I asked him how he knew that the ship was directly in the track of the vortex, and he replied that the facts that the wind was not hauling, but getting steadily worse, with the barometer constantly falling, were sure signs.

And soon after that we returned to the deck.

As I have said, at midday, the seas were truly formidable; but by four p.m. they were so much worse that it was impossible to pass fore or aft along the decks, the water breaking aboard, as much as a hundred tons at a time, and sweeping all before it.

All this time, the roaring and howling of the Cyclone was so incredibly loud, that no word spoken, or shouted, out on deck—even though right into one's ear—could be heard distinctly, so that the utmost we could do to convey ideas to one another, was to make signs. And so, because of this, and to get for a little out of the painful and exhausting pressure of the wind, each of the officers would, in turn (sometimes singly and sometimes two at once), go down to the saloon, for a short rest and smoke.

It was in one of those brief "smoke-ohs" that the Mate told me the vortex of the Cyclone was probably within about eighty or a hundred miles of us, and coming down on us at something like twenty or thirty knots an hour, which—as this speed enormously exceeded ours—made it probable that it would be upon us before midnight.

"Is there no chance of getting out of the way?" I asked. "Couldn't we haul her up a trifle, and cut across the track a bit quicker than we are doing?"

"No," replied the Mate, and shook his head, thoughtfully. "The seas would make a clean breach over us, if we tried that. It's a case of 'run till you're blind, and pray till you bust'!" he concluded with a certain despondent brutalness.

I nodded assent; for I knew that it was true. And after that we were silent. A few minutes later, we went up on deck. There we found that, the wind had increased, and blown the foresail bodily away; yet, despite the greater weight of the wind, there had come a rift in the clouds, through which the sun was shining with a queer brightness.

I glanced at the Mate, and smiled; for it seemed to me a good omen; but he shook his head, as one who should say: "It is no good omen; but a sign of something worse coming."

That he was right in refusing to be assured, I had speedy proof; for within ten minutes the sun had vanished, and the clouds seemed to be right down upon our mastheads—great bellying webs of black vapour, that seemed almost to mingle with the flying clouds of foam and spray. The wind appeared to gain strength minute by minute, rising into an abominable scream, so piercing at times as to seem to pain the ear drums.

In this wise an hour passed, the ship racing onward under her two topsails, seeming to have lost no speed with the losing of the foresail; though it is possible that she was more under water forrard than she had been.

Then, about five-thirty p.m., I heard a louder roar in the air above us, so deep and tremendous that it seemed to daze and stun one; and, in the same instant, the two topsails were blown out of the bolt-ropes, and one of the hencoops was lifted bodily off the poop, and hurled into the air, descending with an inaudible crash on to the maindeck. Luckily, it was not the one into which I had thrust my camera.

With the losing of the topsails, we might be very truly described as running under bare poles; for now we had not a single stitch of sail set anywhere. Yet, so furious was the increasing wind, so tremendous the weight of it, that the vessel, though urged forward only by the pressure of the element upon her naked spars and hull, managed to keep ahead of the monstrous following seas, which now were grown to truly awesome proportions.

The next hour or two, I remember only as a time that spread out monotonously. A time miserable and dazing, and dominated always by the deafening, roaring scream of the Storm. A time of wetness and dismalness, in which I knew, more than saw, that the ship wallowed on and on through the interminable seas. And so, hour by hour, the wind increased as the Vortex of the Cyclone—the "Death-Patch"—drew nearer and ever nearer.

Night came on early, or, if not night, a darkness that was fully its equivalent. And now I was able to see how tremendous was the electric action that was going on all about us. There seemed to be no lightning flashes; but, instead, there came at times across the darkness, queer luminous shudders of light. I am not acquainted with any word that better describes this extraordinary electrical phenomenon, than "shudders" of light—broad, dull shudders of light, that came in undefined belts across the black, thunderous canopy of clouds, which seemed so low that our main-truck must have "puddled" them with every roll of the ship.

A further sign of electric action was to be seen in the "corpse candles," which ornamented every yard-arm. Not only were they upon the yard-arms; but occasionally several at a time would glide up and down one or more of the fore and aft stays, at whiles swinging off to one side or the other, as the ship rolled. The sight having in it a distinct touch of weirdness.

It was an hour or so later, I believe a little after nine p.m., that I witnessed the most striking manifestation of electrical action that I have ever seen; this being neither more nor less than a display of Aurora Borealis lightning—a sight dree and almost frightening, with the sense of unearthliness and mystery that it brings.

I want you to be very clear that I am not talking about the Northern Lights—which, indeed, could never be seen at that distance to the Southward—; but of an extraordinary electrical phenomenon which occurred when the vortex of the Cyclone was within some twenty or thirty miles of the ship. It occurred suddenly. First, a ripple of "Stalk" lightning showed right away over the oncoming seas to the Northward; then, abruptly, a red glare shone out in the sky, and, immediately afterwards, vast streamers of greenish flame appeared above the red glare. These lasted, perhaps, half a minute, expanding and contracting over the sky with a curious quivering motion. The whole forming a truly awe-inspiring spectacle.

And then, slowly, the whole thing faded, and only the blackness of the night remained, slit in all directions by the phosphorescent crests of the seas.

I don't know whether I can convey to you any vivid impression of our case and chances at this time. It is so difficult—unless one had been through a similar experience—even to comprehend fully the incredible loudness of the wind. Imagine a noise as loud as the loudest thunder you have ever heard; then imagine this noise to last hour after hour, without intermission, and to have in it a hideously threatening hoarse note, and, blending with this, a constant yelling scream that rises at times to such a pitch that the very ear drums seem to experience pain, and then, perhaps, you will be able to comprehend merely the amount of sound that has to be endured during the passage of one of these Storms. And then, the force of the wind! Have you ever faced a wind so powerful that it splayed your lips apart, whether you would or not, laying your teeth bare to view? This is only a little thing; but it may help you to conceive something of the strength of a wind that will play such antics with one's mouth. The sensation it gives is extremely disagreeable—a sense of foolish impotence, is how I can best describe it.

Another thing; I learned that, with my face to the wind, I could not breathe. This is a statement baldly put; but it should help me somewhat in my endeavour to bring home to you the force of the wind, as exemplified in the minor details of my experience.

To give some idea of the wind's power, as shown in a larger way, one of the lifeboats on the after skids was up-ended against the mizzen mast, and there crushed flat by the wind, as though a monstrous invisible hand had pinched it. Does this help you a little to gain an idea of wind-force never met with in a thousand ordinary lives?

Apart from the wind, it must be borne in mind that the gigantic seas pitch the ship about in a most abominable manner. Indeed, I have seen the stern of a ship hove up to such a height that I could see the seas ahead over the fore topsail yards, and when I explain that these will be something like seventy to eighty feet above the deck, you may be able to imagine what manner of Sea is to be met with in a great Cyclonic Storm.

Regarding this matter of the size and ferocity of the seas, I possess a photograph that was taken about ten o'clock at night. This was photographed by the aid of flashlight, an operation in which the Captain assisted me. We filled an old, percussion pistol with flashlight powder, with an air-cone of paper down the centre. Then, when I was ready, I opened the shutter of the camera, and pointed it over the stern into the darkness. The Captain fired the pistol, and, in the instantaneous great blaze of light that followed, I saw what manner of sea it was that pursued us. To say it was a mountain, is to be futile. It was like a moving cliff.

As I snapped-to the shutter of my camera, the question flashed into my brain: "Are we going to live it out, after all?" And, suddenly, it came home to me that I was a little man in a little ship, in the midst of a very great sea.

And then fresh knowledge came to me; I knew, abruptly, that it would not be a difficult thing to be very much afraid. The knowledge was new, and took me more in the stomach than the heart. Afraid! I had been in so many storms that I had forgotten they might be things to fear. Hitherto, my sensation at the thought of bad weather had been chiefly a feeling of annoyed repugnance, due to many memories of dismal wet nights, in wetter oilskins; with everything about the vessel reeking with damp and cheerless discomfort. But fear—No! A sailor has no more normal fear of bad weather, than a steeple-jack fears height. It is, as you might say, his vocation. And now this hateful sense of insecurity!

I turned from the taffrail, and hurried below to wipe the lens and cover of my camera; for the whole air was full of driving spray, that soaked everything, and hurt the face intolerably; being driven with such force by the storm.

Whilst I was drying my camera, the Mate came down for a minute's breathing space.

"Still at it?" he said.

"Yes," I replied, and I noticed, half-consciously, that he made no effort to light his pipe, as he stood with his arm crooked over an empty, brass candle bracket.

"You'll never develop them," he remarked.

"Of course I shall!" I replied, half-irritably; but with a horrid little sense of chilliness at his words, which came so unaptly upon my mind, so lately perturbed by uncomfortable thoughts.

"You'll see," he replied, with a sort of brutal terseness. "We shan't be above water by midnight!"

"You can't tell," I said. "What's the use of meeting trouble! Vessels have lived through worse than this?"

"Have they?" he said, very quietly. "Not many vessels have lived through worse than what's to come. I suppose you realise we expect to meet the Centre in less than an hour?"

"Well," I replied, "anyway, I shall go on taking photos. I guess if we come through all right, I shall have something to show people ashore."

He laughed, a queer, little, bitter laugh.

"You may as well do that as anything else," he said. "We can't do anything to help ourselves. If we're not pooped before the Centre reaches us, IT'll finish us in quick time!"

Then that cheerful officer of mine turned slowly, and made his way on deck, leaving me, as may be imagined, particularly exhilarated by his assurances. Presently, I followed, and, having barred the companionway behind me, struggled forward to the break of the poop, clutching blindly at any holdfast in the darkness.

And so, for a space, we waited in the Storm—the wind bellowing fiendishly, and our main decks one chaos of broken water, swirling and roaring to and fro in the darkness.

It was a little later that some one plucked me hard by the sleeve, and, turning, I made out with difficulty that it was the Captain, trying to attract my attention. I caught his wrist, to show that I comprehended what he desired, and, at that, he dropped on his hands and knees, and crawled aft along the streaming poop deck, I following, my camera held between my teeth by the handle.

He reached the companionway, and unbarred the starboard door; then crawled through, and I followed after him. I fastened the door, and made my way, in his wake, to the saloon. Here he turned to me. He was a curiously devil-may-care sort of man, and I found that he had brought me down to explain that the Vortex would be upon us very soon, and that I should have the chance of a life-time to get a snap of the much talked of Pyramidal Sea. And, in short, that he wished me to have everything prepared, and the pistol ready loaded with flashlight powder; for, as he remarked:

"If we get through, it'll be a rare curiosity to show some of those unbelieving devils ashore."

In a little, we had everything ready, and then we made our way once more up on deck; the Captain placing the pistol in the pocket of his silk oilskin coat.

There, together, under the after weather-cloth, we waited. The Second Mate, I could not see; but occasionally I caught a vague sight of the First Mate, standing near the after binnacle, [4] and obviously watching the steering. Apart from the puny halo that emanated from the binnacle, all else was blind darkness, save for the phosphorescent lights of the overhanging crests of the seas.

And above us and around us, filling all the sky with sound, was the incessant mad yowling of the Cyclone; the noise so vast, and the volume and mass of the wind so enormous that I am impressed now, looking back, with a sense of having been in a semi-stunned condition through those last minutes.

I am conscious now that a vague time passed. A time of noise and wetness and lethargy and immense tiredness. Abruptly, a tremendous flash of lightning burst through the clouds. It was followed, almost directly, by another, which seemed to rive the sky apart. Then, so quickly that the succeeding thunder-clap was audible to our wind-deafened ears, the wind ceased, and, in the comparative, but hideously unnatural, silence, I caught the Captain's voice shouting:

"The Vortex—quick!"

Even as I pointed my camera over the rail, and opened the shutter, my brain was working with a preternatural avidity, drinking in a thousand uncanny sounds and echoes that seemed to come upon me from every quarter, brutally distinct against the background of the Cyclone's distant howling. There were the harsh, bursting, frightening, intermittent noises of the seas, making tremendous, slopping crashes of sound; and, mingling with these, the shrill, hissing scream of the foam; [5] the dismal sounds, that suggested dankness, of water swirling over our decks; and oddly, the faintly-heard creaking of the gear and shattered spars; and then—Flash, in the same instant in which I had taken in these varied impressions, the Captain had fired the pistol, and I saw the Pyramidal Sea.... A sight never to be forgotten. A sight rather for the Dead than the Living. A sea such as I could never have imagined. Boiling and bursting upward in monstrous hillocks of water and foam as big as houses. I heard, without knowing I heard, the Captain's expression of amazement. Then a thunderous roar was in my ears. One of those vast, flying hills of water had struck the ship, and, for some moments, I had a sickening feeling that she was sinking beneath me. The water cleared, and I found myself clinging to the iron weather-cloth staunchion; the weather-cloth itself had gone. I wiped my eyes, and coughed dizzily for a little; then I stared round for the Captain. I could see something dimly up against the rail; something that moved and stood upright. I sung out to know whether it was the Captain, and whether he was all right? To which he replied, heartily enough, but with a gasp, that he was all right so far.

From him, I glanced across to the wheel. There was no light in the binnacle, and, later, I found that it had been washed away, and with it one of the helmsmen. The other man also was gone; but we discovered him, nigh an hour later, jammed half through the rail that ran round the poop. To leeward, I heard the Mate singing out to know whether we were safe; to which both the Captain and I shouted a reply, so as to assure him. It was then I became aware that my camera had been washed out of my hands. I found it eventually among a tangle of ropes and gear to leeward.

Again and again the great hills of water struck the vessel, seeming to rise up on every side at once — towering, live pyramids of brine, in the darkness, hurling upward with a harsh unceasing roaring.

From her taffrail to her knight-heads, the ship was swept, fore and aft, so that no living thing could have existed for a moment down upon the maindeck, which was practically submerged. Indeed, the whole vessel seemed at times to be lost beneath the chaos of water that thundered down and over her in clouds and cataracts of brine and foam, so that each moment seemed like to be our last.

Occasionally, I would hear the hoarse voice of the Captain or the Mate, calling through the gloom to one another, or to the figures of the clinging men. And then again would come the thunder of water, as the seas burst over us. And all this in an almost impenetrable darkness, save when some unnatural glare of lightning sundered the clouds, and lit up the thirty-mile cauldron that had engulfed us.

And, anon, all this while, round about, seeming to come from every point of the horizon, sounded a vast, but distant, bellowing and screaming noise, that I caught sometimes above the harsh, slopping roarings of the bursting water-hills all about us. The sound appeared now to be growing louder upon our port beam. It was the Storm circling far round us.

Some time later, there sounded an intense roar in the air above the ship, and then came a far-off shrieking, that grew rapidly into a mighty whistling-scream, and a minute afterwards a most tremendous gust of wind struck the ship on her port side, hurling her over on to her starboard broadside. For many minutes she lay there, her decks under water almost up to the coamings of the hatches. [6] Then she righted, sullenly and slowly, freeing herself from, maybe, half a thousand tons of water.

Again there came a short period of windlessness, and then once more the yelling of an approaching gust. It struck us; but now the vessel had paid off before the wind, and she was not again forced over on to her side.

From now onward, we drove forward over vast seas, with the Cyclone bellowing and wailing over us in one unbroken roar.... The Vortex had passed, and, could we but last out a few more hours, then might we hope to win through.

With the return of the wind, the Mate and one of the men had taken the wheel; but, despite the most careful steering, we were pooped several times; [7] for the seas were hideously broken and confused, we being still in the wake of the Vortex, and the wind not having had time as yet to smash the Pyramidal Sea into the more regular storm waves, which, though huge in size, give a vessel a chance to rise to them.

It was later that some of us, headed by the Mate—who had relinquished his place at the wheel to one of the men—ventured down on to the maindeck with axes and knives, to clear away the wreckage of some of the spars which we had lost in the Vortex. Many a grim risk was run in that hour; but we cleared the wreck, and after that, scrambled back, dripping, to the poop, where the Steward, looking woefully white and scared, served out rum to us from a wooden deck-bucket.

It was decided now that we should bring her head to the seas, so as to make better weather of it. To reduce the risk as much as possible, we had already put out two fresh oil-bags, which we had prepared, and which, indeed, we ought to have done earlier; for though they were being constantly washed aboard again, we had begun at once to take less water.

Now, we took a hawser from the bows, outside of everything, and right away aft to the poop, where we bent on our sea-anchor, which was like an enormous log-bag, or drogue, made of triple canvas.

We bent on our two oil-bags to the sea-anchor, and then dropped the whole business over the side. When the vessel took the pull of it, we put down our helm, and came up into the wind, very quick, and without taking any great water. And a risk it was; but a deal less than some we had come through already.

Slowly, with an undreamt of slowness, the remainder of the night passed, minute by minute, and at last the day broke in a weary dawn; the sky full of a stormy, sickly light. On every side tumbled an interminable chaos of seas. And the vessel herself—! A wreck, she appeared. The mizzenmast had gone, some dozen feet above the deck; the main topmast had gone, and so had the jigger-topmast. I struggled forrard to the break of the poop, and glanced along the decks. The boats had gone. All the iron scupper-doors were either bent, or had disappeared. On the starboard side, opposite to the stump of the mizzenmast, was a great ragged gap in the steel bulwarks, where the mast must have struck, when it carried away. In several other places, the t'gallant rail was smashed or bent, where it had been struck by falling spars. The side of the teak deck-house had been stove, and the water was roaring in and out with each roll of the ship. The sheep-pen had vanished, and so—as I discovered later—had the pigsty.

Further forrard, my glance went, and I saw that the sea had breached the bulkshead, across the after end of the fo'cas'le, and, with each biggish sea that we shipped, a torrent of water drove in, and then flowed out, sometimes bearing with it an odd board, or perhaps a man's boot, or some article of wearing apparel. In two places on the maindeck, I saw men's sea-chests, washing to and fro in the water that streamed over the deck. And, suddenly, there came into my mind a memory of the poor fellow who had broken his arm when we were cutting loose the wreck of the fore-topmast.

Already, the strength of the Cyclone was spent, so far, at least, as we were concerned; and I was thinking of making a try for the fo'cas'le, when, close beside me, I heard the Mate's voice. I turned, with a little start. He had evidently noticed the breach in the bulkshead; for he told me to watch a chance, and see if we could get forrard.

This, we did; though not without a further thorough sousing; as we were still shipping water by the score of tons. Moreover, the risk was considerably greater than might be conceived; for the doorless scupper-ports offered uncomfortable facilities for gurgling out into the ocean, along with a ton or two of brine from the decks.

We reached the fo'cas'le, and pulled open the lee door. We stepped inside. It was like stepping into a dank, gloomy cavern. Water was dripping from every beam and staunchion. We struggled across the slippery deck, to where we had left the sick man in his bunk. In the dim light, we saw that man and bunk, everything, had vanished; only the bare steel sides of the vessel remained. Every bunk and fitting in the place had been swept away, and all of the men's sea-chests. Nothing remained, save, it might be, an odd soaked rag of clothing, or a sodden bunk-board.

The Mate and I looked at one another, in silence.

"Poor devil!" he said. He repeated his expression of pity, staring at the place where had been the bunk. Then, grave of face, he turned to go out on deck. As he did so, a heavier sea than usual broke aboard; flooded roaring along the decks, and swept in through the broken bulkshead and the lee doorway. It swirled round the sides, caught us, and threw us down in a heap; then swept out through the breach and the doorway, carrying the Mate with it. He managed to grasp the lintel of the doorway, else, I do believe, he would have gone out through one of the open scupper traps. A doubly hard fate, after having come safely through the Cyclone.

Outside of the fo'cas'le, I saw that the ladders leading up to the fo'cas'le head had both gone; but I managed to scramble up. Here, I found that both anchors had been washed away, and the rails all round; only the bare staunchions remaining.

Beyond the bows, the jibboom had gone, and all the gear was draggled inboard over the fo'cas'le head, or trailing in the sea.

We made our way aft, and reported; then the roll was called, and we found that no one else was missing, besides the two I have already mentioned, and the man we found jammed half through the poop rails, who was now under the Steward's care.

From that time on, the sea went down steadily, until, presently, it ceased to threaten us, and we proceeded to get the ship cleared up a bit; after which, one watch turned-in on the floor of the saloon, and the other was told to "stand easy."

Hour by hour, through that day and the next, the sea went down, until it was difficult to believe that we had so lately despaired for our lives. And so the second evening came, calm and restful, the wind no more than a light summer's breeze, and the sea calming steadily.

About seven bells that second night, a big steamer crossed our stern, and slowed down to ask us if we were in need of help; for, even by moonlight, it was easy to see our dismantled condition. This offer, however, the Captain refused; and with many good wishes, the big vessel swung off into the moon-wake, and so, presently, we were left alone in the quiet night; safe at last, and rich in a completed experience.

THE MYSTERY OF THE DERELICT

All the night had the four-masted ship, Tarawak, lain motionless in the drift of the Gulf Stream; for she had run into a "calm patch"—into a stark calm which had lasted now for two days and nights.

On every side, had it been light, might have been seen dense masses of floating gulf-weed, studding the ocean even to the distant horizon. In places, so large were the weed-masses that they formed long, low banks, that by daylight, might have been mistaken for low-lying land.

Upon the lee side of the poop, Duthie, one of the 'prentices, leaned with his elbows upon the rail, and stared out across the hidden sea, to where in the Eastern horizon showed the first pink and lemon streamers of the dawn—faint, delicate streaks and washes of colour.

A period of time passed, and the surface of the leeward sea began to show—a great expanse of grey, touched with odd, wavering belts of silver. And everywhere the black specks and islets of the weed.

Presently, the red dome of the sun protruded itself into sight above the dark rim of the horizon; and, abruptly, the watching Duthie saw something—a great, shapeless bulk that lay some miles away to starboard, and showed black and distinct against the gloomy red mass of the rising sun.

"Something in sight to looard, Sir," he informed the Mate, who was leaning, smoking, over the rail that ran across the break of the poop. "I can't just make out what it is."

The Mate rose from his easy position, stretched himself, yawned, and came across to the boy.

"Whereabouts, Toby?" he asked, wearily, and yawning again.

"There, Sir," said Duthie—alias Toby—"broad away on the beam, and right in the track of the sun. It looks something like a big houseboat, or a hay-stack."

The Mate stared in the direction indicated, and saw the thing which puzzled the boy, and immediately the tiredness went out of his eyes and face.

"Pass me the glasses off the skylight, Toby," he commanded, and the youth obeyed.

After the Mate had examined the strange object through his binoculars for, maybe, a minute, he passed them to Toby, telling him to take a "squint," and say what he made of it.

"Looks like an old powder-hulk, Sir," exclaimed the lad, after awhile, and to this description the Mate nodded agreement.

Later, when the sun had risen somewhat, they were able to study the derelict with more exactness. She appeared to be a vessel of an exceedingly old type, mastless, and upon the hull of which had been built a roof-like superstructure; the use of which they could not determine. She was lying just within the borders of one of the weed-banks, and all her side was splotched with a greenish growth.

It was her position, within the borders of the weed, that suggested to the puzzled Mate, how so strange and unseaworthy looking a craft had come so far abroad into the greatness of the ocean. For, suddenly, it occurred to him that she was neither more nor less than a derelict from the vast Sargasso Sea—a vessel that had, possibly, been lost to the world, scores and scores of years gone, perhaps hundreds. The suggestion touched the Mate's thoughts with solemnity, and he fell to examining the ancient hulk with an even greater interest, and pondering on all the lonesome and awful years that must have passed over her, as she had lain desolate and forgotten in that grim cemetery of the ocean.

Through all that day, the derelict was an object of the most intense interest to those aboard the Tarawak, every glass in the ship being brought into use to examine her. Yet, though within no more than some six or seven miles of her, the Captain refused to listen to the Mate's suggestions that they should put a boat into the water, and pay the stranger a visit; for he was a cautious man, and the glass warned him that a sudden change might be expected in the weather; so that he would have no one leave the ship on any unnecessary business. But, for all that he had caution, curiosity was by no means lacking in him, and his telescope, at intervals, was turned on the ancient hulk through all the day.

Then, it would be about six bells in the second dog watch, a sail was sighted astern, coming up steadily but slowly. By eight bells they were able to make out that a small barque was bringing the wind with her; her yards squared, and every stitch set. Yet the night had advanced apace, and it was nigh to eleven o'clock before the wind reached those aboard the Tarawak. When at last it arrived, there was a slight rustling and quaking of canvas, and odd creaks here and there in the darkness amid the gear, as each portion of the running and standing rigging took up the strain.

Beneath the bows, and alongside, there came gentle rippling noises, as the vessel gathered way; and so, for the better part of the next hour, they slid through the water at something less than a couple of knots in the sixty minutes.

To starboard of them, they could see the red light of the little barque, which had brought up the wind with her, and was now forging slowly ahead, being better able evidently than the big, heavy Tarawak to take advantage of so slight a breeze.

About a quarter to twelve, just after the relieving watch had been roused, lights were observed to be moving to and fro upon the small barque, and by midnight it was palpable that, through some cause or other, she was dropping astern.

When the Mate arrived on deck to relieve the Second, the latter officer informed him of the possibility that something unusual had occurred aboard the barque, telling of the lights about her decks, [8] and how that, in the last quarter of an hour, she had begun to drop astern.

On hearing the Second Mate's account, the First sent one of the 'prentices for his night-glasses, and, when they were brought, studied the other vessel intently, that is, so well as he was able through the darkness; for, even through the night-glasses, she showed only as a vague shape, surmounted by the three dim towers of her masts and sails.

Suddenly, the Mate gave out a sharp exclamation; for, beyond the barque, there was something else shown dimly in the field of vision. He studied it with great intentness, ignoring for the instant, the Second's queries as to what it was that had caused him to exclaim.

All at once, he said, with a little note of excitement in his voice:—

"The derelict! The barque's run into the weed around that old hooker!"

The Second Mate gave a mutter of surprised assent, and slapped the rail.

"That's it!" he said. "That's why we're passing her. And that explains the lights. If they're not fast in the weed, they've probably run slap into the blessed derelict!"

"One thing," said the Mate, lowering his glasses, and beginning to fumble for his pipe, "she won't have had enough way on her to do much damage."

The Second Mate, who was still peering through his binoculars, murmured an absent agreement, and continued to peer. The Mate, for his part, filled and lit his pipe, remarking meanwhile to the unhearing Second, that the light breeze was dropping.

Abruptly, the Second Mate called his superior's attention, and in the same instant, so it seemed, the failing wind died entirely away, the sails settling down into runkles, with little rustles and flutters of sagging canvas.

"What's up?" asked the Mate, and raised his glasses.

"There's something queer going on over yonder," said the Second. "Look at the lights moving about, and—Did you see that?"

The last portion of his remark came out swiftly, with a sharp accentuation of the last word.

"What?" asked the Mate, staring hard.

"They're shooting," replied the Second. "Look! There again!"

"Rubbish!" said the Mate, a mixture of unbelief and doubt in his voice.

With the falling of the wind, there had come a great silence upon the sea. And, abruptly, from far across the water, sounded the distant, dullish thud of a gun, followed almost instantly by several minute, but sharply defined, reports, like the cracking of a whip out in the darkness.

"Jove!" cried the Mate, "I believe you're right." He paused and stared. "There!" he said. "I saw the flashes then. They're firing from the poop, I believe.... I must call the Old Man."

He turned and ran hastily down into the saloon, knocked on the door of the Captain's cabin, and entered. He turned up the lamp, and, shaking his superior into wakefulness, told him of the thing he believed to be happening aboard the barque:—

"It's mutiny, Sir; they're shooting from the poop. We ought to do something—" The Mate said many things, breathlessly; for he was a young man; but the Captain stopped him, with a quietly lifted hand.

"I'll be up with you in a minute, Mr. Johnson," he said, and the Mate took the hint, and ran up on deck.

Before the minute had passed, the Skipper was on the poop, and staring through his night-glasses at the barque and the derelict. Yet now, aboard of the barque, the lights had vanished, and there showed no more the flashes of discharging weapons—only there remained the dull, steady red glow of the port sidelight; and, behind it, the night-glasses showed the shadowy outline of the vessel.

The Captain put questions to the Mates, asking for further details.

"It all stopped while the Mate was calling you, Sir," explained the Second. "We could hear the shots quite plainly."

"They seemed to be using a gun as well as their revolvers," interjected the Mate, without ceasing to stare into the darkness.

For awhile the three of them continued to discuss the matter, whilst down on the maindeck the two watches clustered along the starboard rail, and a low hum of talk rose, fore and aft.

Presently, the Captain and the Mates came to a decision. If there had been a mutiny, it had been brought to its conclusion, whatever that conclusion might be, and no interference from those aboard the Tarawak, at that period, would be likely to do good. They were utterly in the dark—in more ways than one—and, for all they knew, there might not even have been any mutiny. If there had been a mutiny, and the mutineers had won, then they had done their worst; whilst if the officers had won well and good. They had managed to do so without help. Of course, if the Tarawak had been a man-of-war with a large crew, capable of mastering any situation, it would have been a simple matter to send a powerful, armed boat's crew to inquire; but as she was merely a merchant vessel, under-manned, as is the modern fashion, they must go warily. They would wait for the morning, and signal. In a couple of hours it would be light. Then they would be guided by circumstances.

The Mate walked to the break of the poop, and sang out to the men:—

"Now then, my lads, you'd better turn in, the watch below, and have a sleep; we may be wanting you by five bells."

There was a muttered chorus of "i, i, Sir," and some of the men began to go forrard to the fo'cas'le; but others of the watch below remained, their curiosity overmastering their desire for sleep.

On the poop, the three officers leaned over the starboard rail, chatting in a desultory fashion, as they waited for the dawn. At some little distance hovered Duthie, who, as eldest 'prentice just out of his time, had been given the post of acting Third Mate.

Presently, the sky to starboard began to lighten with the solemn coming of the dawn. The light grew and strengthened, and the eyes of those in the Tarawak scanned with growing intentness that portion of the horizon where showed the red and dwindling glow of the barque's sidelight.

Then, it was in that moment when all the world is full of the silence of the dawn, something passed over the quiet sea, coming out of the East—a very faint, long-drawn-out, screaming, piping noise. It might almost have been the cry of a little wind wandering out of the dawn across the sea—a ghostly, piping skirl, so attenuated and elusive was it; but there was in it a weird, almost threatening note, that told the three on the poop it was no wind that made so dree and inhuman a sound.

The noise ceased, dying out in an indefinite, mosquito-like shrilling, far and vague and minutely shrill. And so came the silence again.

"I heard that, last night, when they were shooting," said the Second Mate, speaking very slowly, and looking first at the Skipper and then at the Mate. "It was when you were below, calling the Captain," he added.

"Ssh!" said the Mate, and held up a warning hand; but though they listened, there came no further sound; and so they fell to disjointed questionings, and guessed their answers, as puzzled men will. And ever and anon, they examined the barque through their glasses; but without discovering anything of note, save that, when the light grew stronger, they perceived that her jibboom had struck through the superstructure of the derelict, tearing a considerable gap therein.

Presently, when the day had sufficiently advanced, the Mate sung out to the Third, to take a couple of the 'prentices, and pass up the signal flags and the code book. This was done, and a "hoist" made; but those in the barque took not the slightest heed; so that finally the Captain bade them make up the flags and return them to the locker.

After that, he went down to consult the glass, and when he reappeared, he and the Mates had a short discussion, after which, orders were given to hoist out the starboard life-boat. This, in the course of half an hour, they managed; and, after that, six of the men and two of the 'prentices were ordered into her.

Then half a dozen rifles were passed down, with ammunition, and the same number of cutlasses. These were all apportioned among the men, much to the disgust of the two apprentices, who were aggrieved that they should be passed over; but their feelings altered when the Mate descended into the boat, and handed them each a loaded revolver, warning them, however, to play no "monkey tricks" with the weapons.

Just as the boat was about to push off, Duthie, the eldest 'prentice, came scrambling down the side ladder, and jumped for the after thwart. He landed, and sat down, laying the rifle which he had brought, in the stern; and, after that, the boat put off for the barque.

There were now ten in the boat, and all well armed, so that the Mate had a certain feeling of comfort that he would be able to meet any situation that was likely to arise.

After nearly an hour's hard pulling, the heavy boat had been brought within some two hundred yards of the barque, and the Mate sung out to the men to lie on their oars for a minute. Then he stood up and shouted to the people on the barque; but though he repeated his cry of "Ship ahoy!" several times, there came no reply.

He sat down, and motioned to the men to give way again, and so brought the boat nearer the barque by another hundred yards. Here, he hailed again; but still receiving no reply, he stooped for his binoculars, and peered for awhile through them at the two vessels—the ancient derelict, and the modern sailing-vessel.

The latter had driven clean in over the weed, her stern being perhaps some two score yards from the edge of the bank. Her jibboom, as I have already mentioned, had pierced the green-blotched superstructure of the derelict, so that her cutwater had come very close to the grass-grown side of the hulk.

That the derelict was indeed a very ancient vessel, it was now easy to see; for at this distance the Mate could distinguish which was hull, and which superstructure. Her stern rose up to a height considerably above her bows, and possessed galleries, coming round the counter. In the window frames some of the glass still remained; but others were securely shuttered, and some missing, frames and all, leaving dark holes in the stern. And everywhere grew the dank, green growth, giving to the beholder a queer sense of repulsion. Indeed, there was that about the whole of the ancient craft, that repelled in a curious way—something elusive—a remoteness from humanity, that was vaguely abominable.

The Mate put down his binoculars, and drew his revolver, and, at the action, each one in the boat gave an instinctive glance to his own weapon. Then he sung out to them to give-way, and steered straight for the weed. The boat struck it, with something of a sog; and, after that, they advanced slowly, yard by yard, only with considerable labour.

They reached the counter of the barque, and the Mate held out his hand for an oar. This, he leaned up against the side of the vessel, and a moment later was swarming quickly up it. He grasped the rail, and swung himself aboard; then, after a swift glance fore and aft, gripped the blade of the oar, to steady it, and bade the rest follow as quickly as possible, which they did, the last man bringing up the painter with him, and making it fast to a cleat.

Then commenced a rapid search through the ship. In several places about the maindeck they found broken lamps, and aft on the poop, a shot-gun, three revolvers, and several capstan-bars lying about the poop-deck. But though they pried into every possible corner, lifting the hatches, and examining the lazarette, not a human creature was to be found—the barque was absolutely deserted.

After the first rapid search, the Mate called his men together; for there was an uncomfortable sense of danger in the air, and he felt that it would be better not to straggle. Then, he led the way forrard, and went up on to the t'gallant fo'cas'le head. Here, finding the port sidelight still burning, he bent over the screen, as it were mechanically, lifted the lamp, opened it, and blew out the flame; then replaced the affair on its socket.

After that, he climbed into the bows, and out along the jibboom, beckoning to the others to follow, which they did, no man saying a word, and all holding their weapons handily; for each felt the oppressiveness of the Incomprehensible about them.

The Mate reached the hole in the great superstructure, and passed inside, the rest following. Here they found themselves in what looked something like a great, gloomy barracks, the floor of which was the deck of the ancient craft. The superstructure, as seen from the inside, was a very wonderful piece of work, being beautifully shored and fixed; so that at one time it must have possessed immense strength; though now it was all rotted, and showed many a gape and rip. In one place, near the centre, or midships part, was a sort of platform, high up, which the Mate conjectured might have been used as a "look-out"; though the reason for the prodigious superstructure itself, he could not imagine.

Having searched the decks of this craft, he was preparing to go below, when, suddenly, Duthie caught him by the sleeve, and whispered to him, tensely, to listen. He did so, and heard the thing that had attracted the attention of the youth—it was a low, continuous shrill whining that was rising from out of the dark hull beneath their feet, and, abruptly, the Mate was aware that there was an intensely disagreeable animal-like smell in the air. He had noticed it, in a subconscious fashion, when entering through the broken superstructure; but now, suddenly, he was aware of it.

Then, as he stood there hesitating, the whining noise rose all at once into a piping, screaming squeal, that filled all the space in which they were inclosed, with an awful, inhuman and threatening clamour. The Mate turned and shouted at the top of his voice to the rest, to retreat to the barque, and he, himself, after a further quick nervous glance round, hurried towards the place where the end of the barque's jibboom protruded in across the decks.

He waited, with strained impatience, glancing ever behind him, until all were off the derelict, and then sprang swiftly on to the spar that was their bridge to the other vessel. Even as he did so, the squealing died away into a tiny shrilling, twittering sound, that made him glance back; for the suddenness of the quiet was as effective as though it had been a loud noise. What he saw, seemed to him in that first instant so incredible and monstrous, that he was almost too shaken to cry out. Then he raised his voice in a shout of warning to the men, and a frenzy of haste shook him in every fibre, as he scrambled back to the barque, shouting ever to the men to get into the boat. For in that backward glance, he had seen the whole decks of the derelict a-move with living things—giant rats, thousands and tens of thousands of them; and so in a flash had come to an understanding of the disappearance of the crew of the barque.

He had reached the fo'cas'le head now, and was running for the steps, and behind him, making all the long slanting length of the jibboom black, were the rats, racing after him. He made one leap to the maindeck, and ran. Behind, sounded a queer, multitudinous pattering noise, swiftly surging upon him. He reached the poop steps, and as he sprang up them, felt a savage bite in his left calf. He was on the poop deck now, and running with a stagger. A score of great rats leapt around him, and half a dozen hung grimly to his back, whilst the one that had gripped his calf, flogged madly from side to side as he raced on. He reached the rail, gripped it, and vaulted clean over and down into the weed.

The rest were already in the boat, and strong hands and arms hove him aboard, whilst the others of the crew sweated in getting their little craft round from the ship. The rats still clung to the Mate; but a few blows with a cutlass eased him of his murderous burden. Above them, making the rails and half-round of the poop black and alive, raced thousands of rats.

The boat was now about an oar's length from the barque, and, suddenly, Duthie screamed out that they were coming. In the same instant, nearly a hundred of the largest rats launched themselves at the boat. Most fell short, into the weed; but over a score reached the boat, and sprang savagely at the men, and there was a minute's hard slashing and smiting, before the brutes were destroyed.

Once more the men resumed their task of urging their way through the weed, and so in a minute or two, had come to within some fathoms of the edge, working desperately. Then a fresh terror broke upon them. Those rats which had missed their leap, were now all about the boat, and leaping in from the weed, running up the oars, and scrambling in over the sides, and, as each one got inboard, straight for one of the crew it went; so that they were all bitten and be-bled in a score of places.

There ensued a short but desperate fight, and then, when the last of the beasts had been hacked to death, the men lay once more to the task of heaving the boat clear of the weed.

A minute passed, and they had come almost to the edge, when Duthie cried out, to look; and at that, all turned to stare at the barque, and perceived the thing that had caused the 'prentice to cry out; for the rats were leaping down into the weed in black multitudes, making the great weed-fronds quiver, as they hurled themselves in the direction of the boat. In an incredibly short space of time, all the weed between the boat and the barque, was alive with the little monsters, coming at breakneck speed.

The Mate let out a shout, and, snatching an oar from one of the men, leapt into the stern of the boat, and commenced to thrash the weed with it, whilst the rest laboured infernally to pluck the boat forth into the open sea. Yet, despite their mad efforts, and the death-dealing blows of the Mate's great fourteen-foot oar, the black, living mass were all about the boat, and scrambling aboard in scores, before she was free of the weed. As the boat shot into the clear water, the Mate gave out a great curse, and, dropping his oar, began to pluck the brutes from his body with his bare hands, casting them into the sea. Yet, fast almost as he freed himself, others sprang upon him, so that in another minute he was like to have been pulled down, for the boat was alive and swarming with the pests, but that some of the men got to work with their cutlasses, and literally slashed the brutes to pieces, sometimes killing several with a single blow. And thus, in a while, the boat was freed once more; though it was a sorely wounded and frightened lot of men that manned her.

The Mate himself took an oar, as did all those who were able. And so they rowed slowly and painfully away from that hateful derelict, whose crew of monsters even then made the weed all of a-heave with hideous life.

From the Tarawak came urgent signals for them to haste; by which the Mate knew that the storm, which the Captain had feared, must be coming down upon the ship, and so he spurred each one to greater endeavour, until, at last, they were under the shadow of their own vessel, with very thankful hearts, and bodies, bleeding, tired and faint.

Slowly and painfully, the boat's crew scrambled up the side-ladder, and the boat was hoisted aboard; but they had no time then to tell their tale; for the storm was upon them.

It came half an hour later, sweeping down in a cloud of white fury from the Eastward, and blotting out all vestiges of the mysterious derelict and the little barque which had proved her victim. And after that, for a weary day and night, they battled with the storm. When it passed, nothing was to be seen, either of the two vessels or of the weed which had studded the sea before the storm; for they had been blown many a score of leagues to the Westward of the spot, and so had no further chance—nor, I ween, inclination—to investigate further the mystery of that strange old derelict of a past time, and her habitants of rats.

Yet, many a time, and in many fo'cas'les has this story been told; and many a conjecture has been passed as to how came that ancient craft abroad there in the ocean. Some have suggested—as indeed I have made bold to put forth as fact—that she must have drifted out of the lonesome Sargasso Sea. And, in truth, I cannot but think this the most reasonable supposition. Yet, of the rats that evidently dwelt in her, I have no reasonable explanation to offer. Whether they were true ship's rats, or a species that is to be found in the weed-haunted plains and islets of the Sargasso Sea, I cannot say. It may be that they are the descendants of rats that lived in ships long centuries lost in the Weed Sea, and which have learned to live among the weed, forming new characteristics, and developing fresh powers and instincts. Yet, I cannot say; for I speak entirely without authority, and do but tell this story as it is told in the fo'cas'le of many an old-time sailing ship—that dark, brine-tainted place where the young men learn somewhat of the mysteries of the all mysterious sea.

THE SHAMRAKEN HOMEWARD-BOUNDER

CHAPTER I

The old Shamraken, sailing-ship, had been many days upon the waters. She was old—older than her masters, and that was saying a good deal. She seemed in no hurry, as she lifted her bulging, old, wooden sides through the seas. What need for hurry! She would arrive some time, in some fashion, as had been her habit heretofore.

Two matters were especially noticeable among her crew—who were also her masters—; the first the agedness of each and everyone; the second the family sense which appeared to bind them, so that the ship seemed manned by a crew, all of whom were related one to the other; yet it was not so.

A strange company were they, each man bearded, aged and grizzled; yet there was nothing of the inhumanity of old age about them, save it might be in their freedom from grumbling, and the calm content which comes only to those in whom the more violent passions have died.

Had anything to be done, there was nothing of the growling, inseparable from the average run of sailor men. They went aloft to the "job"—whatever it might be—with the wise submission which is brought only by age and experience. Their work was gone through with a certain slow pertinacity—a sort of tired steadfastness, born of the knowledge that such work had to be done. Moreover, their hands possessed the ripe skill which comes only from exceeding practice, and which went far to make amends for the feebleness of age. Above all, their movements, slow as they might be, were remorseless in their lack of faltering. They had so often performed the same kind of work, that they had arrived, by the selection of utility, at the shortest and most simple methods of doing it.

They had, as I have said, been many days upon the water, though I am not sure that any man in her knew to a nicety the number of those days. Though Skipper Abe Tombes—addressed usually as Skipper Abe—may have had some notion; for he might be seen at times gravely adjusting a prodigious quadrant, which suggests that he kept some sort of record of time and place.

Of the crew of the Shamraken, some half dozen were seated, working placidly at such matters of seamanship as were necessary. Besides these, there were others about the decks. A couple who paced the lee side of the main deck, smoking, and exchanging an occasional word. One who sat by the side of a worker, and made odd remarks between draws at his pipe. Another, out upon the jibboom, who fished, with a line, hook and white rag, for bonito. This last was Nuzzie, the ship's boy. He was grey-bearded, and his years numbered five and fifty. A boy of fifteen he had been, when he joined the Shamraken, and "boy" he was still, though forty years had passed into eternity, since the day of his "signing on"; for the men of the Shamraken lived in the past, and thought of him only as the "boy" of that past.

It was Nuzzie's watch below—his time for sleeping. This might have been said also of the other three men who talked and smoked; but for themselves they had scarce a thought of sleep. Healthy age sleeps little, and they were in health, though so ancient.

Presently, one of those who walked the lee side of the main deck, chancing to cast a glance forrard, observed Nuzzie still to be out upon the jibboom, jerking his line so as to delude some foolish bonito into the belief that the white rag was a flying-fish.

The smoker nudged his companion.

"Time thet b'y 'ad 'is sleep."

"i, i, mate," returned the other, withdrawing his pipe, and giving a steadfast look at the figure seated out upon the jibboom.

For the half of a minute they stood there, very effigies of Age's implacable determination to rule rash Youth. Their pipes were held in their hands, and the smoke rose up in little eddies from the smouldering contents of the bowls.

"Thar's no tamin' of thet b'y!" said the first man, looking very stern and determined. Then he remembered his pipe, and took a draw.

"B'ys is tur'ble queer critters," remarked the second man, and remembered his pipe in turn.

"Fishin' w'en 'e orter be sleepin'," snorted the first man.

"B'ys needs a tur'ble lot er sleep," said the second man. "I 'member w'en I wor a b'y. I reckon it's ther growin'."

And all the time poor Nuzzie fished on.

"Guess I'll jest step up an' tell 'im ter come in outer thet," exclaimed the first man, and commenced to walk towards the steps leading up on to the fo'cas'le head.

"B'y!" he shouted, as soon as his head was above the level of the fo'cas'le deck. "B'y!"

Nuzzie looked round, at the second call.

"Eh?" he sung out.

"Yew come in outer thet," shouted the older man, in the somewhat shrill tone which age had brought to his voice. "Reckon we'll be 'avin' yer sleepin' at the wheel ter night."

"i," joined in the second man, who had followed his companion up on to the fo'cas'le head. "Come in, b'y, an' get ter yer bunk."

"Right," called Nuzzie, and commenced to coil up his line. It was evident that he had no thought of disobeying. He came in off the spar, and went past them without a word, on the way to turn in.

They, on their part, went down slowly off the fo'cas'le head, and resumed their walk fore and aft along the lee side of the main deck.

CHAPTER II

"I reckon, Zeph," said the man who sat upon the hatch and smoked, "I reckon as Skipper Abe's 'bout right. We've made a trifle o' dollars outer the old 'ooker, an' we don't get no younger."

"Ay, thet's so, right 'nuff," returned the man who sat beside him, working at the stropping of a block.

"An' it's 'bout time's we got inter the use o' bein' ashore," went on the first man, who was named Job.

Zeph gripped the block between his knees, and fumbled in his hip pocket for a plug. He bit off a chew and replaced the plug.

"Seems cur'ous this is ther last trip, w'en yer comes ter think uv it," he remarked, chewing steadily, his chin resting on his hand.

Job took two or three deep draws at his pipe before he spoke.

"Reckon it had ter come sumtime," he said, at length. "I've a purty leetle place in me mind w'er' I'm goin' ter tie up. 'Ave yer thought erbout it, Zeph?"

The man who held the block between his knees, shook his head, and stared away moodily over the sea.

"Dunno, Job, as I know what I'll do w'en ther old 'ooker's sold," he muttered. "Sence M'ria went, I don't seem nohow ter care 'bout bein' 'shore."

"I never 'ad no wife," said Job, pressing down the burning tobacco in the bowl of his pipe. "I reckon seafarin' men don't ought ter have no truck with wives."

"Thet's right 'nuff, Job, fer yew. Each man ter 'is taste. I wer' tur'ble fond uv M'ria—" he broke off short, and continued to stare out over the sea.

"I've allus thought I'd like ter settle down on er farm o' me own. I guess the dollars I've arned 'll do the trick," said Job.

Zeph made no reply, and, for a time, they sat there, neither speaking.

Presently, from the door of the fo'cas'le, on the starboard side, two figures emerged. They were also of the "watch below." If anything, they seemed older than the rest of those about the decks; their beards, white, save for the stain of tobacco juice, came nearly to their waists. For the rest, they had been big vigorous men; but were now sorely bent by the burden of their years. They came aft, walking slowly. As they came opposite to the main hatch, Job looked up and spoke—

"Say, Nehemiah, thar's Zeph here's been thinkin' 'bout M'ria, an' I ain't bin able ter peek 'im up nohow."

The smaller of the two newcomers shook his head slowly.

"We hev oor trubbles," he said. "We hev oor trubbles. I hed mine w'en I lost my datter's gell. I wor powerful took wi' thet gell, she wor that winsome; but it wor like ter be—it wor like ter be, an' Zeph's hed his trubble sence then."

"M'ria wer' a good wife ter me, she wer'," said Zeph, speaking slowly. "An' now th' old 'ooker's goin', I'm feared as I'll find it mighty lonesome ashore yon," and he waved his hand, as though suggesting vaguely that the shore lay anywhere beyond the starboard rail.

"Ay," remarked the second of the newcomers. "It's er weary thing tu me as th' old packet's goin'. Six and sixty year hev I sailed in her. Six and sixty year!" He nodded his head, mournfully, and struck a match with shaky hands.

"It's like ter be," said the smaller man. "It's like ter be."

And, with that, he and his companion moved over to the spar that lay along under the starboard bulwarks, and there seated themselves, to smoke and meditate.

CHAPTER III

Skipper Abe, and Josh Matthews, the First Mate, were standing together beside the rail which ran across the break of the poop. Like the rest of the men of the Shamraken, their age had come upon them, and the frost of eternity had touched their beards and hair.

Skipper Abe was speaking:—

"It's harder 'n I'd thought," he said, and looked away from the Mate, staring hard along the worn, white-scoured decks.

"Dunno w'at I'll du, Abe, w'en she's gone," returned the old Mate. "She's been a 'ome fer us these sixty years an' more." He knocked out the old tobacco from his pipe, as he spoke, and began to cut a bowl-full of fresh.

"It's them durned freights!" exclaimed the Skipper. "We're jest losin' dollars every trip. It's them steam packets as hes knocked us out."

He sighed wearily, and bit tenderly at his plug.

"She's been a mighty comfortable ship," muttered Josh, in soliloquy. "An' sence thet b'y o' mine went, I sumhow thinks less o' goin' ashore 'n I used ter. I ain't no folk left on all thar 'arth."

He came to an end, and began with his old trembling fingers to fill his pipe.

Skipper Abe said nothing. He appeared to be occupied with his own thoughts. He was leaning over the rail across the break of the poop, and chewing steadily. Presently, he straightened himself up and walked over to leeward. He expectorated, after which he stood there for a few moments, taking a short look round—the result of half a century of habit. Abruptly, he sung out to the Mate. . . .

"Wat d'yer make outer it?" he queried, after they had stood awhile, peering.

"Dunno, Abe, less'n it's some sort o' mist, riz up by ther 'eat."

Skipper Abe shook his head; but having nothing better to suggest, held his peace for awhile.

Presently, Josh spoke again:—

"Mighty cur'us, Abe. These are strange parts."

Skipper Abe nodded his assent, and continued to stare at that which had come into sight upon the lee bow. To them, as they looked, it seemed that a vast wall of rose-coloured mist was rising towards the zenith. It showed nearly ahead, and at first had seemed no more than a bright cloud upon the horizon; but already had reached a great way into the air, and the upper edge had taken on wondrous flame-tints.

"It's powerful nice-lookin'," said Josh. "I've allus 'eard as things was diff'rent out 'n these parts."

Presently, as the Shamraken drew near to the mist, it appeared to those aboard that it filled all the sky ahead of them, being spread out now far on either bow. And so in a while they entered into it, and, at once, the aspect of all things was changed. . . . The mist, in great rosy wreaths, floated all about them, seeming to soften and beautify every rope and spar, so that the old ship had become, as it were, a fairy craft in an unknown world.

"Never seen nothin' like it, Abe—nothin'!" said Josh. "Ey! but it's fine! It's fine! Like 's ef we'd run inter ther sunset."

"I'm mazed, just mazed!" exclaimed Skipper Abe, "but I'm 'gree'ble as it's purty, mighty purty."

For a further while, the two old fellows stood without speech, just gazing and gazing. With their entering into the mist, they had come into a greater quietness than had been theirs out upon the open sea. It was as though the mist muffled and toned down the creak, creak, of the spars and gear; and the big, foamless seas that rolled past them, seemed to have lost something of their harsh whispering roar of greeting.

"Sort o' unarthly, Abe," said Josh, later, and speaking but little above a whisper. "Like as ef yew was in church."

"Ay," replied Skipper Abe. "It don't seem nat'rel."

"Shouldn't think as 'eaven was all thet diff'rent," whispered Josh. And Skipper Abe said nothing in contradiction.

CHAPTER IV

Sometime later, the wind began to fail, and it was decided that, when eight-bells was struck, all hands should set the main t'gallant. Presently, Nuzzie having been called (for he was the only one aboard who had turned in) eight bells went, and all hands put aside their pipes, and prepared to tail on to the ha'lyards; yet no one of them made to go up to loose the sail. That was the b'y's job, and Nuzzie was a little late in coming out on deck. When, in a minute, he appeared, Skipper Abe spoke sternly to him.

"Up now, b'y, an' loose thet sail. D'y think to let er grown man dew suchlike work! Shame on yew!"

And Nuzzie, the grey-bearded "b'y" of five and fifty years, went aloft humbly, as he was bidden.

Five minutes later, he sung out that all was ready for hoisting, and the string of ancient Ones took a strain on the ha'lyards. Then Nehemiah, being the chaunty man, struck up in his shrill quaver:—

"Thar wor an ole farmer in Yorkshire did dwell."

And the shrill piping of the ancient throats took up the refrain:—

"Wi' me ay, ay, blow thar lan' down."

Nehemiah caught up the story:—

"'e 'ad 'n ole wife, 'n 'e wished 'er in 'ell."

"Give us some time ter blow thar lan' down," came the quavering chorus of old voices.

"O, thar divvel come to 'im one day at thar plough," continued old Nehemiah; and the crowd of ancients followed up with the refrain:—"Wi' me ay, ay, blow thar lan' down."

"I've comed fer th' ole woman, I mun 'ave 'er now," sang Nehemiah. And again the refrain:—"Give us some time ter blow thar lan' down," shrilled out.

And so on to the last couple of stanzas. And all about them, as they chaunteyed, was that extraordinary, rose-tinted mist; which, above, blent into a marvellous radiance of flame-colour, as though, just a little higher than their mastheads, the sky was one red ocean of silent fire.

"Thar wor three leetle divvels chained up ter thar wall," sang Nehemiah, shrilly.

" Wi' me ay, ay, blow thar lan' down," came the piping chorus.

"She tuk off 'er clog, 'n she walloped 'em all," chaunted old Nehemiah, and again followed the wheezy, age-old refrain.

"These three leetle divvels fer marcy did bawl," quavered Nehemiah, cocking one eye upward to see whether the yard was nearly mast-headed.

"Wi' me ay, ay, blow thar lan' down," came the chorus.

"Chuck out this ole hag, or she'll mur—"

"Belay," sung out Josh, cutting across the old sea song, with the sharp command. The chaunty had ceased with the first note of the Mate's voice, and a couple of minutes later, the ropes were coiled up, and the old fellows back to their occupations.

It is true that eight bells had gone, and that the watch was supposed to be changed; and changed it was, so far as the wheel and look-out were concerned; but otherwise little enough difference did it make to those sleep-proof ancients. The only change visible in the men about the deck, was that those who had previously only smoked, now smoked and worked; while those who had hitherto worked and smoked, now only smoked. Thus matters went on in all amity; while the old Shamraken passed onward like a rose-tinted shadow through the shining mist, and only the great, silent, lazy seas that came at her, out from the enshrouding redness, seemed aware that she was anything more than the shadow she appeared.

Presently, Zeph sung out to Nuzzie to get their tea from the galley, and so, in a little, the watch below were making their evening meal. They ate it as they sat upon the hatch or spar, as the chance might be; and, as they ate, they talked with their mates, of the watch on deck, upon the matter of the shining mist into which they had plunged. It was obvious, from their talk, that the extraordinary phenomenon had impressed them vastly, and all the superstition in them seemed to have been waked to fuller life. Zeph, indeed, made no bones of declaring his belief that they were nigh to something more than earthly. He said that he had a feeling that "M'ria" was somewhere near to him.

"Meanin' ter say as we've come purty near ter 'eaven?" said Nehemiah, who was busy thrumming a paunch mat, for chafing gear.

"Dunno," replied Zeph; "but"—making a gesture towards the hidden sky—"yew'll 'low as it's mighty wonderful, 'n I guess ef 'tis 'eaven, thar's some uv us as is growin' powerful wearied uv 'arth. I guess I'm feelin' peeky fer a sight uv M'ria."

Nehemiah nodded his head slowly, and the nod seemed to run round the group of white-haired ancients.

"Reckon my datter's gell 'll be thar," he said, after a space of pondering. "Be s'prisin' ef she 'n M'ria 'd made et up ter know one anuther."

"M'ria wer' great on makin' friends," remarked Zeph, meditatively, "an gells wus awful friendly wi' 'er. Seemed as she hed er power thet way."

"I never 'ad no wife," said Job, at this point, somewhat irrelevantly. It was a fact of which he was proud, and he made a frequent boast of it.

"Thet's naught ter cocker thysel on, lad," exclaimed one of the white-beards, who, until this time, had been silent. "Thou'lt find less folk in heaven t' greet thee."

"Thet's trewth, sure 'nuff, Jock," assented Nehemiah, and fixed a stern look on Job; whereat Job retired into silence.

Presently, at three bells, Josh came along and told them to put away their work for the day.

CHAPTER V

The second dog watch came, and Nehemiah and the rest of his side, made their tea out upon the main hatch, along with their mates. When this was finished, as though by common agreement, they went every one and sat themselves upon the pin-rail running along under the t'gallant bulwarks; there, with their elbows upon the rail, they faced outward to gaze their full at the mystery of colour which had wrapped them about. From time to time, a pipe would be removed, and some slowly evolved thought given an utterance.

Eight bells came and went; but, save for the changing of the wheel and look-out, none moved from his place.

Nine o'clock, and the night came down upon the sea; but to those within the mist, the only result was a deepening of the rose colour into an intense red, which seemed to shine with a light of its own creating. Above them, the unseen sky seemed to be one vast blaze of silent, blood-tinted flame.

"Piller uv cloud by day, 'n er piller uv fire by night," muttered Zeph to Nehemiah, who crouched near.

"I reckon's them's Bible words," said Nehemiah.

"Dunno," replied Zeph; "but them's thar very words as I heerd passon Myles a sayin' w'en thar timber wor afire down our way. 'Twer' mostly smoke 'n daylight; but et tamed ter 'n eternal fire w'en thar night comed."

At four bells, the wheel and look-out were relieved, and a little later, Josh and Skipper Abe came down on to the main deck.

"Tur'ble queer," said Skipper Abe, with an affectation of indifference.

"Aye, 'tes, sure," said Nehemiah.

And after that, the two old men sat among the others, and watched.

At five bells, half-past ten, there was a murmur from those who sat nearest to the bows, and a cry from the man on the look-out. At that, the attention of all was turned to a point nearly right ahead. At this particular spot, the mist seemed to be glowing with a curious, unearthly red brilliance; and, a minute later, there burst upon their vision a vast arch, formed of blazing red clouds.

At the sight, each and every one cried out their amazement, and immediately began to run towards the fo'cas'le head. Here they congregated in a clump, the Skipper and the Mate among them. The arch appeared now to extend its arc far beyond either bow, so that the ship was heading to pass right beneath it.

"Tis 'eaven fer sure," murmured Josh to himself; but Zeph heard him.

"Reckon's them's ther Gates uv Glory thet M'ria wus allus talkin' 'bout," he replied.

"Guess I'll see thet b'y er mine in er little," muttered Josh, and he craned forward, his eyes very bright and eager.

All about the ship was a great quietness. The wind was no more now than a light steady breath upon the port quarter; but from right ahead, as though issuing from the mouth of the radiant arch, the long-backed, foamless seas rolled up, black and oily.

Suddenly, amid the silence, there came a low musical note, rising and falling like the moan of a distant æolian harp. The sound appeared to come from the direction of the arch, and the surrounding mist seemed to catch it up and send it sobbing and sobbing in low echoes away into the redness far beyond sight.

"They'm singin'," cried Zeph. "M'ria wer' allus tur'ble fond uv singin'. Hark ter—"

"'Sh!" interrupted Josh. "Thet's my b'y!" His shrill old voice had risen almost to a scream.

"It's wunnerful—wunnerful; just mazin'!" exclaimed Skipper Abe.

Zeph had gone a little forrard of the crowd. He was shading his eyes with his hands, and staring intently, his expression denoting the most intense excitement.

"B'lieve I see 'er. B'lieve I see 'er," he was muttering to himself, over and over again.

Behind him, two of the old men were steadying Nehemiah, who felt, as he put it, "a bit mazy at thar thought o' seein' thet gell."

Away aft, Nuzzie, the "b'y," was at the wheel. He had heard the moaning; but, being no more than a boy, it must be supposed that he knew nothing of the nearness of the next world, which was so evident to the men, his masters.

A matter of some minutes passed, and Job, who had in mind that farm upon which he had set his heart, ventured to suggest that heaven was less near than his mates supposed; but no one seemed to hear him, and he subsided into silence.

It was the better part of an hour later, and near to midnight, when a murmur among the watchers announced that a fresh matter had come to sight. They were yet a great way off from the arch; but still the thing showed clearly—a prodigious umbel, of a deep, burning red; but the crest of it was black, save for the very apex which shone with an angry red glitter.

'Thar Throne uv God!" cried out Zeph, in a loud voice, and went down upon his knees. The rest of the old men followed his example, and even old Nehemiah made a great effort to get to that position.

'Simly we'm a'most 'n 'eaven," he muttered huskily.

Skipper Abe got to his feet, with an abrupt movement. He had never heard of that extraordinary electrical phenomenon, seen once perhaps in a hundred years—the "Fiery Tempest" which precedes certain great Cyclonic Storms; but his experienced eye had suddenly discovered that the red-shining umbel was truly a low, whirling water-hill, reflecting the red light. He had no theoretical knowledge to tell him that the thing was produced by an enormous air-vortice; but he had often seen a waterspout form. Yet, he was still undecided. It was all so beyond him; though, certainly, that monstrous gyrating hill of water, sending out a reflected glitter of burning red, appealed to him as having no place in his ideas of Heaven. And then, even as he hesitated, came the first, wild-beast bellow of the coming Cyclone. As the sound smote upon their ears, the old men looked at one another with bewildered, frightened eyes.

"Reck'n thet's God speakin'," whispered Zeph. "Guess we're on'y mis'rable sinners."

The next instant, the breath of the Cyclone was in their throats, and the Shamraken, homeward-bounder, passed in through the everlasting portals.

GREY SEAS ARE DREAMING OF MY DEATH

I know grey seas are dreaming of my death,
Out on grey plains where foam is lost in sleep,
Where one damp wind wails on continually,
And no life lives in the forgotten air.
Ayhie! Yoi! but oh! the mood doth change,
The sea doth lift me high on living mountains;
As a mother guards her babe
So the fierce hills round me range,
And a Voice goes on and on in mighty laughter—
The joyous call of Strength which doth enguard me.
Ayhie! Yoi! All the splendour of the sea
Doth guard me from the slaughter.
Oh! Men in weary lands
Lift up your hearts and hands,
And weep ye are not me,
Child of all the sea
Out upon the foam among the fountains
And the glory
And the magic of this water world
Where in childhood I was hurled,
Weep, for I am dying in my glory;
And the foam swings round and sings,
And the great seas chaunt; and the whitened hills are falling;
And I am dying in my glory, dying—
Dying, dying, dying—

FOOTNOTES:

[1] This is evidently a reference to something which Mr. Philips has set in an earlier message—one of the three lost messages.—W.H.H.

[2] Captain Bolton makes no mention of the claw, in the covering letter which he has enclosed with the MS.—W. H. H.

[3] I suggest the existence of smaller air vortices within the Cyclone. By air vortices, I mean vorticular air whorls—as it might be the upper portions of uncompleted waterspouts. How else explain the naked mizzen and fore topmasts and t'gallant masts being twisted off (as later appeared to have been the case), and yet the great spread of the lower topsails and the foresail not suffering? I am convinced that the unequal force of the first wind-burst is only thus to be explained.

[4] It occurs to me here, as showing in another way the unusual wind-strength, to mention that, having tried in vain every usual method of keeping the wind from blowing out the binnacle lamps; such as stuffing all the crevices with rags, and making temporary shields for the chimneys, the Skipper had at last resorted to a tiny electric watch light, which he fixed in the binnacle, and which now enabled me to get an odd vague glimpse of the Mate, as he hovered near the compass.

[5] A description absolute and without exaggeration. Who that has ever heard the weird, crisp screaming of the foam, in some momentary lull in a great storm, when a big sea has reared itself within a few fathoms of one, can ever forget it?

[6] The Second Mate, who was holding to the rail across the break of the poop, gave me this information later; he being in a position to see the maindecks at the time.

[7] Possibly, our being pooped at this time, was due chiefly to the fact that our speed through the water had diminished, owing to our having lost more of our spars whilst in the Vortex, and some of the gear still towing. And a Mercy our sides were not stove a thousand times!

[8] Unshaded lights are never allowed about the decks at night, as they are likely to blind the vision of the officer of the watch.—W.H.H.

William Hope Hodgson - A Short Biography

William Hope Hodgson was born in Blackmore End, Essex, England on November 15th, 1877.

He was the second of twelve children to father, Samuel Hodgson, an Anglican priest and mother Lissie Sarah Brown.

Three of his siblings died in infancy and it is a theme he returns to many time in his later writings.

Samuel Hodgson was the priest at 11 different churches over 21 years necessitating frequent moves for the family.

By the age of 13 William had determined that his future lay as a sailor and so ran away from his boarding school. He was found and returned swiftly to his family. After much effort William's father agreed that he could be apprenticed as a cabin boy and so began, in 1891, a four year apprenticeship.

Sadly within a few months Samuel had succumbed to cancer of the throat and died leaving his family to live an impoverished life dependent on charity handouts. William returned from sea in 1895 to study in Liverpool and earn his mate's certificate before he once more took to life as a sailor.

William was a very handsome man but quite short. He was thus prone to be bullied on ship and sought some way to defend himself. He embarked on a personal training programme which ensured that an attack on him would end in failure and the bullies being pummelled unmercifully.

This theme of bullying of an apprentice by older seamen and the enacted revenge also appears frequently in William's later writings.

At sea William developed many interests. He practised photography, created a stamp collection and became a fine marksman, all the while developing his writing skills and committing his experiences to memory.

In 1898 the Royal Humane Society awarded him a medal for heroism for saving another sailor who had fallen overboard in shark-infested waters.

In 1899, at age 22, he opened W. H. Hodgson's School of Physical Culture, in Blackburn, England, offering personal exercise regimes for personal training. Some of his clients were members of the Blackburn Police force. A visit to their department was made by the famous escapologist Harry Houdini, who allowed himself to be incarcerated and then escaped.

In 1902, William appeared on stage with handcuffs and other restraining devices supplied by the Blackburn police department and applied the restraints to Houdini. Houdini had more than usual difficulty in removing the restraints, and complained that he had been deliberately injured and that the locks of his handcuffs had been jammed.

William revelled in his flair for publicity; even riding a bicycle down a street so steep that it had stairs, an event that produced an article in the local paper. However none of this enabled him to acquire sufficient clients to stop his personal training business from failing.

He did again however make wise use of the experience and wrote a series of articles including "Physical Culture versus Recreative Exercises" (published in 1903). Another of these articles, "Health from Scientific Exercise," featured photographs of Hodgson demonstrating his exercises.

But again it was a limited market and he now moved into a career for which he would be defined by; fiction writer.

The Royal Magazine published his first short story, "The Goddess of Death", in 1904, in which a statue of Flora which stood in Corporation Park, Blackburn, was used as the focus of a tale in which a Hindu statue, seized from an Indian temple, stood in a small English town. The statue comes alive to take its revenge on the people who stole it. It was the beginning of a stream of popular short stories from his pen and fertile mind.

Although he wrote a significant number of poems, only a handful were ever published in his lifetime. Several, including "Madre Mia", appeared as dedications in his novels. In 1906 he published an article in The Author magazine, proposing that poets could earn money by writing inscriptions for tombstones. (His widow did however publish two volumes after his death).

In 1906 the American magazine The Monthly Story Magazine published "From the Tideless Sea", the first of Hodgson's Sargasso Sea stories. Hodgson continued to sell stories to American magazines as well as British magazines for the remainder of his career. Although easy to sell he never really managed the level of comfort that his works should have generated.

His first published novel, The Boats of the "Glen Carrig", appeared in 1907, to positive reviews. That same year also came "The Voice in the Night", and "Through the Vortex of a Cyclone", a realistic story inspired by Hodgson's experiences at sea and illustrated with tinted slides made from his own photographs.

In 1908 Hodgson continued to explore the subject of ships and cyclones in his story "The Shamraken Homeward-Bounder", and published his second novel, "The House on the Borderland", again to positive reviews.

Also worth noting from this period is the satirical science fiction story, "Date 1965: Modern Warfare", a Swiftian satire in which proposes that war should be carried out by men fighting in pens with knives, and the corpses carefully salvaged for food.

In 1909, he published "Out of the Storm", a short horror story about "the death-side of the sea," in which the protagonist drowning in a storm rants about the horrors of a storm at sea.

That same year came another novel, "The Ghost Pirates". In the foreword, he wrote that it ... completes what, perhaps, may be termed a trilogy; for, though very different in scope, each of the three books deals with certain conceptions that have an elemental kinship. This book, the author believes that he closes the door, so far as he is concerned, on a particular phase of constructive thought.

Despite the critical success of his novels, Hodgson remained relatively poor. To try to increase his income from short story sales, he began wrote the first of his recurring characters, Thomas Carnacki, who featured in several of his most famous stories. The first - "The Gateway of the Monster", was published in 1910 in The Idler.

His last novel to see publication, "The Night Land", was published in 1912, although it is likely to have its roots from some years before. Hodgson also worked on a 10,000-word novelette version of the novel, now known as The Dream of X. The original was much longer and the shorter version was easier to sell and retain copyright over for the American market.

Hodgson continued to expand his writing into related genres, publishing "Judge Barclay's Wife", a western adventure, in the United States, as well as several non-supernatural mystery stories and the science fiction story "The Derelict", and even war stories.

In 1912, Hodgson married Betty Farnworth, known also as Bessie, a girl from Cheadle Hulme, who wrote the 'agony' column for the women's magazine Home Notes. Both were aged thirty-five.

Betty gave up her job when they married on 26 February 1913, in the London borough of Kensington. They moved to the south of France and took up residence there, owing in part to the lower cost of living.

Here Hodgson began a work entitled "Captain Dang (An account of certain peculiar and somewhat memorable adventures)" and continued to publish stories in multiple genres, although financial security continued to elude him.

When war broke out in Europe, the Hodgsons returned to England and William joined the University of London's Officers' Training Corps and received a commission as a Lieutenant in the Royal Artillery.

In 1916 he was thrown from a horse and suffered a broken jaw and a serious head injury; he received a mandatory discharge, and returned to writing.

Refusing to remain on the sidelines, Hodgson recovered sufficiently to re-enlist. His published articles and stories from the time reflect his experience in war.

After volunteering for a forward observation role he was killed by an artillery shell at Ypres in mid-April 1918.

William Hope Hodgson - A Selected Bibliography

In common with many writers of this period the volume of work was large and accurate records were not always kept. We have listed below the main works and categorised for easier reference those published during his lifetime or shortly after by efforts of his widow.

Novels

The Boats of the "Glen Carrig" (1907)
The House on the Borderland (1908)
The Ghost Pirates (1909)
The Night Land (1912)
The Dream of X (1912) (abridgement of "The Night Land" primarily for the American market)
Captain Dang (unfinished)

Fiction Series

Carnacki
Carnacki, the Ghost Finder (abridged) (1910) [SF]
The Gateway of the Monster (1910)
The House Among the Laurels (1910)
The Whistling Room (1910)
The Horse of the Invisible (1910)
The Searcher of the End House (1910)
The Thing Invisible (1912)
Carnacki, the Ghost-Finder (1913)
The Haunted Jarvee (1929)
The Find (1947)
The Hog (1947)

Captain Gault
Contraband of War (1914)
The Diamond Spy (1914)
The Red Herring (1914)
The Case of the Chinese Curio Dealer (1914)
The Drum of Saccharine (1914)

From Information Received (1914)
The German Spy (1915)
The Problem of the Pearls (1915)
The Painted Lady (1915)
The Adventure of the Garter (1916)
My Lady's Jewels (1916)
Trading with the Enemy (1917)
The Plans of the Reefing Bi-Plane (1996)

Captain Jat
The Island of the Ud (1912)
The Adventure of the Headland (1912)

D.C.O. Cargunka
The Bells of the Laughing Sally (1914)
The Adventure with the Claim Jumpers (1915)

Sargasso Sea
From the Tideless Sea Part One (1906)
The Mystery of the Derelict (1907)
From the Tideless Sea Part Two: Further News of the Homebird (1907)
The Thing in the Weeds (1913)
The Finding of the Graiken (1913)
From the Tideless Sea (1914)
The Voice in the Dawn (1920

Short Fiction
The Goddess of Death (1904)
A Tropical Horror (1905)
The Valley of Lost Children (1906)
The Boats of the Glen Carrig (excerpt) (1907)
The Weed Men (excerpt) (1907)
The Weed Men (excerpt) (1907)
The Terror of the Water-Tank (1907
The Voice in the Night (1907)
The Noise in the Night (1908)
The Shamraken Homeward-Bounder (1908)
The Ghost Pirates (abridged) (1909)
The Silent Ship (1909)
Out of the Storm (1909)
The Captain of the Onion Boat (1910)
The Smugglers (1911)
Bullion (1911)
My House Shall Be Called the House of Prayer (1911)
The Mystery of the Water-Logged Ship (1911)
The Albatross (1911)
In the Wailing Gully (1911)
The Ghosts of the Glen Doon (1911)
The 'Prentices' Mutiny (1912
Mr. Jock Danplank (1912)

On the Bridge (1912)
Judge Barclay's Wife (1912)
The Getting Even of Tommy Dodd (1912)
The Derelict (1912)
The Girl with the Grey Eyes (1913)
The Sea Horses (1913)
How the Honourable Billy Darrell Raided the Wind (1913)
Kind, Kind and Gentle is She (1913)
Jack Grey, Second Mate (1913)
The Island of the Crossbones (1913)
Senator Sandy Mac Ghee (1914)
The Dumpley Acrostics (1914)
The Last Word in Mysteries (1914)
The Stone Ship (1914)
We Two and Bully Dunkan (1914)
The Getting Even of "Parson" Guyles (1914)
The Regeneration of Captain Bully Keller (1914)
The Friendship of Monsieur Jeynois (1915)
Inn of the Black Crow: Extract from the Travelling Notebook of John Dory, Secret Exciseman (1915)
The Mystery of Missing Ships (1915)
Captain Gunbolt Charity and the Painted Lady (1916)
What Happened in the Thunderbolt (1916)
An Adventure of the Deep Waters (1916)
Jem Binney and the Safe at Lockwood Hall (1916)
The Haunted "Pampero" (1916
The Real Thing: 'S.O.S' (1917)
The Mystery of Captain Chappel (1917)
Diamond Cut Diamond with a Vengeance (1918)
A Fight with a Submarine (1918)
The Home-Coming of Captain Dan (1918)
In the Danger Zone (1919)
The Waterloo of a Hard-Case Skipper (1919)
The Baumoff Explosive (1919
By the Lee (1919)
Old Golly (1919)
The Storm (1919)
A Timely Escape (1922)
Demons of the Sea (1923)
Merciful Plunder (1925)
The Wild Man of the Sea (1926)

Poetry Collections
The Calling of the Sea (published posthumously by Hodgson's widow in 1920)
The Voice of the Ocean (published posthumously by Hodgson's widow in 1921)

Essays
Is the Mercantile Navy Worth Joining? (1905)
Through the Vortex of a Cyclone (1907)
Author's Introduction to the Manuscript (1907)

Date 1965: Modern Warfare (1908)

www.ingramcontent.com/pod-product-compliance
Lightning Source LLC
Chambersburg PA
CBHW051258170626
46809CB00004B/1699